TOO COOL

BY DUFF BRENNA

Waking in Wisconsin (poems)

The Book of Mamie

The Holy Book of the Beard

Too Cool

DUFF BRENNA

TOO COOL

NAN A. TALESE

DOUBLEDAY

New York London

Toronto Sydney

Auckland

PUBLISHED BY NAN A. TALESE

an imprint of Doubleday

a division of Bantam Doubleday Dell Publishing Group, Inc.

1540 Broadway, New York, New York 10036

DOUBLEDAY is a trademark of Doubleday, a division of

Bantam Doubleday Dell Publishing Group, Inc.

Grateful acknowledgment is made to Borealis Press to reprint ''Shipping Curious Cow''

from *Pastoral Symphony* by V. J. Chouinard.

Library of Congress Cataloging-in-Publication Data

Brenna, Duff.

Too cool / Duff Brenna.—1st ed.

p.   cm.

PS3552.R377T66   1998

813'.54—dc21   98-12924

CIP

ISBN 0-385-48971-4

Printed in the United States of America

August 1998

FIRST EDITION

1 2 3 4 5 6 7 8 9 10

FOR BRENDAN DUFF NEILAN

Perhaps some of us have to go through dark and devious ways before we can find the river of peace or the highroad to the soul's destination.

—JOSEPH CAMPBELL, *The Hero with a Thousand Faces*

CHAPTER 1

TRIPLE E IS BROKE. He cruises the streets of Gunnison searching for someone to roll. Jeanne has a buck and some change. Ava has two dollars. Tom has three. The car is almost out of gas. It has been a jittery day moving through the mountains, the tires skidding on patches of ice, slipping toward guardrails, jagged canyons. The radio has warned of another storm coming. They need to get gassed up and out of the Rockies, get to the plains of Utah before the storm hits.

"What should we do?" says Jeanne, trusting Triple E to have an answer. "Should we just get as much gas as we can and keep movin? Maybe we can find someone to roll in Utah. There are rich Mormons in Salt Lake, Triple E." She shivers and looks away from him. "God, it's cold. I can feel the cold pressin on the glass." She touches the window. Leaves the imprint of her fingers on the moist glass. "I should've stopped and got me some pants," she says. "This skirt is dumb." She tugs at the hem. Her kneecaps poke out smooth and brown. She is wearing a fur jacket. She has on ankle-top boots made of white suede. Her gaze wanders to Triple E, her eyes seeking assurance. He turns the heater up and she turns back to the window. "So cold," she says. "We gotta get outta here." She is not in her element. She is playing at being bad, doing her best to measure up to him, her love, her Triple E.

From the back comes Ava's tiny voice. "This isn't workin," she says. She and Tom have been arguing and now they are both slumped at opposite corners of the seat, glaring out the windows at the ghastly snow. Tom says she is smothering him, why can't she lay off? Their lives at stake and all Ava wants to do is suck-face. Doesn't she know there's a time and place for everything? The goddamn car jerking all over the ice, six inches from death, cops looking for them, money running out, and she wants what? to make out? wants to talk about love and babies and shit?

"What the fuck wrong with you, girl?"

Ava has taken the hint. She has squashed herself up, her arms crossed, her face turned away, and she says it again, "This isn't workin."

"What isn't workin?" says Triple E.

"Me and Tom nor nothin," she says. "I don't know why I come. We don't know where we're goin, we don't know what we're doin, cept running round creation with you, Triple E. You're the one fought the law, you're who they want, not me, not us guys."

He can't argue with her. He nods, his eyes on her in the mirror—petite bit of a thing, fragile as a sparrow. She is fourteen years old and his cousin and he should be looking out better for her; but there is this thing she has about Tom Patch. And when he jumped in the car at school and said he was going with Triple E and Jeanne, Ava hopped in with him, eyes bright, ready for adventure. Triple E knows he should have made her get out of the car right then. But he didn't.

"Nobody's makin you stay," he tells her. "I'll let you out anytime you say, Ava. You can go on home."

"Like how?"

"Like, just call your mom. She'll come get you."

Ava is quiet a second or two, then she tells him to forget it, she is staying.

Parking next to a grocery store, Triple E watches as customers come out and get into their cars and drive away. A woman, hunched in a heavy coat and carrying a grocery bag in her arms, comes out of the store. Her purse dangles at her elbow. She walks past the parking lot and keeps going up the street.

"There," says Triple E. "You guys wait here."

HE GETS OUT OF the car and walks behind her. The street is packed with houses on both sides, but just a few blocks away is white prairie wilderness. The sun is setting. Distant mountains huddle shoulder to shoulder like conspirators, their peaks lost in ashen clouds. Bitterbrush and trees and sage meander over the slopes fanning out beyond the town. Trees are scattered over yards and terraces. The sidewalks are gray, icy. Snow hardens along the curbs and against the wheels of parked cars. Icicles hang from the edges of peaked roofs. Lights in windows glow in a yellow haze of frost.

Past a streetlight on the corner there are shadows beneath the black trees. When she enters the shadows, Triple E will go for her purse. He watches her carefully as she crosses the street, then moves into the gloom. He can see she is being careful, trying not to slip on the ice. He, too, is unsteady. Salt grips the soles of his shoes, but he feels like he might bust his ass any second. Hurrying close behind the old woman, he is about to snatch the purse from her arm, when she turns around. Looks at him.

"My-my," she says, her voice raspy, "isn't it just freezing to death out here? Where's your hat, honey? You should have a hat on."

"Uhnnh," he mutters.

"You'll get frostbit ears."

"Ummm," he says.

They walk together across the street. He sees a wrinkled patch of face bunched inside a knit cap and a scarf tied beneath her chin. He takes her arm and helps her up the curb. She is shaky and leans on him trustfully. His fingers are inches away from her purse.

"Thank you," she says. And then she says, "You're Masterson's boy, aren't you? I thought I knew you. You're Billy Masterson."

"Uhhh," he says.

"It's me, Ida."

"Oh, uhhh."

"How's your dad, Billy?"

"Okay."

She looks him up and down. "You been to military school or something?" she says. She has a crooked lip. It lifts at one corner and slopes downward at the other. Lots of vertical lines encircle her mouth. Her breath steams. His too.

"Uh-huh, military school," he says, running his hand over his buzzed hair.

"Those are parade shoes you're wearing, aren't they." She

points at his shoes. The shoes are buffed a very shiny black, the edges are laced with snow.

"Yes, ma'am."

"I know parade shoes when I see them. Wilfred was thirty years in the army."

Ida talks fast, like she is afraid he'll go away if she doesn't keep talking. She says she knows military school is hard on boys, but it's good for them in the long run, builds character, gives a boy proper American values and self-discipline. If she had her way all boys would go to military school soon as they turned twelve. "Too many boys running on the streets where they're nothing but trouble. Denver especially," she says. "I'm glad I don't live there no more. What those people do to one another, it's criminal. Give me the country, give me the mountains. How old are you now, Billy?"

"Sixteen."

"Ah-yes," she says. She settles her gaze on him. "It's what I like about Gunnison. Nice kids like you. Been taught the values." She pauses a moment to clear her throat. She keeps squeezing Triple E's arm, yanking lightly on the sleeve of his jacket as they walk along. "The worse thing Nixon ever did, you know, was take away the draft. Young men and all their excess energy, they need a place to burn it off. Draft them in the army. Give them pride in themselves and pride of country, that's what Wilfred always said."

"I guess," says Triple E.

"I miss my Wilfred," says Ida, her voice small. She turns at the walkway in front of her house. The house is pillowed in snow. It looks rumpled, homey, like something from a fairy tale. The porch light is on. Smoke rises from the chimney. "Nice seeing you again, Billy," she says. "Tell your dad hi from Ida."

"Sure will, Ida," says Triple E. He watches her mount the porch, her gloved hand carefully gripping the rail. After she goes inside, he stands in front, stamping his feet, trying to decide what to do. The kitchen light comes on, and he can see her moving around, putting groceries away. The sky lowers around him, and he finds himself wishing he could go inside Ida's house, not to rob her, but to sit with her beside the fire, warming his feet, watching TV, safe from winter and everything.

WHEN HE GETS BACK to the car, Jeanne and Tom are just coming out of the store. They have a bag of groceries: two packages of Oreo cookies, a box of vanilla wafers, some Twinkies, a gallon of milk, and Dentyne chewing gum.

"You bust the old bitch?" says Tom.

"She got to her house too soon. Where's Ava?" Triple E says.

Ava isn't in the car. He scans the parking lot for her.

Nobody knows where Ava is.

"She's havin a snit," says Tom. "She'll be back."

They eat some cookies. They wait and wait, but Ava doesn't show up. Finally they drive around the streets looking for her, up one, down another. No Ava.

"Shit, what happened to her?" says Triple E. "Goddammit, Ava."

"Maybe she moto-vated," says Tom. His arms are draped over the seat, his face half-wedged between Jeanne and Triple E. It is an angry face, smoky brows and black eyes, an aggressive nose and chin. Triple E can smell vanilla wafer on Tom's breath.

Jeanne agrees that Ava has moved on. Triple E pulls the

car to the curb and sits awhile idling, watching the gas gauge, trying to figure out what to do.

"Let her fly-away home," says Tom. "Let her go. We got more important things to worry about right now than that little birdbrain."

"She's my cousin, man. I can't just leave her here in the middle of nowhere," says Triple E.

"You told her she could go," says Jeanne.

"I guess," he says.

So finally he is forced to leave her. The car is almost out of gas, the clouds are slithering in darker, meaner, spitting snow.

"Let's just keep on," says Jeanne. "I want out of this, it's scary."

HE DRIVES BACK TOWARD the highway and stops at a gas station near the edge of town. He pulls up to the full-service pump and an attendant comes out. He is a boy in overalls and a backwards baseball cap, shuffling along, hands in his pockets. He smirks at Triple E and says, "This is full-service here, dude."

"Fill'er up," Triple E tells him.

The kid shrugs. He grabs the nozzle and stands there kicking his boots together, his breath smoking, while the tank fills. When he is done and has hung up the hose, Triple E starts the car and drives away. The kid gapes after him a second, then takes off for the office, his arms waving.

A man comes out. The kid points. The man runs toward a car nearby and jumps in it, tears out onto the highway.

Says Tom, "He's after us."

Triple E speeds up. Rock walls fly by on one side, the frozen Blue Mesa Reservoir on the other. Snow is falling again.

The car behind them is gaining. The man is flashing the lights on and off and blowing his horn. Triple E rounds a long curve and feels the Oldsmobile drifting, the engine straining. He knows if they hit any ice now it is all over, they will fly into the lake, break through. Drown.

"Whoa!" says Jeanne. "Jesus, Triple E, look out! Look out!"

The rear of the Oldsmobile shucks loose, fishtails. The car drifts. Gravel spews behind them as Triple E hits the passing gear and muscles the car through the curve. The fishtailing stops and they head into another curve, snaking to the right this time, gravitating in the direction of rock that climbs crookedly into the gray sky. Again the rear of the car lets go. It slams the rock face, bounces back. A hubcap flies off. It skitters over the pavement and shoots onto the ice, keeping pace with the car for twenty or thirty yards before spinning out. Jeanne has one hand on the dashboard, the other on the seat back. She keeps muttering, "Oh God, oh God."

Triple E can see in the mirror that the car behind them is falling back.

"We're losin him," he says.

THE SNOW IS THICK as floating wool. White walls enclose the car. The walls soak up sound, creating an eerie tunnel of peace that goes on mile after mile. The motor purrs. The windshield wipers work back and forth. Triple E and his friends are quiet, watchful, expectant. The highway leaves the canyon and the river and starts climbing. Evergreens thicken. The road winds, climbs, curves. Triple E pushes speed to the edge. The tires slip now and then, but always catch in time to keep the car from rocketing into the void. The wipers can barely keep up with the snow. It's all a blur of white.

At one point, red lights abruptly flash in front of them. A

police car swishes by, slams on its brakes. Triple E can see it in the mirror, skidding as it tries to come to a stop and turn around.

"Somebody's phoned ahead," he says. "If they got our license, they know this puppy's stolen."

"Let's just stop," says Jeanne. She clutches his arm. "This isn't worth it, Triple E. Remember what happened last time we tried to outrun the cops?"

There is a scar on his forehead, where bullet fragments had knocked him down one night when the beginning of the end began. He sees the night and the long alley. He hears shots cracking in the air, the warnings to halt and then more shots and the sense of being punched, and he falls, his rifle clattering away from him. This time he and Jeanne might not be so lucky. He imagines the two of them dying in a hail of bullets à la Bonnie and Clyde. He presses harder on the gas pedal. There is no going back. All the stuff he has done, they will lock him up forever this time, throw away the key. He looks in the mirror and can no longer see the red lights.

Tom is looking too. "He quit," says Tom.

Triple E takes the next two-lane going north. He eases off the gas. The snow is letting up a bit. The car is cruising. Things are looking better.

After a few minutes of hopeful watching, Jeanne relaxes on the seat. She lights a cigarette and passes it to his lips. When she hands it to him, he can see her hand trembling. "It's gonna be okay," he says. "We'll be outta these mountains in an hour. It'll be warmer in Utah. No snow on the highways. We got it made now. Right, Tom? Two hours at the most and we can kiss Colorado goodbye." He glances over the seat at Tom.

"Fuckin cars these days, the metal's too thin, too light. There's not enough weight to hold roads like this," says Tom.

They start down. The grade is steep at first. There are some tight curves bordered by pines and broken granite. Deep gorges to fall in. A few miles on, they enter Black Canyon, the facings rising like tomahawks on both sides, craggy edges at queer angles as if threatening to fall forward and slice the road or the car in half. Flickers of light cling to the clouds above.

Once past the canyon the grade is easier. They climb and then descend. They are gradually leaving the mountains, moving toward washboard rolls of lesser hills, gentler curves. Triple E turns on the headlamps and sees snowflakes doing kamikaze dives through the beams. The road turns slushy, the tires make a sizzling sound.

As the miles accumulate, everybody starts feeling better. Jeanne's hands no longer tremble. She and Tom and Triple E laugh about the look on the attendant's face. Major geekboy. They discuss the stability of the car on the river curves. Triple E says he should have stopped early on and put some heavy rocks in the trunk to keep the back tires from slipping. He had noticed it before, how the ass-end tended to drift. Tom is right, thin metal no good.

Triple E doesn't tell them, but long before he stole the Oldsmobile, it gave him premonitions of death. He believes he will die in an Oldsmobile because when he was a little boy he saw one slip over black ice and roll into a ditch, and his father stopped to help. He and other men jumped in the ditch and started pulling on the driver, pulling him out of the wreckage and laying him on the snow, and then Triple E's father returned to the car and said the driver was dead. Triple E took it as a sign from heaven—*stay out of Oldsmobiles.* When he became a car thief at twelve, he took anything available, but not Oldsmobiles. Until this one. Two-tone green, brand new, and owned by Renee Bridgewater. There had been other makes in the Goodpasture lot, but the keys to the Olds were in his hand and he was in a hurry.

"When we get to Salt Lake, we'll trade this in on a road-hugger," he tells Tom.

"Firebird," says Tom. "Pontiac Trans Am."

Jeanne slides over and snuggles up to Triple E. He runs his hand up her skirt and they fool around. Just the feel of her smooth thigh and her head on his shoulder, the smell of her hair, makes his heart quicken. In the deepest pockets of his soul flows the essence of Jeanne, Jeanne, Jeanne, and he is awful happy she came with him. He squeezes her leg some more. She turns herself around so that she is face to face with him, half in his lap, and she kisses him, while he keeps one eye on the road.

"Watch your drivin, man," says Tom. "I don't want to die a fool."

THEY BREAK OVER A rise and can see miles down a long, slow grade. Far away are tiny red lights winking. Jeanne turns around and sits up straight. She puts her hands over her eyes, like if she can't see the red lights they don't exist.

Tom says, "A roadblock. We're big-time now." He is leaning over the seat again, his elbows between Triple E and Jeanne.

The barrier of light is a mile or so away, dinky in the distance, like lights on a Christmas tree, but there is no doubt that what they see is a roadblock. They stop the car and sit for a time staring as the wipers beat back and forth and Jeanne makes groaning noises and Tom cusses. Triple E thinks about punching the Oldsmobile and flying at the roadblock at a hundred miles an hour. Would the cops pull back? Would they shoot? Would they leave their cars in place to see if he chickens out?

Jeanne says that maybe they had better cool it. Cops in front, cops behind, what choice do they have?

Tom says they should turn around and go back. Wait for dark and then slip through Gunnison and over Monarch Pass, go to Salida or something.

Triple E remembers an access road he saw a few miles back. He wonders where it goes. "I think you should get out," he says to Jeanne. "Just walk down there and they'll take care of you. Tell them we kidnapped you."

"What're you gonna do?"

"I'm not goin back, that's for sure."

She puts her arms around him. She says, "What can they do to you, huh? Put you back in reform school? When you're eighteen they'll have to let you out. That's not so long, Triple E. It's just two years. Once we're eighteen, we can do what we want and nobody can stop us, not the law even can stop us when we're eighteen."

"Two years is forever, Jeanne. Two years. No way."

"You gonna grow wings and fly outta here?" says Tom.

Triple E chuckles. He says, "I might just grow wings if I have to, but for now I'm gonna try some road I saw back there. Maybe it has an outlet somewhere. I'm gonna find out."

Jeanne leans her head on his chest. She squeezes him. "You," she says.

"I'll send for you when I get where I'm goin," he says.

She hesitates a few seconds, then she sits up and says, "All right then let's do it."

"Is it what you want?" he says.

"Where you go, I go," she says.

"What about you, Tom?"

"I don't care. Get us the fuck outta here," says Tom.

———

TURNING THE CAR AROUND, he drives to the access road and goes north-northwest as the road winds up-down-through a clutter of hills. The car knocks against boulders and the branches of evergreens, its tires whirling in the snow and sometimes nearly stopping, but somehow he keeps the car from getting stuck, his foot to the floor, the engine roaring. He feels caught up in the grip of movement for its own sake, as a kind of pledge against the dead-white badlands all around.

He thinks about what could happen, and he curses all the wrong moves he has made and the danger he has brought to Jeanne and Tom and Ava. He glances at Jeanne, her hands on the dash again, her perfect profile like sculptured wood— Jeanne Windriver, his Indian princess, first love. She is so fine—soul-cool. She has rebelled against her parents, turned her back on them and home and every lesson she has ever learned, all for love of car thief Triple E. And now she is in the kind of trouble she couldn't have imagined only twenty-four hours before, snug in her robe, watching *Cheers* on TV, while her mother made popcorn in the kitchen and her dad in his easy chair spat tobacco juice into a coffee can.

Safe and adored then, but now her foundations are all overthrown. Triple E's destiny is her destiny, and he has no idea what his destiny will be, no idea where he is going, what he is doing. He has no plan, has no notion of what he will do if the road plays out at a ranch house or, worse yet, plays out in the middle of nowhere. In some corner of his mind, a little voice is speaking to him, telling him to give it up, that he is putting Jeanne and Tom in an impossible position, hurrying faster and faster toward zero-nada-nothing. For her sake, if you love her, go back, surrender, apologize for what you did to Mrs. Bridgewater, get back on the boxing team, go back to the barn and the Goodpasture cows, be with your buddies, your fellow j.d.'s in the dorm. What had been so bad about that? It hadn't been so bad.

But he knows he can't go back. Not there, no way. They all hate him really, they all want to beat him up, make him pay for what he did to them. What buddies? None, not any. And escaping from Goodpasture the way he did, it was the point of no return. Too many points of no return in his life. If the cops catch him, they'll fix him good, send him up to Golden or the correctional school at Buena Vista, where they know how to deal with incorrigible criminals like bad bones Triple E.

He rams the Oldsmobile up one hill and down another, unwinding from the mountains, finding the trees playing out and the car lights breaking over rolling prairie in the distance. He sees black brush and powdery snow. He sees stunted trees, and he sees some cattle. At one point he stops the car and watches a small herd nuzzling fresh bales of hay.

"We're close to somethin," he says. "There's a ranch around here."

"I feel lost," Jeanne says. "I don't know where I am."

"Just a little more," he says, trusting in luck.

"I don't like this," says Tom, his voice a whisper. "It's spooky."

They go on and pretty soon the snow is getting thicker on the road and Triple E is having to plunge the car through drift after drift, breaking a trail, following the bare outlines of the road as it winds beside some whitened arroyos. The car becomes a bulldozer sending surge after surge of powder in front of the lights.

They descend into a shallow ravine, the bottom so obliterated by snow there doesn't seem to be a road. Triple E thinks about stopping and trying to back out. He knows he will need the chains to get moving from a dead stop at such a steep angle. The chains are in the trunk, where he put them after bottoming out at Monarch Pass. He and Tom can put them on again. It would be the safe thing to do, but he decides to throw the dice. He guns the engine. The car dives into a sea of white and lurches sideways and stops. He tries reversing and rocking the car. The tires whirl.

When he and Tom get out to look, they see snow covering the rocker panels. The car is high-centered. There is nothing for the wheels to grab on to.

"We're fucked," says Tom and goes back inside.

Walking to the top of the ravine, Triple E looks around for lights in the distance, a ranch house, another car, anything; invisible flakes tick at his face. Shielding his eyes he looks and looks, but all he sees is darkness thick as pudding.

When he gets back to the car, Jeanne asks him what they are going to do, and he says he and Tom will dig the car out in the morning. He turns the lights off. The heater is on and it is warm enough. They still have plenty of gas. They can hear the wind howling and making zithering noises at the edges of the windows. The snow sweeps in front of them in ghostly sheets. Sometimes a gust of wind makes the car shudder.

THEY SIT IN THE dark eating Oreo cookies and drinking milk. They smoke cigarettes. Triple E thinks about Mrs. Bridgewater having so much faith in him, telling him he could move mountains. He wonders what she thinks about him now.

After what he did to her, she probably wants him dead, he figures. He knows he went a little crazy, a little nuts. But he's much better now. And he doesn't blame anybody who hates him. His father long ago said he was too much trouble and it's true.

"I think we should go to Idaho, don't you?" says Jeanne.

She is chewing a cookie, her breath smelling of chocolate. "I hear Idaho is God's country. People go there to start over. It was in a magazine I read. 'The Zealots of Idaho' it was called." She waits for him to say something, but he keeps quiet. "You guys could get jobs as lumberjacks. Lots of logging in Idaho."

He likes the word *lumberjack,* feels it fits the kind of rugged guy he is, a guy meant for forests and mountains, an explorer type like the men who opened the West. The old breed of *real* men. Triple E the lumberjack. And Jeanne, she could get a job as a waitress somewhere. They would get a cabin in the country. They would settle in, go to the city now and then for movies and dances and parties. Goodpasture Correctional Facility would become just a peculiar dream. The city of Stone Garden creeping like a tentacle over the prairie land, the open spaces yielding to a sprawl of houses, none of that would matter much. One day maybe he would write home and send pictures and shock hell out of all those who had written him off. It's a cheery thought.

"Yeah, Idaho maybe," he says.

LATER, AFTER TOM FALLS asleep, Triple E and Jeanne make slow, painful love, going all the way for the first time, no hesitation on Jeanne's part anymore, she's ready. No mention of the oath she swore to her parents that she would stay a virgin until she got married. Triple E penetrates her and she gives a little cry and then she lies there, her hands on his shoulders, her mouth open, her eyes closed.

Afterwards there is blood. He takes off his undershirt and gives it to her. She sits there, holding the undershirt between her legs and they talk about love, how it was probably love at first sight, only they didn't know it right away, it took some time to wake up. Triple E tells her about seeing her at school, how she was wearing her white shoes and tight blue skirt and a blue sweater and long, loopy earrings. Her hair black like blindness. And he heard somebody say, "There she is, that's Jeanne Windriver, whoa baby."

She says she remembers him always in his fatigue jacket, jeans, and tennis shoes, and his hair over his forehead, and his eyes following her, coaxing something extra into her walk.

LATER, JEANNE SLEEPS WITH her head in his lap, her legs curled on the seat. She looks like a little animal all bunched up in her furry jacket, and Triple E feels soft, feels a tenderness that settles in his chest and throat. He wants to take care of her. He wants to love her. He strokes her hair, bends down and kisses the side of her head. Then he leans back, closes his eyes, tries to sleep.

Sleeps.

HE WAKES WITH A start. He is sweating. The car is too hot. Reaching over he turns the ignition key and the hum of the motor dies. He cannot see out the windows, but he can hear what is going on. Angry gusts of wind buffet the Oldsmobile. There is a teasing, sadistic whine leaking through the car's imperfections. A sense of submerging, of suffocation, fills him. He feels the deep pool of snow rising. He looks at the ceiling and wonders how high it is now. Can he swim to the top of it? Will there be a way out in the morning?

Primitive fear. He is so puny, a bug in the grip of the storm, and his heart is inadequate and he will not be able to cope with what is coming. It is God's judgment on him for what he has done. He's not sure if there is a God, but he makes a little plea anyway. He says, "C'mon, man, what did I ever do to you?" He closes his eyes.

THE TINK OF BBs on tin cans, the shattering of glass bottles. Triple E and Chuck Pump got in some practice before turning their BB guns on each other.

The great dirt bluffs at Sand Creek. A forty-foot drop to the bottom, and Triple E wanted to push Pump off and see if he bounced. Below was the valley carved by a million years of running water. There were cattle grazing on the lush grasses. There were huge trees, their branches pasted with leaves. The wind hit the cliffs, rising upward, blowing dirt in Triple E's face.

He and Chuck played war, shooting at each other from behind brush and hills. At noon they took a rest, sitting with their legs over the edge as they surveyed the valley. Triple E had thought for some time about making a parachute and jumping off the cliffs. Once when he was younger, he made a chute of his bed sheet and got Chuck Pump to jump off the roof of the house, with the sheet tied under his armpits. Triple E held the chute open, letting the wind fill it while he urged Pump on. Pump leaped and broke his ankle that day, and Triple E got beat with the peachwood paddle and his butt was so sore he waddled like a duck.

Triple E backed away from the cliff, whirled like a gun-slinger and shot Chuck Pump in the forehead, and Pump hopped around, yowling, nearly going over the edge, until Triple E yanked him back. And Pump said, "Yeah, that'd be real funny, you turd!"

Pump rubbed his finger over the BB stuck in his forehead, shiny as a new penny. He dug it out and looked at it. "You tried to blind me," he said. Chuck grabbed him and they wrestled in the soapweed. Triple E ended up on his face in a hammerlock. And Chuck said: "The day I can't whip your ass is the day I'll

18

suck the head of your peter in the middle of Colfax Avenue on the Fourth of July!" It was something he would say a number of times over the years, but at the bluffs that day was the first time Triple E heard it. "You'll what?" he said.

When the two of them were little they were best buddies. That was before Tom Patch came along. Before then, Chuck would follow Triple E everywhere, his hand always on Triple E's shoulder, possessive. He would do what Triple E would do, say what Triple E would say, believe what Triple E believed. And that was all fine, until Tom saw them one day and said they looked like fags walking arm in arm like that. Then Triple E made Chuck keep his hands off and started snapping at him, calling him plumhead like the others did, making fun of the plum-colored birthmark on his temple.

One day Chuck went up to Tom Patch and said, "Hey you, Tom Patch. I hear you think you're bad." And Tom stepped on Chuck's foot and shoved him on his can and said, "That's right." Chuck followed Tom from then on, dogging his footsteps, hitching his pants low like Tom, wearing his shirtsleeves up like Tom, checking out the girls and leering at them the way Tom did. Chuck got heavy and bad, and that day at the cliffs when he got Triple E in a hammerlock and said he would kick his ass or suck the head of his peter, Triple E, laughing and yet almost crying from the pain in his arm, told Chuck that he sounded like a butt-bopping faggot. The words had given Chuck pause, relaxing his grip just long enough for Triple E to break away and slug him in the nose. Chuck bled all over and swore vengeance. He took off for home, holding his nose, blood pouring through his fingers.

And then there it was: the cat. It was a stray thing somebody had dumped. It came up to Triple E giving him soft cat mews, whining, begging to be friends. Triple E pet the cat until it purred. Then he thought about the roof and Pump and the parachute. The roof hadn't been high enough. Hadn't been time for the chute to open.

Triple E took off his undershirt and made holes in it for the cat's legs. He knotted the neck. He dressed the cat in the undershirt and held it where the wind shot up the bluff face. The undershirt ballooned and Triple E let the cat go. It wriggled around and tried to climb the parachute. Cat and undershirt plummeted forty feet down and hit and bounced, creating a small brown cloud. The cat got up and ran a few feet and collapsed.

Triple E hurried down and got the cat. It was bleeding from its mouth and ears. He wrapped it in the undershirt and jogged all the way to Stone Garden, to the veterinarian. The vet asked him what happened to the cat and Triple E said he had no idea, he just found the thing starving out on the prairie by the bluffs. When the vet said it was dying and there was nothing to do, Triple E's chin started trembling and he felt like he might cry. It was awful, the damned thing coming along and tempting him that way. "And look what happens to you," he said, rubbing the cat's soft ear.

"What did you say?" said the vet.

"I'm bad luck," said Triple E.

"GEEZ, I THOUGHT I had forgotten that," he whispers.

Jeanne stirs. "What, honey?" she says.

"Go to sleep," he says. "It's nothin." He strokes her arm, her hair. Kisses her hair. Her hair smells smoky, sexy.

Another gust of wind slams into the car and the snow is swept from the windshield for a moment, but there is nothing much to see, ghost-flakes licking at the glass. Triple E starts the car, welcomes the heat. The digital clock says 1:48, a tiny pulse of red light counts the seconds ticking away.

"God, listen to that wind," Jeanne whispers.

AFTER THE WIND DIES down and the snow piles up, insulating the car, it stays warm for longer and longer periods. Triple E falls into a deep sleep around two-thirty with the gas gauge near the three-quarter mark. When he wakes five hours later, the car is like a sauna inside. He hurriedly shuts the motor down and cracks a window, putting his mouth to the crack and sucking crisp, clean air. He sucks some snow into his mouth and feels it melting, trickling down his hot throat. The gas gauge is now a tick above one-half.

Tom Patch coughs and he says, "I gotta headache, I gotta piss." And he tries to open the door, but can't. "Christ, what's this?" he says. "Are we buried alive?" He rolls down the window and starts digging a way through the snow wall. He plunges into it, wiggling his way out of the car.

"I gotta go too," says Jeanne.

Triple E rolls his window down and pushes aside the snow and climbs out. He sees clouds touching the earth from horizon to horizon, the clouds closing round them like walls. The wind nibbles at his face. He can feel snow settling on his stubble hair, wetting his scalp.

"It's scary," Jeanne says as she comes out behind him and looks around.

"Tom and me will get us outta here," he tells her.

"You think so?" says Tom, his voice scornful. He is pissing in the snow, writing his name. tOm PAtcH.

Jeanne squats while Triple E holds her hand to keep her from falling over. He sees the snow melting yellowish beneath her bottom. Her ass touches the snow and she squeals. When she is done he takes his turn. Then they climb back into the car.

Jeanne uses Triple E's blood-spotted undershirt to dry herself. He lies down, his knees up, his head in her lap, while she rubs her thumb round and round the indentation on his forehead. The indentation is white and oblong and shiny, an emblem of when he nearly got his head blown off.

"We're gonna need help," says Tom, his tone filled with annoyance. "No way we're unstickin this piece of Cutlass Ciera crap by ourselves." He is leaning over the seat, eating a Twinkie and slurping milk from the jug, setting the jug on Triple E's stomach after each drink. Between bites he tells them he is going back to the highway and flag somebody down. Everybody in these parts has a four-wheel drive. That's what they need to pull the car out, a four-wheel drive.

Triple E tries to talk Tom out of it, saying it is too far to the highway, and even if he got there, no one will want to drive a four-by down some treacherous, lousy road and risk getting stuck. The cops are probably still sniffing around too. They will catch Tom.

But Tom won't listen. He is going and that's that. He doesn't think it's far.

"I'll be back in no time," he says. He stuffs some cookies in his pocket and gets out. He is wearing a leather jacket with chrome studs and a black knit cap. He has good boots on. Triple E and Jeanne watch him bend his head into the wind and climb to the top of the ravine. He turns and waves and shouts something, his words scattering in the wind. Snow swirls around him playfully and then he disappears.

"Tom Patch, you can't talk to that mungo," says Triple E. "He thinks he knows everything."

"No, he *knows* he knows everything," says Jeanne, her voice catty.

Triple E looks at the tracks and the spot at the crest where Tom sunk away. The seconds tick by. The wind erases Tom's footprints, and the snow shifts around, making restless patterns that come and go. It's as if live things are crawling underneath, giant snow worms or something.

CHAPTER

THE WIND. ALWAYS THE wind. Piercing, threatening, deadly cold. On the other side of the mountains is Gunnison. West is Utah, rolling plains, more snow, then the desert and dirt and sea-level salt. East onward are more mountains, Monarch Pass, the Continental Divide, the eastern slope, Goodpasture, Denver, Aurora, Stone Garden. Safety. Punishment.

More snow has piled up since Tom Patch went in search of help. The Oldsmobile is encased in snow. Triple E rolls down the window and tunnels out again, and what he sees makes his pulse hammer. The snow has filled in the hollow of the road, burying everything, chaparral and all, creating gnomish shapes and a wispy white marshmallow pond all around. It is as if time has stopped, as if now everything will age frozen and unchanged until the universe eats itself.

He kicks his knees high, bulldozing his way through powder to the top of the ravine, where the road crests. At the edge
of the incline, he looks back at the car, its green shafts of color
showing, like shadows bleeding through the snow. He lowers
his eyes, looks down at his snow-encased ankles and calves.
His Goodpasture shoes are already soaked. His toes are already
freezing. Wherever he looks he sees nothing but pale desola-
tion. The wind snatches at his hair and coat, plasters his pants
to his thin legs. Snow patters his face. Squinting his eyes
against the wind, he searches the clouds pressing down on him
and feels trivial. He looks in the direction that Tom took and
wonders if he should go after him, or maybe try the other
direction, where logic tells him there is a rancher, the one who
feeds the cattle.

"What am I gonna do?" he says. He looks with resignation
at the car. Hopelessly stuck. Wading back, he begins sweeping
his arms over the trunk, throwing powder into the wind. He
cleans behind the bumper, makes an exhaust chimney for the
smoke. Once the lid is cleared, he has Jeanne pull the inside
release and the trunk pops open.

He sees the spare and a jack, the tire chains, a set of golf
clubs, a piece of Astroturf. There is a toolbox too. And a box
filled with books. *Art and Soul: A Search for Spirituality in a
Technocratic World* is the title of the book on top. Its author is
Renee Bridgewater. He hands the book through the window to
Jeanne. "This is the lady from Goodpasture," he says. "Told you
she was smart." He takes another book from the box: *Pastoral
Symphony,* a thin volume of poems by someone named V. J.
Chouinard. The little book has a holstein on the cover and a
man in a baseball cap with his arm wrapped around the cow's
neck. Cow and man have faraway eyes. He hands the poems to
Jeanne, then goes back to the trunk. He takes the golf clubs

out and the piece of Astroturf, closes the trunk, then bulls his way back up the hill and stomps a spot in the snow where he can set the turf and a golf ball. Choosing a wooden-headed driver, he starts whacking golf balls, shooting them like bullets into the sky, sending them with the wind. He sees the balls climb, then disappear white on white.

"Maybe I should'a been a golfer," he says. Mrs. Bridgewater had asked him once about his ambitions, and he told her he had no ambitions. She gave him books, and he read them and he learned about Franz Kafka and others and he started wondering if words knew the way. Ambition hooked him briefly, little daydreams about being like her, a smart-ass Ph.D. But then he lost faith. Words coming from her mouth wandered over him empty as air, unable to *do* anything, unable to physically take hold and change anything.

And he shifted his thinking toward Coach Tozer Douglas instead. Few words, lots of action: teach tough kids how to box, how to do it fair, how to do it like a game with rules, and not like it was life or death in the streets. Triple E started seeing himself as a prizefighter, a middleweight, or maybe even a heavyweight, battling his way to the top. A hero. The champ. Women falling all over him. Men backing off, lowering their eyes with respect. Here comes the champ, that's Triple E, the champ. *Triple E, Triple E,* his name echoing through the ages.

He had always been willing to mix it up, no matter how scared he was. Ever since he was little at school in Stone Garden and cats messing with him to see if he had anything or was he going to be a baby and run home to mama. He learned early to swallow the fear and not mind the pain. He learned to go for the face, for the nose especially. He learned to use his hands, to use his speed and give five for one, tattoo the nose, make the bastard's eyes water, make him blind and afraid. He had learned to get his punches in first, to let loose fast and furious at any hint of a fight coming, take the heart out of the other guy. He had made himself a reputation by the time he was ten. Big guys like Chuck Pump might still mess with him, but nobody his own size, not unless it was some rival from another school or somewhere else who didn't know how bad Triple E was. It had seemed to him by the time he was fifteen and the vacant lots east of Stone Garden had turned to houses and stores that there was nothing more to life than fighting and fucking and smoking dope, playing it cool, hanging out, looking for trouble, building the rep.

Looking around at the rolling world in front of him bitter as salt, he shakes his head and wonders how he went from bone-bad, streetwise badass boy from Stone Garden, Colorado, to a speck of nothing, a stinkbug wandering in the wilderness.

"How did this happen?" he says aloud.

"What you doin, Triple E?" says Jeanne, calling from the car.

"I'm figurin!" he tells her.

"Figuring what? You got a plan? I hope to God you got a plan, Triple E."

"I've always got a plan," he says.

He tosses the golf clubs in the drift beside the car and climbs back inside. He strips his shoes and socks off, sets them on the floor in front of the blower. He shimmies out of his pants and shakes the snow off, drapes his pants over the seat, legs hanging in back to drip dry. Fiddling with the radio, he finds a station playing an oldie called "In the Still of the Night."

. . . *I held you . . . he-eld you ti-ight . . .*

"Look at your legs," says Jeanne. His legs are red and goose-pimply. He flips them across her lap and she massages them and his feet. Her hands feel smooth and gentle. Her touch reminds him of the times when he was little and his stomach ached and his mother would rub it round and round, soothe the pain away. He got ulcers by the time he was nine and had to take a medicine that made his mouth feel like cotton.

"Rub my stomach," he tells Jeanne.

Jeanne runs her hand under his shirt and rubs his stomach. She rubs low in circles, the circles going down, down, until she is rubbing his hairs. She has a naughty smile on her face. "What's that thing there?" she says.

"Blind Mole Joe," says Triple E.

She turns his skivvies down and examines him. "How can somethin so little get so big?" she says. She turns it this way and that. She looks under the testicles, lifting them, searching out each ball with her fingertips. "Smooth," she says. "Does it hurt?"

"Feels good," he tells her.

She lifts his penis, stares into its blind eye. She lays her cheek on it, rubs it back and forth. "Funny weird," she says.

He listens to the song on the radio saying what he is thinking, that he will never let her go in the still of the night. The wind whips the car, tears at the windows, makes his heart nervous. He can hear a bee-like buzz coming from the heater fan.

"Guys call him joebuck?" she says.

"Joebuck. Yeah, that's one of its names."

"How come?"

He thinks about the origin of joebuck. He learned it from some older kids and had used it for years before he found out that joebuck came from a movie called *Midnight Cowboy*. In the movie there was a stud and his name was Joe Buck. He tells her about it and she nods. She's not really interested, he can tell. Her attention is elsewhere. He watches her hand move. It is a small, dark, Indian hand, fine bones, the faintest trace of blue veins running from the middle knuckle toward her wrist. Red polish on the nails. A sweet young hand.

"Like what I'm doing?" she asks.

"Mmmm," he murmurs.

Her voice gets serious and low, a bit husky. "The things we've done, Triple E. I mean, who would believe it? Some people live their whole lives and it's all the same humdrum stuff, but not us. We've had somethin special, I think, don't you? My mom said I'm too young to know what real love is, but I don't think so. I know I love you, and I don't care about nothin as long as I'm with you. I'm glad I came no matter what happens." Her words are wobbly. Triple E can see sudden tears glistening on her lashes.

"Don't worry, Jeanne, I'll get us outta here," he says. "I'm not lettin nothin happen to you. Come here."

She bends to him and they kiss. He moves his hand up inside her sweater and massages her breast. Over her shoulder he can see the snow pressing against the glass, like jagged stars mashed together, plastered to all the windows, separating them from a frozen world by a mere quarter of an inch. The music fades on the word *night.* And they look at each other and the wind moans and the small heater buzzes like a hive.

THEY MAKE LOVE SO desperate hard that morning that Jeanne gets sore. She says she has to rest, and so they sit up and eat cookies and drink milk. Then they smoke and go through the books from the trunk. Jeanne opens Mrs. Bridgewater's *Art and Soul* and reads aloud from its introduction:

30

For the majority of people in the late twentieth century, *Enlightenment* has proved chimeric. And why shouldn't it? The mind's limit for understanding its own *raison d'être* has been reached and has found (especially in science) an abyss where it hoped answers would be. We grudgingly acknowledge the need for science, but its stifling materialism saddens us and fills us with anxiety. We turn desperately toward the world of the body, briefly solid and able to give us an experience of being alive, which is what we want—and which only the flesh *knows* in certain intense moments that are routinely connected with sex and/or violence. Jesus gives way to the Marquis de Sade and we wallow in our passion for *nature* omnipotent, which relieves us, as the gods once did, of all responsibility for what we do to one another. In the name of passion and procreation, we forgive ourselves for all our sins.

In a time of spiritual emptiness and angst and acting out, what stands between us and the disintegration of the soul and a life spent metaphorically running on all fours? Nothing but the habit of art. Which is why we who hang on however tenuously to the life of the mind drag our flesh forward to the altar of the world's art and make *it* our god. And we say God is Art, or Art is God. It is an inner call and an outer doctrine that keeps us going. We cling to the divinity of art as others cling to Jesus or Mother Mary, Krishna or New Age crystals—because we know in our hearts that those who live without an inner call or an outer doctrine are hopelessly desperate and lost. They are the doomed children of nature, crucified by an indifferent world and condemned at last to the same ageless, meaning-less oblivion that rolled over the universe long before they were ever born. The plurality and iconography of art can circumvent such a dismal destiny of the mind. Art is . . .

Jeanne stops reading and looks up from the page. "What do you think of this?" she asks.

"That's her. She said a million times we'd all behave better if we were taught to love art. She said it would make us sensitive to evil and more likely to do good. She had some right-minded ideas, I suppose. For a different world. If it was a different world from what it is. If people weren't such god-damn assholes." He pauses to puff on his cigarette, his mind busy. Then he adds: "She believed way too much in books. Faith in the *Words*, know what I mean? Like words had this power to fix everything. It's . . . I don't know, she wasn't in touch with mean mother-earth, the reality. Smart in some ways, dumb as a dick in others."

Jeanne tosses the book on the backseat and picks up the poetry by V. J. Chouinard. She reads to herself, while Triple E stares at the snow on the windshield and thinks about his last moments with Renee Bridgewater, her eyes wide-horrified, her pants down, pubic patch and fleshy legs exposed. His fists like clubs above her, ready to play Humpty Dumpty with her head.

"Oh, listen to this," Jeanne says. "You'll like this, I bet. It's called 'Shipping Curious Cow':

> *Young cow, just ripening teenager*
> *in human terms, loam black except for a*
> *heart-patch of white between her eyes—*
> *bulging curious eyes wondering*

why she stands before the barn door—
leans her muzzle against my wrist
and roughly licks.
    I pat her neck and say,
      "Forgive me, girl."
The shipper comes with his electric prod
and forces her to climb
the ramp.
    "She wouldn't settle," I tell him
for the umpteenth time, nervous and guilty,
wishing I could think
of a way to save her.
    "Can't keep them
if they don't make babies," he says.
    He hands me a check
      which I fold in my pocket.
Four days pass and then my
shirt comes through the wash—
the check still there.
    Faded and flaking, I pull it out
and think of Curious unsettled
and see my name on the line
faint as the veins
in a young girl's breast.

Jeanne says, "How sad, gee, he must be a nice man to write a poem about his cow."

Says Triple E, "Yeah, well, every cow eventually has to go. That's the thing: Burger-King is waitin."

"I don't want to think about it," says Jeanne. And then she says, "I'm gonna become a vegetarian. Let's be vegetarians, Triple E. Let's raise our kids to hate meat."

"Okay," says Triple E.

She is leafing backward through the poetry. She stops and points and says, "Hey, look at this. Renee Bridgewater signed this book to you, Triple E. Look, here's your name. She must've been gonna give you this."

He takes the book from Jeanne and looks at the dedication:

For Elbert Earl Evans—"Triple E"—
who has more poetry in his soul than he knows—
RENEE BRIDGEWATER

"Oh, Christ no," he says. "She was gonna give me this." He runs his hand over her name. "Jesus, I bet she wishes she'd never met me now, after what I did to her."

"Did you hurt her?" says Jeanne.

For a second he wonders if he should tell the truth. But a lie comes much more natural. "Am I the kinda lowlife motherfucker would hurt a woman?" He flips through the book, turning the pages, reading a line here, a line there. The poems are all about a farm and how tough it is to survive the winters in Minnesota. Triple E likes the book. He slips it inside the breast pocket of his jacket.

AROUND ELEVEN THAT MORNING the storm breaks up. The clouds start coming apart, letting rays of sunshine through. Triple E says no more waiting for Tom, it is time to get help. He crawls out the window. Jeanne follows him. They go to the crest of the road and look around at the glittering mounds of wasteland, snow-mist slithering on the wind toward the curve of the horizon.

"This is godawful," she says, kicking her suede boots together and hugging herself. Her hair keeps blowing across her face, her furry coat collar flaps against her cheek. "How you suppose Tom is doing? Should we wait for him some more?"

"You better go back to the car," Triple E says. He looks at her skirt and her white boots with the little leather ears slapping against her shins. Her exposed legs show the heart-shaped scar on her left calf. "I'll go this way and check it out," he tells her, pointing north. "If Tom comes back, tell him to wait, I'll be back in a couple hours. I'll see if I can find that rancher who dumped the hay we saw. He's gotta have a four-wheel drive or a tractor. He'll pull us out, that's what. I got this feelin."

"I'm numb," she says. "It's even colder than when it was snowing. God, I wish I had worn my jeans," she says.

He embraces her, reaches down with grateful hands and squeezes her lovely butt. "You're prime," he tells her.

She nods. She puts her arms around him and they kiss and their lips are cold. "Don't take long," she tells him.

He watches her wade back to the car and go through the window and roll it up tight. The exhaust curls cleanly from the back of the car. He wants to go with her. He wants to be in the car, kissing her soft lips. He looks again in the direction Tom took, and he gets this shuddering premonition that Tom isn't coming back and that nobody will be out looking for himself and Jeanne and there won't be anything to eat once all the cookies are gone. The gas gauge is just below the half mark and will probably be empty by nightfall. It is up to him, he thinks. It is do or die. The window comes down again and she looks out.

"Come kiss me!" she cries.

He wades back through the snow, to her mouth.

HE GOES WEST ALONG what seems to be the outlines of the road. Before him the landscape glistens gold in the slant of the sun, swirling like a sea of sunburnt wheat. The wind makes his eyes ache, they water and the water freezes on his lashes and he has to brush it off with his fingers. He stomps through the snow, stopping often to scoop snow into his mouth, gobs of it. He is so thirsty, he can't eat enough snow. Before very long he is panting and the moisture from his mouth is freezing to his lips, his nose, his eyebrows. He keeps taking his hands from his pockets and slapping his face and ears to get the blood moving.

Within an hour or so, he can hardly feel his feet. He actually walks out of one shoe and it is several yards before he notices it and retraces his steps. The shoe tongue is stiff as a knife. His hands are too cold to tie the strings together. He beats his hands on his thighs until some feeling comes back. He makes a knot in the shoestring. His fingertips pulse with pain, like invisible needles are jabbing them.

"This is real bad," he tells himself. Again he searches the shifting fields, the implacable horizons. There has to be a rancher somewhere to put out hay for the cows he saw. Has to be. He pictures a house: smoke rising from the chimney, warmth blasting him as the door opens and a lady with kind eyes invites him in. Maybe over the next rise. Maybe only one more and there it will be. He thinks of eggs frying in a pan sunny-side up, some toast and jelly, some hot, creamy coffee.

Each rise shows him nothing but more snow and more rolling land. He keeps pushing himself, fighting frostbite, thinking that his toes might have to be chopped off, that his fingers might have to go too—if he doesn't find some warmth *soon*. His lashes freeze again and he can't see well and he limps off the road, finds himself tumbling down an embankment. A little avalanche buries him when he hits bottom.

In a panic he thrashes around. He digs himself out and gasps for air. He shakes snow off his head, clears his nostrils and ears, slaps his face until it stings. He makes spitting noises, and he cries out, "Mama . . . Mama-Mama!" Looking into the pale sky, the cold sun, he searches for a sign, an omen of some kind that will tell him not to worry, that everything is going to be all right. He can't die. He is way too young to die. A kid like him has to have a future. Isn't he special? Mrs. Bridgewater said he was special, a Kafka kind of guy, she said. The special ones don't die till they've done what they came for. He frowns at the word *special*.

Nobody is special. He talks himself out of it, tells himself he isn't special, best to face the truth. Like everyone else, he is in the grip of forces way beyond his control and they will decide on a whim just what his fate will be.

Triple E looks longingly toward the sky. Far away he sees a speck crossing the universe, leaving a trail of vapor behind. It is an airplane. He watches it float along like a fairy. He wonders how many people are up there comfy in their seats, having drinks, eating lunches, looking out the plane's windows at the terrible earth, none of them suspecting that a human being is freezing to death in a ditch on the western slope of the foothills of Colorado.

He sees the snow burying him until spring, until the rains and the warm winds wash it away, exposing him to crows and coyotes working him over like they did Too Far Tim, the boy from Goodpasture who lost his way in the woods, gnawing him to bits, the animals spreading him through the bushes and the underground dens. He watches rain and wind erode the earth, creating slides to cover what is left of him. Over eons of time the earth hardens into rock. A million centuries pass and ten thousand species become extinct. Then some living thing with a digging tool digs up his bones and calls him a scientific name. His bones are put in plaster, dried in an oven, mounted in a museum. Creatures come to see him and give guesses as to who he was and how he died.

TRIPLE E FORCES HIMSELF to climb back to the road and go on. He stumbles to the next ridge and the next and at its crest he sees a wall of hills closing him in, and endless body rising, sagging, like a giant sleeping on its side. He turns away disheartened, falls again and rolls onto his back. A pair of birds fly by. He watches as they dip close, skimming over the snow, doing a three-sixty overhead to check him out. Then they go away, full of freedom, picture-perfect white on a blue canvas sky, little puffs of practically nothing.

He thinks about his father, about when his father showed up at the jail one time drunk, smelling of cow blood and old sweat, his eyes leaking sorrow. He had taken Triple E's hand through the bars, his touch as delicate as an eyelash, and he said, "God's curse. You're not the son I asked for. Why can't you be? Why can't you?"

Triple E struggles to his feet and stands in the wind, blinking his eyes. As he looks toward a valley far away he thinks he sees something shaped like a house. A tiny, snow-blotted rectangle, and beside it is another building, something larger, a barn. There is a broad, downward slope in front of him, leading to a valley, mounds of snow-choked brush, bitterbrush, sage, all of it stretching onward toward a distant rise that flows into more hills and eventually into the teeth of the mountains.

The sight of the buildings makes him laugh out loud. "Told you!" he shouts. "Told you! Hah!" His voice is unrecognizable.

It sounds like his father's voice. It sounds gruff. He waves his arms. "Here! Here I am!" He hurries toward the buildings, trotting, jogging, falling. Oh yes, oh yes! He will knock on the door and explain what has happened. The good people will bring him inside, put him by a fire, bring him hot soup. Phone calls will be made. Rescue teams assembled. He wants fried eggs and bacon and toast and coffee, that's what he wants! Everything's all right now, Jeanne. Didn't Triple E tell you?

He sees her looking at him with cooing eyes. He has saved her life. She is proud of him, loves him, loves him unto death us do part. She knows there is no one like Triple E anywhere else on the face of the earth. *God bless you, Triple E. God bless you, my love.*

"Run," he tells himself. "Hurry, hurry." It's something he can do. He's a runner, a runner, a runner.

"Move your ass," says his father. "You save that girl and I'll forgive you everything you done."

"Watch me, Dad. Just watch me!"

He is running, stumbling, running. His father's voice keeps coaxing, keeps telling him things, keeps after him as it always has—as it always will.

CHAPTER 3

IT IS A LONG way. A lot farther than it looked. The house in the valley still seems tiny as a toy. Triple E is tired. He is hungry. He rests against a snow drift, burrows into its softness and eats snow. He can't get enough of eating snow. Above him clouds go by swift and broken. The sun is still in the east, climbing toward noon.

He coughs. He searches his pockets for cigarettes, finds one and lights it. He is calmer now. More confident. He will rest, have a cigarette, eat more snow, and then get to the bottom of the valley and let himself be rescued. He thinks about his parents, about what they must be saying, his friends in school, his teachers, the j.d.'s at Goodpasture—everybody hates him: not worth the powder it would take to blow his bony ass to bits.

He is one of those rags on a stick you see hanging out on corners, loitering in alleys smoking dope, prowling through stores with sticky fingers. Slouching shoulders. Scuffed Converse blacktops padding along cat quiet—that is Triple E in Stone Garden, before he got locked up at Goodpasture Correctional Facility. Low-class teen typical, he catches the stares of passersby, who shake their heads and wonder what the world is coming to. *Look at that. Why don't somebody just shoot him and get it over with? Is that the future of America? God help us.*

He knows it's true, not many people would miss him if, like a bad cold or the flu, he was to fade away at last. He knows he is worthless. He knows that his kind never grows up, never becomes *respectable,* never manages to support the system. The only thing he has going for him as far as he can tell is the swiftness of his hands and feet. He can fight like a badger. He can move like a prairie wind. Nature itself does not abhor a Triple E.

He got started running early, running from gangbangers, running from his father, running from the cops, running from his life. And by the time he was fourteen, he was such an accomplished runner that he set a junior high school record for the 440-yard dash. So he had that going for him, he was a runner and he was good with his fists. The basics needed to survive.

He is from Stone Garden, east of Denver. The people who live there like to call it the "City in the Country." They have an ordinance that every store fronting East Colfax Avenue has to have a facade of flagstone. Red, like the reddish rocks in the Garden of the Gods and Red Rocks Theater. The same sort of rock breaks out around Estes Park and over Vail Pass and other places where Triple E has been with his father hunting and fishing. He remembers learning in school how Colorado got its name—from something Spanish that meant "color red." Nature's blood and sun, veins of it jumping up all over the west, breaking through granite and packed clay old as the earth itself, the same thin crust of soil mile after mile—red rock jutting from it suddenly, like a sock in the eye.

HE LIES ON THE snowbank and sees the red storefronts on the street he has walked ten thousand times. He sees himself stealing from those stores, running off with his loot, pretending that he has been spotted and people are chasing him. He likes the story of a boy who runs. He likes being chased. He thinks he will run until he catches himself, until in running he discovers who he is. Not just under his clothes, but at the core, where the real Triple E is waiting to be discovered. He recalls his father once calling him a hollow boy. Saying to him: "If I poked a hole in you with my finger nothing but dust would come out. You're a hollow boy, a boy made of dust." He wonders about that, if it's true. He sees his father at the slaughterhouse, killing-wand in hand, leaning over the cow closure, and the wand popping on the cow's head and the cow falling instantly dead. And another one forced up the ramp. It too dispatched. And another. And another. And his father's eyes are flat and lifeless, the soul in hiding.

"Who is hollow? Who has dust coming out?" says Triple E, scooping snow into his mouth, melting it on his dry tongue.

Behind the drift, he is out of the wind, and the sun's rays are actually warming him. The weather is not so bad behind the drift. He knows he should get up and get on to the farmhouse and save Jeanne. But he wants to think a minute. He has just had an insight, a brief revelation about the night L.D. got gangbanged and how that act led to consequences that ultimately got him six months in Goodpasture. A little beam of truth has come to him about that night. It was the jumping-off point. Geronimo.

TRIPLE E AND TOM Patch were riding around in a stolen Chevy looking for trouble, when Triple E told Patch what was going down with cousin Ava, and Patch complained that Ava wanted him to marry her and what a joke, Jesus Christ. Cats his age can't be talkin no marriage. He never said he loved Ava, never promised anything. She was the one practically forced him to put his arrow in her quiver.

Triple E told him he ought not put the wood to Ava.

"Why?" Tom said.

"Cuz she's my cousin, man."

"Cuz she's my cousin, man," said Tom Patch. And he said Triple E didn't know Ava, that Ava was like her mother, a big slut, slutty to the gills. A fellow didn't have to work for it, Ava jumped his bones. And so what can a girl like that expect?

Triple E knew it was true enough, that Ava in her hunger for love would let a guy do anything he wanted. Ever since her parents had gotten divorced, she had been chasing boys. She opened herself for whoever she was with, her whole attitude begging for something that she never really got. Triple E had always liked her, and he felt sorry for her, but felt revulsion too. She was a nervous little bird, chin trembling, tears available at the first harsh word. Way too needy. Way too much desperation in her eyes. She wasn't going to get what she wanted draping herself all over an outlaw like Tom Patch.

Triple E considered punching him, but Tom was driving. And also he thought Tom might be able to kick his ass. It was in the realm of possibility. He had seen him in action plenty of times, and he knew Tom didn't let up with just a few punches. He liked to get a mungo down and kick him, work his head and

44

his ribs, he liked that. He wanted broken bones, busted noses, cracked teeth. Triple E had his own wild style, but it was upright, *mano a mano,* and when a guy went down, Triple E usually let him get up to fight some more if he wanted. It was the skill, the *sweet science* as someone called it, that Triple E admired. He figured if he ever got into it with Tom, it would have to be all-out, fists, feet, knees, elbows, teeth, fight him to the death.

He wasn't in the mood to get himself killed over Ava. People had these lives they *had* to live. It was written in the stars, his mother said. The stars and the eclipses of the sun and moon making us villains or heroes by heavenly compulsion.

THEY PICKED UP CHUCK Pump and Jasper John, and the four of them went over to Liquor Barn, bopping down the aisles, and while the other boys provided cover, Triple E put a quart of ouzo inside his army fatigue jacket and walked out with it. They drove around the backstreets of Stone Garden, passing the bottle back and forth. Chuck Pump grinned his evil ways at them, claiming that ouzo stuck to his lips like pussy juice and the fine fellows all agreed it did. They discussed what they should do and Jasper John said he had talked to L.D. and she was babysitting at a house not far away. So they went over there because L.D. was heavy prime and she put out. They drove over and talked their way inside, and it wasn't only L.D. Jeanne Windriver was there too. The girls had some pot, a baggy of it.

EVERYBODY GOT LOOSE. PUMP flopped on the couch between L.D. and Jeanne, and fed them ouzo. He took over the conversation, telling them dirty jokes, making them squeal with laughter. Jeanne was wearing her trademark short-short denim skirt and a sweater, and Triple E kept seeing flashes of panty as she leaned back on the sofa, wiggling her knees in and out like her legs were laughing at Pump's jokes too.

Chuck Pump had his arm possessively draped over L.D.'s shoulder. He told the joke about the guy standing outside a window and eating corn on the cob, which a woman was throwing out after using it as a dildo up her snatch, and the guy kept saying, Pass me some more of that hot-buttered corn! L.D. and Jeanne made faces over that one and said Pump was disgusting. He leaned back satisfied. He turned serious eyes on L.D. and told her the word was she stuffed socks in her bra.

L.D. looked at her breasts thrusting seriously against her father's shirt she was wearing and she said her mambas were one hundred percent trueblue bonafidee L.D.

Chuck said, "Well the word is they ain't. Tell her, man."

The others agreed *ain't* was the word, though they all knew it wasn't the word and that everyone knew L.D. was genuine.

The boys, and even Jeanne, were staring at L.D.'s breasts.

"Let me find out if they're real," said Chuck. "I'm foreman of the truth squad." He reached for her, and she knocked his hand away, said it was no way she was letting him touch her beauties. She was laughing when she said it, but Chuck got mad. He didn't think she was funny. He said it was her dad's socks for sure. He said he knew a girl who cut the tips off turkey basters and cupped them over her tits and it made them look pointed as anvils. He asked L.D. did she want everybody talking trash like that about her? "Let me lay the hand of man on you, clear things up once and for all," he said.

L.D. looked at Triple E, her head cocking to the side, a little smile creasing her lips. She said she would let only him verify her anvils.

Triple E said, "Hunh?"

46

Chuck's jaw clenched. He spoke through his teeth, asking, "Why goddamn Triple E, man? Ain't the Pumper good enough?"

TRIPLE E CACKLES, HIS breath visible in the air as he thinks about Chuck Pump, sees Chuck Pump as he looked that night, Pump at seventeen, the oldest. His skin reddish, his face permanently flushed as if he has a sunburn. Marine-style haircut. Birthmark near his temple looking like a squished grape. Piggish eyes and upturned nostrils. Mouth and jaw like a bench vise. Pump's ambition is to become a porno star. He says he is a natural for porno movies and that one day everyone will see his joebuck on the screen and he will be famous. Girls don't like Chuck very much, not even L.D., who has a murky reputation herself.

WORKING UP A SNIT, snarling at L.D., Pump made out that he was a bad hombre to cross, but she kept googie eyes pasted on Triple E, and she said only he could do it, only Triple E could give her the truth test.

Triple E went woozy with her looking at him. L.D. was big. All that flesh unnerved him. He glanced over to Jeanne, who appealed to his sense of beauty much more. She was pure prime in a lean way. But she had crossed her legs tight and had put on a stony face when Pump started in on L.D. Jeanne looked different with her face scrunched. She made Triple E think of a hide-chewing squaw squatting in front of a teepee. Pressed lips and pissed-off eyes. He wondered if she was mad because L.D. was getting all the attention, or because of the subject matter. Jeanne, the army brat. Her father stationed at Fitzsimmons Army Hospital in Aurora. She was new to school back then, untested territory. Triple E had heard she was a virgin, which in itself made her more interesting than the other girls he knew.

HE SMILES TO HIMSELF and rolls the cigarette between his finger and thumb, watches the smoke waver and rise like L.D. getting up from the couch, holding out her hand to him. He remembers how he took her hand, how eager for it, taking her hand and going with her into the bedroom to check her anvils.

AS SOON AS THE door closed, she wrapped him up in her big arms, kissed him, her mouth open, tongue probing and drooling and a little overwhelming. Dutifully he put his hand on her breast, gave it a squeeze. She moved her lips to his neck and sucked up a hickey, and then told him to be careful because her breasts were tender.

"How come?" he asked her.

"They get that way," she said.

He put his hands over them. It was nice, it was fun. New flesh.

HE TAKES A HANDFUL of snow and rubs his face with it. "Geez," he says, "I wonder what she saw in me?" He can't imagine what it was. Big L.D. Willowy Jeanne Windriver. The other girls in his life who came along smiling and giving him the eye, giving him their lips, their bodies to play with. Whatever did they see? He looks at the palm of his hand, then its backside. His palm is callused, the backside is red, veiny, rough. There are cold cracks in the first and second knuckles, like the tiny red mouths of baby snakes. His hand is like an old man's hand. It amazes him that this ugly hand ever dared fondle the fine soft skin of girls.

———

HE OPENED HER SHIRT and looked at her bra and the bloat of flesh pressing against it. Putting his palm under first one breast, then the other, he lifted them, guessing their weight, guessing maybe two pounds of pure bovinity. When he let go, her breasts settled downward like bags of bread dough.

She led him to the bed, pulled him down on top of her and kissed him some more and said she loved the kissing part most of all and she could kiss him all night because he had the nibbliest mouth.

He looked at her face. She had small eyes, a small nose, and duck lips that all but hid her teeth. Her hair was fluffy, it smelled of marijuana. She undid her shirt all the way and lifted her bra over mountains of vanilla. He could see tiny blue veins in them and the nipples were smooth and very pale. She pushed his face against one and told him to go ahead.

She smelled mildly of stale day-old sweat. Her nipple tasted salty. He didn't really like it. He didn't really like her.

So he was somewhat relieved when Pump walked in and said: "Well, what's the verdict, mungo man?" The other boys were standing behind Pump, looking over his shoulders. Eager. Silly. Serious. Pump's eyes had fastened onto L.D.'s breasts. "Yo, she gots em good," he said, rubbing his hands together, warming them for her.

She was getting up, adjusting her bra. Pump stopped her. Told her not to hide those *purty thangs,* not to be so selfish with them. Nature's gifts were meant to be shared. She stood beneath the overhead light, round-shouldered and covering her breasts with crossed arms. There was vacillation in her eyes. She studied Triple E. He looked at her, trying to read what she wanted.

Pump called her star-stuff and asked her how old she was, but she didn't answer. Pump said she looked eighteen and ready for the pornos. She licked her big lips, then let them hang cretin-like glistening, while Pump shoved her forearm aside and ran fingers round and round a nipple. "It's getting hard," he said.

"C'mon, don't," she said. "Be nice, Chuckie." But she wasn't moving, she wasn't doing anything to stop him. She was passive, docile, almost paralyzed.

Pump told her he was planning to be nice. He said she had great skin and the sweetest ass and the sexiest lips. Porno star material. They could get gigs as a couple. There was major coin in it. And fame. He named some porno stars who had made it big.

And he said, "Stick with me you'll be fartin through silk." His hand slid down and started playing with her ass.

He said: "You like a man who takes charge, baby?"

She kept looking at Triple E. "I meant for just you and me," she told him. Her lower lip was trembling. "We were bein so nice, Triple E. Don't you like me?"

The other boys had surrounded her and were using their hands. Tom was kissing the back of her neck. Jasper was rubbing her belly down and down. Chuck was on his knees kissing her bottom, whispering something in her rear.

"Get off me," she said, but her voice was quiet and she didn't move an inch. Her eyes flashed at Triple E. "Stop them," she murmured.

"Nobody's gonna hurt you," said Tom. "You know you wanna, L.D."

"Triple E," she said, her voice almost weepy.

He held up his hand, his mouth open, ready to say something. But he didn't say anything. These were his buddies. He couldn't tell his buddies not to bone L.D. What the hell business was that of his? Nobody ever told nobody not to. He shrugged his shoulders.

HE SQUIRMS AT THE memory of it. Fine fellow, Triple E.

Sitting up, he flips the butt of his cigarette away, watches it smolder in the snow, weak smoke rising, and he hears the echoes in his head of L.D.'s words and Pump's hoarse coaxing and Tom's assurances to her. Jasper seems mesmerized by her breast. He looks like somebody sucking a Popsicle. The boys cling to L.D.'s body. He watches again as they stretch her over the bed, manipulate her with their hands and mouths. She is like a cold engine they are trying to start. Pull the choke, turn the key, press the starter, cup the carburetor, pump the gas. Do something. Try a shot of ether. There—do that again. L.D. closes her eyes and her breath quickens. Triple E watches her weaken, watches her legs spread.

HE WENT BACK TO the living room. He didn't want to be part of sharing her, going places where the others had just been. It was gross. She was gross. Everybody knew what L.D. did when she was in the mood. Everybody knew she said no when she meant yes. It occurred to Triple E that cousin Ava was that way too, except she loved just one at a time, didn't take them on in bunches like L.D. Noises were coming through the door, grunts, little cries. A sound that was nearly a sob.

Jeanne came out of the baby's room. "He was fussing," she said. Then she looked around and she said, "Where's everybody?"

Triple E jerked his thumb toward the noises.

Jeanne made a face. "All of em?" she said.

"That's not my style," he said. "Like a bunch of monkeys." He felt his cheeks flushing, his ears burning.

She giggled at him. Her eyes looked nervous. She tugged at her sweater sleeves, pushing them down at first, then yanking them back above her elbows. "I'm told you're nicer than Tom or Chuck," she said as if trying to reassure herself. "That's what L.D. said."

"Yeah?"

"Are you?"

"I don't know," he said, cracking a grin, hoping Jeanne would tell him more about himself. He wanted definitions. He thought maybe he should kiss her, but she broke eye contact and backed away. "L.D. used to chase me at school when we were little," he told her. "I was always scared she would crush me." He winked at Jeanne, chuckling, trying to be *nice*. "She was always big. 'Bomba Mama,' the guys called her."

Flickering smiles played over Jeanne's lips. She moved close, and he could see chips of ginger floating in her eyes, her lips moist and pouty, promising things. He wondered if he could get her on the couch, get a finger in the rim of her panties and do some work. Would she let him do what L.D. would? He looked at her skirt, her strong, dark legs. Was she really saving herself for marriage as he'd heard? He wanted to ask her about it. Was Jeanne Windriver an old-fashioned girl?

She kept shuffling her feet, closing in, moving away. Biting her lip. Her eyes restless. He offered her a cigarette. She lit up and then put on some music. Bass guitar pulsing. He watched her blow smoke and bob her head, her hair rippling like midnight over Sand Creek.

She called him a funny thing.

"Who's a funny thing?" he said.

"You."

"Why?"

"Because you blush. Boys never blush about anything."

"I'm just hot, it's hot in here," he said. He took a step toward her, ready to wrap her up.

She folded her arms and turned her back to him and looked toward the bedroom, where they could hear the headboard banging the wall. His eyes roamed over Jeanne, the skirt pulling tight across her hips.

"I heard you're a virgin," he said. The rumors had been all over school, like it was a really big deal, hot-looking fox like her and never been laid. It was a tantalizing notion. A virgin. He didn't know if he knew any virgins. There were some girls he suspected, but he didn't really know. None of them ever admitted it. "If I'm out of line, just say so," he told her.

She looked at him over her shoulder. He couldn't tell what she was thinking, whether she was mad or amused or what. Ashes fell from her cigarette, hitting one white shoe and scattering. Her smile flickered. She walked to the love seat, sat down, crossed her legs. She looked at her knee, her eyes narrowing, her brows a straight, uncompromising line.

"What's wrong with being a virgin?" she asked him.

"Nothing wrong with it, not a thing," he said. It was a moment in his life he would never forget, her intense eyes, one hand prim on her lap, the other over her breast, cigarette smoke throwing signals. And the knowledge solid in his fine fellow brain that what was between her legs was intact, had never been mucked with. He liked her a whole lot then. He wanted to touch her. Touch her hand, that was all, just touch her hand. Maybe a kiss, a soft, slow one. He looked at her face, trying to read her.

He remembered her in the hall at school, her slightly pigeon-toed prance, the way her ass bucked when she walked. "I see you all the time," he said, "wearing those bunny boots, and you prance so fine, it's like watchin a thoroughbred walk."

She tittered. "Thoroughbred?" she said.

He felt his ears warming as he told her about a guy saying it on TV, about seeing a woman walking like a thoroughbred, and it made Triple E think of her, of Jeanne Windriver.

"You thought of me?" she said.

"Yeah," he said. "All kinds of things go on in my head. I'm a thinker, you know."

"A stinker, more likely," she said.

He hadn't really been thinking of her that much, but now he was, most definitely. Close up and with the memory of L.D. still on his fingers and lips, his blood hadn't yet cooled. It seemed to him he could smell Jeanne's skin, like a warm orchid, like something wet and misty. Her hair was so black it was almost blue. It bounced as she moved her head, leaning forward to pick tobacco off her skirt. She rolled the tobacco shred into a little ball between her thumb and finger and flicked it at him. She was looking him over carefully, taking him in, making calculations.

Then she said: "Lonesome eyes."

"Huh?" he said.

"It's like you have some sad secret, the way your eyes look. Do you?"

"What?"

"Have sad secrets."

"I dunno." He wanted her to go on. Secrets? Lonesome eyes? Jesus, girls were silly. But then again, maybe they knew something he didn't know. He studied her face. Tell me about myself, *tell me who I am,* he wanted to say.

Her upper lip curled and she showed a tooth the way Elvis

did in the movies. He flopped into a chair. He crossed his leg and kicked his foot and squirmed. He stood up and walked to the door of the bedroom and listened a second, then paced around looking at the crummy furniture and a box of toddler toys in a corner. He had to keep moving. It was something that had always driven his parents crazy, that he couldn't sit still. Even as a baby in his highchair he had to rock and roll. His mother used to give him tranquilizers to calm him down. Even with tranquilizers, he slept at most six hours a night. He had boundless energy. *You're exhausting me, Triple E!* was his mother's constant complaint.

Jeanne was watching him, her mouth so friendly.

He wondered if she was a prick-teaser. He had seen prick-teaser smiles many times, girls he knew at school, flirts trying out their powers. Maybe that was her thing, get a guy hot, then act like there was nothing meant by it, being friendly was all. Only a sicko would get nasty ideas just because a girl was being friendly. That's the way some were when a guy made his move, copping a feel: *What's the matter with you? What made you do that?*

He looked out the window, at the dewy lawns and trees and houses closing in, killing the prairie, leaving a guy no room for running wild. Something stirred in him. He felt an impulse to burn Jeanne, to throw a match into her goddamn sexy hair.

When he turned from the window, she was still looking at him, her eyes like tractor beams pulling him in. He tried to feel indifferent. He told himself she was just another flaky brat. "What did you mean about my eyes being lonesome eyes, what's so lonesome?" he said.

"You know," she said.

He thought she might be sneering at him. But maybe not.

He didn't know. He couldn't read her face. Faces were the barrier. There was no way to tell what kind of mind was hiding behind a face. Faces were foolers.

"You know what lonesome means," she said, turning from him, crushing the stub of her cigarette in an ashtray.

He wanted to yell at her, he wanted to say: *Tell me what you see! Tell me what I am for you! I gotta know!* She had the power. Just sitting there that way, looking way too cool, those legs and hair and everything.

"Want another cigarette?" he said, shaking the pack at her, popping one up for her white and stiff.

The boys came out of the bedroom. They were fussing with their clothes and looking around as if suddenly the furniture had become interesting. L.D. followed later. She went into the bathroom and stayed awhile, then came out sulky and sat on the seat next to Jeanne. The air smelled uncomfortable. Tom Patch sipped ouzo and stared at the stereo like he was mad at it. Jasper John draped his long body near the door, bit his fingernails, and studied the far wall. Chuck Pump was his same self, flushed and sweaty, his birthmark glowing like a wound. Triple E's stomach felt queasy. He was burping the ouzo. He was glad when Jasper said he had to get home. Jasper kept glancing at Triple E. There was shame in Jasper's eyes.

Triple E knew the feeling. He had done it once with a Colfax floater in the back of a stolen station wagon, paid the woman thirty bucks for a blow job just to find out how it felt, and gotten antsy when it was over, wondering what the hell had gotten into him giving her thirty dollars for such a thing. All he had wanted was to be rid of her.

Tom Patch, too, one time, drunk and talkative, talking about his first fuck, eleven years old with a teenager named

Kay, boned her in a portable potty and couldn't stand her after. It was the smell, he said.

But there was something mysterious about aftersex. The way it made you want to run.

"You want to go?" said Jasper.

The girls sat with their legs tucked up. L.D. glared at Triple E. "I hate you," she said as he walked toward the door. Her words mixed with the music. Some raspy-voiced woman singing *My baby's got a love weapon—love weapon* . . .

THEY RODE AROUND AND Pump told about a girl named Judy Wolf, how he and four cats from Derby gangbanged her out by the arsenal, and she was just like L.D., eating it up, wanting more and more. Triple E had heard the story before. He knew Judy Wolf. Everybody knew Judy Wolf. He had boned her one time himself.

"L.D. wanted it real bad," said Jasper. "What were we supposed to do, man? It's not our fault."

"Man, we should name her Creamy, she was sopping," said Pump.

"Creamy, yeah, that's her name."

"You could see it in her eyes," said Tom.

"Bedroom eyes," said Pump.

"If she didn't want it, why'd she let us?" said Jasper. "We didn't rape her, that's for sure."

"I'm the woodmaster," said Pump.

"We're all woodmasters," said Tom.

Pump continued talking, telling tales of conquest, spinning images out that Triple E had seen before, gotten from Pump or from a movie, or from some porno book Pump was always passing around. Triple E scowled and rubbed his stomach, soothing it. Tom drove and now and then chuckled at something Pump said. Jasper John drifted silent in the backseat, his face a morose study. Triple E got tired of listening to Pump running off the mouth.

"Shut up, Pump, will you, for five seconds?" said Triple E.

"What's with you, man? You could've had your turn. Don't be gettin pissed at me, Triple E, just cuz you didn't get laid, you could'a knocked off some, she wouldn't have missed it."

Triple E rolled down the window and took gulps of air.

"What's the matter now?" said Pump.

"It's that goddamn L.D.," Triple E said, gasping. "She's a pig."

"You drank too much ouzo," said Pump. "L.D. be prime."

"Pull over Tom," said Triple E. "I'm gonna walk home."

Tom pulled up to the curb and Triple E jumped out and slammed the door.

He strolled down East Colfax Avenue. His head was hurting. His stomach was surly. The aftertaste of everything was in his mouth—ouzo and pot and the memory of L.D.'s nipple clinging like a cobweb. He saw her hate-filled eyes and hated her right back.

"Like it's all my fault, you bitch. Like you couldn't have walked the hell outta there. Ain't my motherfuckin fault."

He started running up the hill toward his house, the cool air cleaning him, his legs pumping faster and faster, winning the 440 again, leaving the whole pack of mungos gasping. Getting the blue ribbon at assembly, crossing the stage while the principal held out the ribbon and everybody applauded. Pretty neat.

"I got legs," he said, looking down at his legs with appreciation. Fast feet. So fast nothing could catch him. So fast that if he wanted to, he could leap at the crest of the hill and his momentum would carry him into space and he would be like a meteor dazzling the eyes of all the puny earthlings. A fiery light, an omen. On high, up, up, up. *Look! Look there in the sky!*

I hate you, she had said. Hate you . . . hate you. And she had meant it, the bonehole.

Lots of people hated Triple E. It was nothing new.

HIS LEGS ARE STIFF. They ache with cold. He kicks his feet a bit, stomps around, then sets out again for the toy house at the bottom of the valley. He thinks he sees smoke rising from the chimney, but it could be the wind kicking up a snow haze. He walks carefully, sidestepping brush, taking little steps. His feet are clumsy. There's no feeling down there. It's like walking on blocks of ice. He can't get into his stride.

Jeanne is the one for stride. If there is anything about her he will always remember, it is her walk. It is strange—the things a fellow focuses on: a high-stepping walk, hips shifting, cheeks jiggling in a sheath of skirt. It's the focus-total, an obsession. It's like he was born with it, a hunger so huge the whole world couldn't fill it.

He is puffing, blowing steam from his mouth. The steam

settles on his jacket and freezes into ice crystals. Looking down he can see his jacket is white. The front of his pants is white too. He runs his hand down and dusts himself off a little, but in seconds he has turned white again. He wonders what he would look like to other people. Are his eyebrows white? His hair? His whole face. Is he like a ghost walking?

At the bottom of the valley the little house and outbuildings seem to wobble in the air. Maybe they're not even real, he tells himself. Maybe we're all ghosts. He turns and looks back at the spot where he had settled and smoked a cigarette. He half expects to see himself sitting there frozen dead, but the space is empty.

"Knock it off," he tells himself. "Don't start playin tricks. No time for it, man. Get your ass in gear before you end up dead and everybody dead and all your fault!" This energizes him. He picks up the pace.

AFTER THE L.D. GANGBANG, Triple E didn't see her or Jeanne for a couple of weeks. Then he saw them both the night he got shot for stealing a car.

He always tried to steal his cars in Arapaho County. It was bad luck to steal them in Adams County north of Colfax. All the guys he knew who got caught for stealing cars stole them in Adams County, so he kept himself confined to the other side, to Arapaho, if he could. But there was nothing doing on the Arapaho side of Colfax. All the cars he wanted were in busy areas too risky to try.

After walking around for two hours in the frosty air, his breath smoking and the tools of his trade in his fatigue jacket dragging him down, he decided to take a chance on Adams County. He crossed Colfax near IM BLUE, where the Blacks hung out, listening to funky guitar and old blues buddies. Inside he heard some soul-cool cat singing about how whiskey and women done him wrong. He peeked in the window. The bartender was tall, thin, and black. He looked right at Triple E. He looked resentful, defiant. Triple E was reminded of someone he had seen on TV. It was a documentary about the civil rights movement back in the sixties, and they showed an athlete raising his black-gloved fist as the flag rose and the national anthem played. It had taken a lot of guts to do that, raise your fist to the whole world like that. Triple E stiffened his arm and made a fist to show the man they were brothers. The man waved him away from the window.

"Fuck you then," mouthed Triple E.

He headed down the street and went north at the corner, walking between patches of dirty snow left over from the last storm. On both sides of him were brick houses and huge trees, the trees stripped ugly, twigs plastered against the moon like alien fingers. Branches rattling in the wind. Cars grating over the salted pavement. There were plenty of cars along the curbs. Porch lights were on, and he could see the fluorescent glow of televisions smearing windows here and there. Above him clouds drifted toward the moon, and he could smell the possibility of more snow. He hated winter. He hated snow, cold toes, cold fingers, frost-nipped ears. Falling snow was filled with silence. Snow was dead rain. His feet were already freezing. He could never keep his feet warm in winter, no matter how many pairs of socks he wore.

He was deep in thought, and for a few moments didn't notice a car trailing him, but finally the tick of the engine caught his attention. He glanced over. A pale Buick with chrome hubcaps and white walls was inching along beside him. Inside were three or four guys. The one riding shotgun was looking at him like he was a mysterious insect or something. There had been lots of shootings, total strangers getting gunned down on the streets, cats blowing each other away in bars. A tot on a tricycle was killed by a stray bullet, a kid from Washington High arrested for it and they were trying to get him tried as an adult. The dead tot's father showed up at the police station with a gun, waving it around and bawling about his baby. A commentator on TV had said that Denver was worse than Tombstone in the days of Wyatt Earp, setting new records for anarchy and murder every year. The city was becoming unlivable. It was becoming Los Angelized.

Triple E slipped his hand into the pocket of his jacket and gripped his baby juke-bar, the one he used for popping ignitions. He moved it against the material, so it would look like he had a gun. His heart was racing hard. His breath quickening. He had a reputation of not fearing anything; but truth was he knew lots of fear. He walked around with a bellyful of fear gnawing holes in his gut, but no one knew it. He looked at the car. The guy riding shotgun looked big. He had lots of hair and a mustache and a goatee. He was older than Triple E by quite a bit, in his twenties somewhere.

When the car stopped, Triple E stopped too. He hung back. The terrace and a mound of gray snow between himself and the car. He was ready to run. He wished he was really crazy, a berserker who could leap on the car, smash the windows with his juke-bar, whale on the cats inside, get at them, kill them, rid the earth of them—so he could quit being afraid of them. It was always his way when a fight was coming. No finesse, his fists going like pile drivers.

He mourned his nakedness. He needed a gun. Hardly anyone bothered with duke city anymore, but went right for the real thing, to endgame. He saw a flash in the car and his heart yo-yo'd. Then he saw the flame of a match. The shotgun rider lit a cigarette. The window came down, a face leaned out, smoke blew toward Triple E. Lips curled at him.

"Boy, where you think you goin?"

"Yo, man, what's happenin?" said Triple E.

The guy's mouth opened wide, teeth flashing. "What's happenin? What you mean, what's happenin?"

It was like the guy had never heard such a lame word as *happenin*.

Someone inside the car was chuckling softly. Triple E drew hope from the sound. He smiled. He shrugged. He said he didn't know what he meant.

"He don't know," said the guy, looking toward the driver.

"I say bone the motherfuckah," said a voice in the back.

"Take him out," said another one.

"Hey, hey, be cool, nigger," said the driver. He had a deep, barking voice. It made Triple E think of the Doberman that lived next door always warning him to stay away from the fence. He bent over slightly and could see in the glow of the streetlight that the driver calling the others "nigger" was one himself. There were two white guys in the car and two blacks. It passed through his mind that he could run down the hill and into traffic on Colfax, dodge cars, take his chances. He hated the way the guy was looking at him, an arrogant grin on his face, his face saying, suck shit *cockroach*.

"What you think is in its pocket, Melvin?" said the driver.

The one named Melvin leaned out the window again, and in his hand was a semiautomatic something and he said it was time for show and tell.

Triple E pulled the juke-bar out. Melvin laughed. They all laughed. They said he was an entertaining little motherfucker and what was he doing with a juke-bar?

"Knock your brains out," said Triple E. "Except you got heat, so I guess I won't."

"Otherwise you would, except we got heat." They all chuckled at the notion. Triple E was real funny.

He considered his situation. He knew things were on the verge. What he said would bring them piling out the doors, or maybe make them back off. He knew he had to bluff hard, had to win their respect. Any sign of weakness and they would tear him apart. He hunched his shoulders, felt his biceps stiffen.

"I'm not looking for trouble, man," he said, his voice steady and low, a touch of anger in it. "But if that's what you want, here I am. I ain't goin nowhere."

There was silence inside the car as they looked at each other. Then somebody said, "Got balls."

"What he say?"

"Macho scarecrow standing there ready to rock and roll."

"Hey, sucker, how old are you?"

"Fifteen."

"You fuckin fifteen and choosin bad motherfuckers like us? You a fuckin kamikaze, man!"

"I ain't choosin nobody. But if it's got to be, let's get it the fuck over with. I'm freezin my ass off standin round here waitin on you motherfuckers. I got more important things to do than standin round here, man." While he was talking, Triple E took out his switchblade, held it in the folds of his jacket. He was wishing he had stayed home, that he was in bed warm with a *Mad,* giggling it up about some goofy Alfred E. Newman thing. Anywhere but here, he told himself. *Hup-hup, ho-ho, here we go.* He made a quick plan to go after the Melvin one, before he could get out the door, go for the veins on the back of his wrist and lay the bar over his nose, do it one-two. His upper lip was threatening to tremble. He hoped he could control his voice.

"What makes you so sassy, little shit like you?" said Melvin.

"Just me, don't give fuck bout nothin."

They asked him his name.

Triple E told them.

"Triple E what?"

"Triple E Evans."

"Triple E Evans, what kind of name is that?"

"We know an Evans," said one of them.

The guys in the car leaned their heads together and talked it over. He couldn't make out what they were saying. Felt like he'd been pricked with a pin and the air was running out. He pasted on a stiff, contemptuous mouth. Tried to make his eyes scary, hot-killer crazy-mean. Lonesome eyes, Jeanne had called them. Jesus, he hoped not. Lonesome eyes was no good.

Melvin said he knew a Bonnie Evans working at Samsonite. "Any relation?"

"That's my mother," said Triple E.

"No shit? Bonnie is your mother?"

"Yeah."

"Your old lady's mint," Melvin told him.

"Yeah, she is," Triple E said.

Somebody asked him what he was doing icing his ass in the middle of downtown Denver.

Triple E didn't answer right away.

"Juke-bar," said the driver.

"Car thief," said somebody.

"Say what?" said Melvin. "Is that right, Triple E? Fess up, son, we ain't tryin to save your soul."

Triple E admitted he was looking for wheels.

They got friendly all of a sudden, snorting and laughing and checking him out. Melvin asked him if he wanted some cannabis. Triple E bought a stick from Melvin and put it in his pocket. Then the driver told him to get on his white-thief way and give the man some grief. They all repeated it like a mantra: "Grieve the motherfuckin man, grieve the motherfuckin man."

Triple E started walking. He could hear them talking, laughing about him. Somebody said, "Kamikaze talking bad shit to bad motherfuckers!"

"The tools of his trade, man. Dig it, juke-bar and switch-blade."

"Check it out. Melvin almos off that skinny motherfucker."

"Yeah, almos."

"Man, that hoe, his old lady, she got hair down to here, got tits like footballs, man. Heavy prime, ain't she, Melvin?"

"I told you about her workin at Samsonite agitating her ass for us brothers. Didn't I tell you that?"

"No you didn't. Look here, man, I want to know mo bout this bitch!"

They were insulting his mother, but Triple E wasn't about to risk himself for her honor. Let her dress different if she wanted respect. Laughter shot out of the car, like a thunder-bolt aimed at the middle of his back. He leaned away from it, ambling along, showing them cool, that he was not hurrying to get away, just bopping off to grieve the *man*. At the first inter-section he turned east and shifted to a jog that moved him four blocks in two minutes.

At a crossroads, he came upon a Ford Thunderbird double-parked and idling in the street, no one in it. There were skis strapped to the roof. Some people were talking on a porch close by, silhouetted against light coming through a doorway.

He walked by, jumped in the car, sped away. Behind him he heard yelling, then it faded.

ON THE WAY TO the party, he dumped the skis and racks in some bushes in a nearby park, then he drove to Aurora. Music was loud in the street when he arrived, the whole place throbbing with noise. Triple E recognized the Sex Pistols and their horseshit sound: cats with their tails on fire, Mau Maus beating on barrels. There were cars filling the lawn and the street. He double-parked and went inside. He smelled pot and beer fumes. Kids from school were there, some of them dancing, some of them lounging over the furniture, making out, some of them listening to the music, their eyes catatonic. He searched for Tom Patch but couldn't find him. In the kitchen he saw Jasper John sitting on the counter, nursing a bottle of beer. Jasper asked Triple E where he had been so long.

Triple E took the weed from his pocket, lit it, dragged the smoke deep into his lungs, handed it to Jasper, then told him what had happened with the guys in the Buick. Jasper grinned and said trouble was always following Triple E.

"For sure," said Triple E. "Where's Tom, ain't he comin?"

Jasper said Tom was at the Shift with Jeanne. They wanted some privacy.

Triple E felt like running his head into the wall. If Jeanne was with Tom at the Shift, she was done for. Girls in Tom's clutches didn't have a chance. He would get rough with her if she didn't come across.

The Shift was an old house on Zenith Street that had once belonged to the Shift family. Roy Shift had cut his wrists in the bathtub and it was said his ghost still haunted the place. It had been empty for three years. It was run-down. No one would buy it. Triple E and his friends used it as a clubhouse. They had taken over an upstairs bedroom, hauling in a mattress and a kerosene stove and a portable radio. They had papered the walls with naked models from *Playboy, Hustler, Penthouse*. When the wind blew, they could hear moans coming from the attic. Sometimes there was a sound like an ax chunking into wood. Sometimes footsteps could be heard pacing the hall. It was a good place to take girls and make out. The noises made girls clingy. Triple E had never seen Roy Shift's ghost, but he kept his mind open to the possibility. He wanted there to be ghosts. He wanted to see Roy and have a talk with him. Ask him about death. Like, was death bad or not? Was there a god, and if so why did he make such a fucked-up world? Did he have a plan? Did Jesus tell you all the formulas of the universe when you died? Did he really know everything that was going to happen? Did he really send souls to hell? Was Satan real? Was anything? Triple E had his suspicions that God or Jesus was no more real than Santa Claus, but he wasn't sure. Willing to keep an open mind just in case.

Pump and L.D. came into the kitchen arm in arm. Pump asked him what the fuck he was doing, and Triple E told Pump to eat a big one.

Pump showed his I.Q.

Triple E held out the stick of weed and told Pump to take a hit, it would sweeten him up. Pump had shaved his head bald and was wearing a loop earring in his left ear. His face looked on fire, the birthmark glowing like reflective tape. He wore a sleeveless denim jacket, camouflage pants, and camouflage boots. He got nose to nose with Triple E.

"What's this shit I hear you callin me fag," said Pump.

Triple E glanced at L.D. Her lips sulked. Her eyes were saying no more checking out her anvils. He backed away from Pump. "Who called you a fag? I never called you a fag."

"You sayin I'm a homosexual fat faggot queer."

Triple E had no idea what he was talking about.

"Ask L.D.," Pump said.

"I heard you," she said.

He knew what she was doing. L.D.'s revenge for letting his buddies bang her, for him not wanting it, her, or her goddamn *anvils*.

"A homosexual fat faggot queer," repeated Pump, smacking his lips, seeming to savor the words.

Triple E wasn't sure what to do. He wasn't sure how serious Pump was. He looked mad. But then, he always sort of looked mad.

"I'm gonna kick your ass," said Pump.

Triple E told him he could try.

L.D. kept insisting he had called Pump a faggot. She stuck her chin out, like she was daring Triple E to take a poke. She said it was in Graham's Café and he said Chuck sounded faggy, saying he would suck Triple E off if he couldn't kick his ass. L.D. had heard it and Triple E was a liar if he denied it.

Triple E remembered the occasion. A long time ago. Six months maybe. He had been hacking Pump and told the girls the suck your peter story and everybody thought it was funny.

"Ah, man, is that all it is?" he said. "You say it all the time, Pump. You say if I can't kick your ass I'll suck the head of your peter—"

"—on the Fourth of July in the middle of Colfax Avenue!"

"Yeah, that's it."

"You think I'm queer?"

"Hell no, you're just stupid."

Chuck hit him then, a Sunday sucker punch. He wasn't expecting it. He thought all things considered, that Chuck and he were tight, were good-enough buddies, had been for years and years and Chuck hadn't slugged him since they were small fries out at the bluffs shooting BBs at each other. Triple E felt his head go hollow, as if a vacuum had sucked his brain out, leaving him with nothing but space in his skull. His limbs were paralyzed. He found himself on the floor, helpless, unable to cover up or anything, and Chuck stomping on him, doing bad things to his face and ribs. He heard shouting and the music thumping.

Jasper came off the counter and shoved Chuck away. Chuck swung on him and missed and Jasper picked up a Coors bottle and swore to God he would break Chuck's face if he didn't back off. L.D. took his arm and said that he had fixed the little turd, fixed him good. She pulled him toward the doorway, where all the other kids had gathered in a bundle, watching like vultures as Triple E got stomped.

Crooking his arm around L.D.'s neck, Pump said, "See, tole you he was a *punk.*"

JASPER SPONGED TRIPLE E'S face with a wet towel. After a minute, he could control himself a little, but he still felt like his muscles were made of mush. Jasper helped him up and pushed the dish towel in his face to catch the blood that was running from his nose. They went out the back door, Triple E stumbling in the freezing air. He was furious. Shamed, humiliated, disgraced. He couldn't understand it, how Chuck could let all the years go, give up their friendship, for L.D., just to give her some false justice for Triple E not giving a damn about her, letting her idea of romance—*Triple E can feel my anvils*—turn into a gangbang.

She could've said no.

It was a crazy world, the stars were messing with him, the

moon was shuffling forth loony vibrations. War rays from Mars. He told Jasper to take him home. He was going to get his .30-30 and kill that cocksucker.

JASPER DROVE HIM IN the Thunderbird. Triple E sat forward, nose bleeding, mouth swelling, jaws locked, his mind drenched in anger and depression. He would never live it down, not if he was a hundred. Pump had decked him, kicked his guts in, called him a punk in front of everybody, and got nothing in return, not so much as a split lip. Caught off guard, Triple E's body had failed him, had gone numb and worthless. There was an awful, gnawing sensation of vulnerability in his heart. He was such a nothing, such a rag, it seemed to him like the slightest thing, a breeze, a microbe, a defining word—*punk, punk, punk*—could carry him away, blow his atoms into the void. He touched his nose and winced at the pain and told Jasper it was broken. Jasper made sympathetic noises.

When they got to the house, it was empty, his parents off somewhere tooting. Triple E washed his face and changed his shirt. He stuffed toilet paper up his nostrils to stop the bleeding. His nose and eyes were swelling. His lip looked like it had half a cherry glued to it. He cussed in front of the mirror, cussing Pump, cussing L.D., calling her a fat syph twat.

"What a mess," said Jasper.

Triple E got the Marlin .30-30, loaded it, and went back to the car. He told Jasper to drive him over to the Shift to get Tom. He wanted Tom there as more backup.

"It ain't worth killin Pump," said Jasper. "He's Mr. Retardo. He was a waterhead, you know."

Triple E didn't give a fuck.

———

AT THE SHIFT, HE went inside and yelled for Tom. Tom came to the head of the stairs and looked down through the shadows and asked what was up.

"Did Roy Shift show?" said Triple E.

Tom claimed that Roy had been there fussing in the attic. "Come on up, man, we got some Irish Creme, and we got Wolfman Jack all the way from California."

When Triple E got inside the room, he hardly looked at Jeanne except to notice she had her clothes on and was sitting on the mattress on her shins. She looked down at her knees when he entered. The radio was loud. Triple E heard Jim Morrison's hypnotic voice. He was waiting for the sun. The place was warm, the kerosene heater on, flickers of yellow light dancing on the walls. Nude glossies shimmered like they were catching fire. He went over by the window and looked at the backyard. He saw an old engine hanging on a rusted A-frame, there were five-gallon paint cans piled in a pyramid, pieces of a chain-link fence rolled up and entwined with dead weeds, some stepping-stones led to a pair of T-shaped pipes holding remnants of a clothesline. Here and there were sooty patches of snow. It all made a design like an abstract painting. Sad shapes on canvas. Worn out figures in shadowy blues. The trash bin of Roy Shift's life. Triple E spit blood on the floor. The music ended. Wolfman Jack howled.

Jasper was busy telling Tom what had happened. Tom came over and turned Triple E's face to the light. Triple E said he hadn't seen it coming. His defenses had been down. Pump had suckered him. Triple E checked out Jeanne again. She was on her feet and looking at him, her brows curved in sympathy. He wondered if she was still a virgin. He looked at her skirt. He knew her skirt had been up. The lap was wrinkled. He thought he saw spots of virgin blood on her knee, something dark there. He looked at her and she jerked her eyes away. He hated her and hated Tom Patch too. He hated and hated.

"What's with that bitch L.D.?" said Tom, turning on Jeanne.

Jeanne said she didn't know shit about it.

THEY LEFT THE SHIFT and got into the car, Jasper driving, Triple E riding shotgun, the other two in back. They went a few blocks and as they turned a corner, some rolling reds hit them. The car lit up inside like a brothel. Jasper's eyes went wild. "Holy Christ!" he said. "Fuckin fuzz!"

Tom told him to stay cool, and told Triple E to hide the rifle.

"Should I pull over?" asked Jasper.

Triple E and Tom looked at each other. They didn't know what to do.

"Oh man, they're gonna know this mother's stolen. I'm royally fucked, man. I'm fuckin-fucked," said Jasper.

Triple E tried stuffing the rifle under the seat. He jammed it barrel-first into the opening and when it wouldn't go, he started shaking it, wiggling it, until, abruptly—boom! it exploded. It was like the inside of the car blew up. There was a two-second stunned pause, the smell of gunpowder rising around them like an unbathed soul. Then Jeanne said she was shot. Her voice was breathless, like someone was choking her.

"Oh, Jeanne, oh no!" Triple E cried.

Jasper stomped on the gas and the Thunderbird burned rubber. Behind them the red lights rolled, the siren chased them.

Triple E tried to explain that the gun just went off. He was aghast at what he had done. He pulled the rifle out and looked at it as if it might tell him why it had done such a stupid bad thing.

"Bleedin major blood!" shouted Tom.

Triple E craned his neck over the seat, hanging on with one hand as the car swerved and darted. He saw blood running down Jeanne's calf, the left one. It looked black. There was a lot of it.

Jeanne sat slumped in the corner, her eyes amazed. She said her parents were going to kill her. She sucked in her breath, a long sob following.

"It's starting to burn. It's starting to burn bad!" she said.

Triple E took off his jacket, ripped off his shirt and threw it to Tom, yelling at him to wrap Jeanne's leg, stop the bleeding. He took off his undershirt too and threw that back to Tom. Tom bent down, fumbling with her leg. Both of them bounced up and down and side to side as the car went airborne over dips and laid its frame on the pavement, throwing sparks into the night. Behind them the sirens were constant. Jasper missed a turn and the car flew over a number of lawns, sideswiped some parked cars and lurched back onto the street.

Triple E wiggled into his jacket and turned around. He sat with the rifle in one hand and his other hand on the dashboard. On the radio Rod Stewart was asking if he was sexy, and Triple E found himself madly singing the refrain over and over. The Thunderbird slid onto East Colfax and went winging through Aurora, where more police cars joined the chase. Their sirens paved the way, making other cars pull over. Jasper didn't stop for anything, cross traffic, pedestrians, red lights. He had pedal to metal, doing eighty-five. Near Stone Garden, he turned off East Colfax. He zigzagged north and east along the backstreets, not very far from where Triple E lived.

Triple E yelled at Jasper to head for the bluffs over Sand Creek. They could all hide down there in the dirt caves.

But nobody knew what to do with Jeanne. She couldn't run. She was bleeding to death. She needed a doctor.

"I know a vet!" shouted Triple E, his voice sounding weird to him, sort of screechy like a trapped skunk.

Jeanne looked at him like he was crazy.

A police car was coming toward them. There were one or two, maybe three, behind them. Jasper whipped the car into an alley, glanced the left fender off a cinderblock fence, then lost control. The car plowed over a snowmobile, hit the corner of a garage and spun sideways, stopped. The engine died, steam shot up. Triple E flew out the door, rolled onto the ground, scrambled to his feet, and took off. He heard sirens dying behind him and voices yelling, warning him to stop. Spotlights hit him, night became day. A megaphone voice ordered him to drop his weapon. *Drop your weapon! Drop your weapon!* But he didn't drop it. He whirled around to see them, how far away they were. Shots barked. Something hot hit him in the forehead, knocking him sideways. The rifle flew from his hands. He rolled once, stood up, and kept running. Blood was pouring into his left eye. He wiped at it with his fist. It occurred to him that he had been shot in the head and shouldn't be able to run at all. Was it a dream? Was he really lying back there in the alley dead and done for, and this was his ghost running away? *I'm dead,* he told himself. Where was the tunnel and the white light and the relatives waving? Where was Papa and Nana? Where was Roy Shift? Where was Jesus with the formulas?

He leaped over fences and ran through yards and down alleys. When he found a vacant lot, he ran into it, hoping to hide himself in the weeds. As he hurried toward its center, he found himself mysteriously flying. It was as if the world had hit an air pocket and was diving from beneath his feet. He thrashed his legs for one or two seconds before the ground came back again. Tumbling and rolling, he finally came to rest on his back. He lay panting, trying to get his bearings. Around him was a block foundation. He was lying in a basement. Everywhere were relics of an old house, broken stairs, hanging pipes, foundation beams askew. He listened for voices, for sirens, heard nothing but his own sobbing breath. He rested his gaze straight above him, on heaven, where ragged clouds flew across the moon and stars.

HIS NOSE FELT BIG with pain. He moved carefully, not wanting to jar his face anymore. Warm blood trickled over his eye and cheek and over his lips. In the silence he measured his plight and found it bigger than he could handle. He closed his eyes and thought of when he was little and stupid and things were easy. A memory rushed through his head, a vision of his mother brushing her hair and smiling at him in the mirror, calling him her little man. And then he saw himself in a wheelbarrow and his father wheeling him around, running up and down the lawn going *zoom! zoom!*. Had that ever happened? Had things been nicer once, or was it all a myth? He saw his father's fist, saw anger, hatred, felt the blows, felt himself being lifted and thrown into the wall, felt the wall crack behind him, his bladder letting go. The concussion that followed, the huge headaches.

"That motherfucker. One of these days," he said.

Sitting up he pulled the twists of toilet paper from his nose. He tried to breathe through his nostrils but couldn't. Blood was seeping down the left side of his face, trickling under his jaw. There was a rhythmic pounding somewhere behind his eyes, like his heart had floated up and nested there.

Daintily, with trembling fingers, he reached to feel the wound in his head and touched two tiny holes, two rips in the skin. Something sharp pricked his finger. He nipped it out and held it in his palm, a wee piece of lead, a bit of shrapnel that had ricocheted off of something, the road, or maybe a rock or the brick garage. A little different angle and it might have cracked his skull and killed him. He giggled. A giddiness ran through him. He was filled with immortal longings and an odd notion that he was being saved for some purpose, some grand thing yet to do. He had a destiny to fulfill. There was no other way to explain why the angle of the ricochet had hit him just so, why it hadn't made his head explode. He realized for the first time that he wanted very badly to live, and he wanted very badly to believe that Jesus was real and everything had a purpose and that the course of his life would show it, that there would be white light and meaning and answers at the end of his journey. His fingers explored the wound. The skin had a flap in it, like a tiny, wet, ragged mouth.

A few minutes later, he was breathing easier and he left the basement hole and went home.

When he got there, the police popped out of the dark and told him to interlace his fingers behind his head. A cop pushed him against a car and started patting him down, poking hard against his testicles.

He growled at the cop, told him: "Get your goddamn hands off my ass, you faggot bastard."

"What you call me?" said the cop.

Recklessly Triple E told him that all cops were faggot bastards.

The cop punched him in the kidney and Triple E's knees buckled and he almost threw up.

"Who's a faggot bastard? Who?" said the cop.

"Me . . . I am," babbled Triple E.

"Who? Who's a faggot bastard?"

The cop was twisting Triple E's ear. "I'm a bastard, I'm a bastard!"

"Damn right you are."

Neighbors were out, standing on their porches across the street. No one asked questions. They all seemed to understand what was going on. Everybody had been waiting for it, a night filled with cops and Triple E in trouble. Who couldn't have predicted it? Who didn't know this moment would come?

The cops wanted to know where his parents were. He told them he didn't have any parents. His hands were twisted behind his back. He was cuffed. And in his ear came the cop's voice again asking who was a faggot bastard. The cop pinched him on the upper arm, pinched his triceps so hard Triple E cried out.

They took him to a hospital and got him stitched up and bandaged. Then he was driven to the Adam's County Jail at Brighton and locked in a cell.

TRIPLE E TRIPS AGAIN, falls, gets up, dusts the snow from his sleeves and does a little dance, pounding his feet up and down. The wind swipes at his ears and nose. He wishes now he had the undershirt that he gave to Jeanne to wipe the blood off her quiver. He wishes he had his Siberian boots and his hat with the earflaps. He wishes he had remembered to take a pocketful of Oreos.

Ahead of him as far away as ever, it seems, is the tantalizing vision of the farmhouse. It makes him think of Monopoly, the little houses on the board. He wonders if his mind is playing tricks on him again, if the farm is a mirage that will vanish as he closes in. He checks the circumference of his universe, vast and white and indifferent, able to swallow life the way the sea can swallow ships and even whole civilizations. A smothering dream: he becomes the last living thing, his head bobbing on the surface of an empire made of snow.

CHAPTER 5

WITHIN A HUNDRED YARDS or so, he knows he has made a mistake. Snow shrouds the buildings. No smoke rises from the chimney. Ice lies blue in the shadows and lights up the sun-spanked walls like a transparent skin.

There are three outbuildings—a small barn with a tack room in back, a pump house twisted with age, and a machine shed. Inside the machine shed he finds a scattering of junk: rusted corrugated roofing, an old harrow, a broken plow, a sickle, a bench vise, the flywheel of an engine. There is a transmission covered with sludge, its shift lever pointing like an accusing finger toward the ceiling. The blade of a shovel juts from the floor like a grave marker. There is a small water tank too, and the frame of a boy's bicycle. There are dozens of Folger coffee cans strewn over the carcass of an ancient Studebaker, which lies on its back looking very much like a giant dead beetle.

Triple E tries to imagine the machinery and implements oiled and humming. The people working the land. The door opening. The wife calling her man to dinner. Cattle lowing to one another in summer evening. Birds plucking at insects. Kids playing in the yard. The sun sets red as fire over the mountains.

And then something happened. Somebody died. Or a crop failed. Or the cows sickened. The weather wouldn't cooperate. Or maybe the people just got worn out and couldn't go on. Everything turned ugly and they ran away. Let the bank have it.

He feels eerie standing amid their mess, their scraps all over the place, the exfoliations of a lifetime. People turn over like furrows beneath the plow. He, too, is turning over, leaving bits of himself here and there. He touches this, touching that, weaving in and out like a searcher in a graveyard peering at every tombstone, trying to find the images that will make the dead live again. Their story is here, like a book with the pages torn out and scattered.

HIS MIND IS TANGLED with ghosts, bits of people he would purge if he could. His naked mother draped over a strange man's knees. His father's shoes in a puddle of blood, a white hardhat on his head, a cow-killing wand in his hand. Perversions of his grandparents too: Nana in her last days, eyes bulging, the rest of her face folding like a wilted flower. And Papa on the kitchen floor, his dark mouth arrested in the midst of a fatal exhalation. The dampness of the old man's hand, the quick coldness of it. *Goin to find Nana.*

Triple E shakes his head. He turns from the shed. He

walks toward the house. It is a small house. The door is weathered gray, with chips of white paint clinging in spots. There is a sagging porch. Icicles hang long as spears from the porch roof.

Putting his shoulder to the door, he forces his way inside. It is like entering a snow cave. The floor is bare and covered with frost. The walls are glazed with frost. There is a stone fireplace, a pile of frozen ashes in its mouth. He lifts the ash block in one piece and throws it outside and closes the door. He searches the house for something to burn and finds a dry room with yellowed newspapers tacked to the walls. MAN ON THE MOON! shouts a headline. He tears off some papers, then rips up pieces of rotting floorboard, setting them at an angle on the wall, stomping them in half. Soon he has a pile of sticks and paper in the fireplace. He strikes a match, lights another cigarette, then touches the match to the paper and watches it climb after the wood. He gets a nice fire going. As it burns, he rips up more flooring and adds it to the flames.

He lifts first one foot then the other to the fire and after a while he feels his feet slowly thawing, filling with pain, as if someone is poking needles into his toes. He knows the blood in his toes is frozen and that if he cut the skin open, the blood would ooze forth as purple slush. He does not dare take his shoes and socks off. He doesn't want to see his feet.

He keeps feeding the fire and it crackles and climbs, flushing him with heat. Steam rises off his clothing. Water runs in rivulets from his hair. The walls and ceiling begin to melt. Drops of water fall on him. After a few minutes of piling wood, he sits down to rest. His cheeks and ears burn. He has chills and muscle tremors. He is sure he has a fever. He spins on his fanny in front of the fire, going in circles, cooking himself like a side of beef on a spit. He hallucinates Goodpasture, the mess hall and hot pancakes and butter and syrup and sausages. Coffee with cream and sugar. He sees the cows in the Goodpasture barn, hears the milk machines wheezing, the cows snuffling into their hay, the warm feel of their udders and teats as he massages the last drops of milk out. He hears panting and the slap of leather, the grunts and growls of boys in a gym. He hears Coach Tozer telling him he has the goods to be a fighter. He is swift, he hits hard, he can take a punch, he has heart.

He sees Mrs. Bridgewater. Her eyes behind thick lenses glisten like crystal balls. He ponders the phrase *smart as a whip*. He heard her call him that once. "Smart as a whip," she said. What does it mean? How can a whip be smart? Is it because the touch of a whip smarts? Is the crack of a whip smart? How can he be smart as a whip and not understand what smart as a whip means? This is the thing, the problem with his peculiar kind of brain. People know all this stuff, like smart whips, that makes no sense to him at all. Maybe Mrs. Bridgewater was just blowing smoke up his ass. It was her job to *repair* him.

She told him he had to get past himself. He had to stop being selfish, and he had to forgive those who hurt him. *Forgive life itself,* she told him.

Forgive life itself.

He doesn't understand. He doesn't understand its value or anything. What is there to value? What does *life* do that is good? You get to get laid, maybe. Get drunk, smoke dope, and feel fine for a few hours. Watch some crud on TV that makes you laugh. But it all ends up heavy pain one day. It all comes to disease or accident. And death. In one way or another you turn mental in order to protect yourself from life. Looked at coldly, life is a raw deal, a place where you get your nuts cracked and where you get to watch yourself decay, your teeth fall out. Your whole body go gnarly. Old people implode like baked apples.

And afterward . . . oblivion. Except if God is real, if Jesus is waiting with a beacon in his hand. Or the devil with a pitchfork. His bet is that the earth will swallow him soon enough and he will still be muddleheaded, still be wondering to the last what it was all about.

"Bout nothin," he says. "Thank you very much, Jesus."

His mother was always saying that instead of Jesus, people should thank the chicken, and thank the cow, and thank the poor pig or the fish, when they sat down to eat. She was soft-hearted where animals were concerned, but people were another story. People are mean, she said, most of them get what they deserve.

"The slaughterhouse worker and his T&A wife," says Triple E. "She could have been an actress, a star. Just ask her, she'll tell you." His mother got pregnant in her teeny-bop years. Married before she was eighteen. He wonders how she ever let it happen—Denver girl with big dreams, going big places, gets herself knocked up. Goes nowhere. Old, stupid story.

Once when he was twelve or thirteen his parents were sitting at the table in their cups, talkative, and she said, "I don't ever want to see you without rubbers in your wallet, Triple E. Don't you go screwin some girl and gettin married like me and your dad. We were young . . . and too damn dumb to live," she said. "Don't be young and dumb, Triple E."

"Your mother was an accident waiting to happen," said his father.

"Oh, drop dead," she said. And then her eyes narrowed and she said, "I didn't know I was marryin a man so mean he could kill for a livin. When your father got that job, I wanted to die."

"You know nuttin bout it, whad a man has to do to make a livin."

"You enjoy it. You like killin defenseless animals."

His father ground his teeth and he said, "Fuckin hypo-crites, that's whad people like you are. I do your killin for you, and you got the balls to talk shit to me?" He spread his hands, palms up, looking at them as if searching for bloodstains. "You think I wanna? You think these hands and me enjoy it? Stupid drunken bitch."

"Then why do it?" she said. Her eyes were full of hate.

"Make a livin somehow," he told her. "The pay is good. Good pension plan. Free fuckin steaks."

"Poor cows," she said, working up some tears.

"You juss a dumb cunt," he said.

She stood up, knocking her chair over, weaving in front of him. Her fist was cocked. She threatened him with her fist, but he just grinned at her, and he said to Triple E, "Get a load of your mama."

"Bastard!" she said. "Bastard . . . bastard . . ."

"Never get married," said his father.

A jittery woman. Flighty and nervous, hungry-eyed. On the go. No Friday or Saturday night at home for her, as if she has to live it all in a minute, in a hurry, the moment, *now,* passion, feeling, because the sun might not come up tomorrow. Actu-ally Triple E understands that part. He gets the same way—restless and wired and feeling like life is going 186,000 miles a second, sixteen today, sixty tomorrow, and saying *Where did it go?* He had heard his nana say it, looking at the candles on her birthday cake, *Where did it go?* And she made gestures with her fingers, like puffs of smoke, and she said, *Poof, poof . . .*

His back is freezing, his face roasting. He has chills upon chills. He turns and lets the fire massage his back.

"I got a fever for sure," he tells himself. "I could get pneu-monia and die and nobody would ever know." He has done too much, been too bad, too mean. He wishes it weren't true, but what the hell.

TOO LATE. EVERYTHING IS too late. He looks around at the decrepit house and thinks again about the people who lived in it and how they must have come to the realization finally that everything was too late. Finally there were no options left. So they skedaddled. Or they died. It was the end. They had no options. Everybody must come to it one day—out of options.

Looking out the window he can see white fields stretching to forever. There is no beauty in it, no beauty in the glitter of the earth. His feet hurt awful, sending waves of pain into his ankles and calves, and he wishes he hadn't tried to thaw them out.

The sun is almost directly overhead. It is noon, or maybe a little later. He has three or four hours before dark, depending on if it doesn't cloud up again. He wonders how Jeanne is doing. He wonders if he should go back and get her, bring her to the house and keep a fire going all night. It is a plan. The gas in the car will be used up by nightfall. The car will turn into a tomb. He can get Jeanne and bring her to the house. There is enough material around the yard, old tin, and twelve-bys, which they could use to plug the broken windows, and there is plenty of wood to keep a fire going until they can get a weather break and make it out of the valley, make it back to the highway and civilization.

In the meantime it will be all right. They will make a cozy nest for two. They will melt snow for water. He will use his shoestrings for a snare and catch some rabbits and they will cook them over the fire. Maybe he can find some things in the barn to make a bow and arrow. He will go hunting like the

Indians who once roamed these mountains, these valleys. He will come back with meat and feed his woman, and they will fuck and sleep and eat and fuck. And one day they will walk out alive and amaze the hell out of everybody.

His heart warms. He builds the fire up again to get himself hot before going back to Jeanne. He takes wood for a pillow, lies down, and keeps his feet to the fire, grimacing from the pain in his toes.

AS HE GAZES AROUND the room, he notices a strange spot on one wall. The frost is almost gone. The wall sweats. Drops of water patter the floor. There is some sort of growth beneath the frost. He investigates and finds an old beehive. Chunks of honeycomb remain between the boards. In their six-sided cells is the residue of honey. It is no longer syrupy. It is almost pure, frozen sugar. He tears a piece off and stuffs it into his mouth and chews. Sugar, yum. He sucks it from the wax, spits the wax out and takes another bite, and another.

When he has had enough, he fills his pockets with honeycomb and sits down dreamily in front of the fireplace. The honey in the wall is a good omen.

IN A MOMENT OF serenity he thinks of Roman candles bursting, glittering in the sky, drifting back to earth. Fourth of July was fun. Summer was a great time. Warm nights. Out the window at midnight he would go a'roaming with Tom Patch and Jasper John and Chuck Pump, the four of them with cherry bombs in their pockets, lighting them on porches, throwing them at cars.

They had stolen their first car on a Fourth of July, a Volkswagen so easy to hotwire it was sinful. And they had driven it to death, gotten themselves stuck out near Derby and had to walk home. But it was a start. Twelve years old and already a major criminal. Nothing like it, the excitement of it. Cars roared to life under his knowing fingers, stolen cars, cars that became piles of junk, parted out for money, fifty bucks for a Toyoto engine, twenty bucks for a Honda door, ten bucks for the heater out of an old Bel Air.

Fishing pole and
a pocketful of worms,
he glides down the cliffs
to sanctuary—

A buzz wakes him. He coughs and realizes he was snoring, his own snoring sounding like a bee.

Images flicker and he sees the pond, the bees zipping, the dragonflies hovering over green water. He is stepping in the present, falling into the past, and it is as if they are one and the same dimension circling each other, never out of one but in the other, like a snake with its tail in its mouth.

It is the day of Ava and Tom:

He closes his eyes and pictures the pond, the cupped hole he made in the mud, the leaves he put inside, and then the worms from his pocket, squirming in the cool hole.

HE PICKED A NIGHTCRAWLER and made it eat the hook.

The pond was shaped like a soft-edged diamond, triangular: wide in the middle and V-curved at both ends. The ends were trimmed in pussy willows. There were pinkish sands along the border between the water and the grass. In the center, the water was dark, secretive, a color reflecting the green of the cottonwood leaves that rose overhead. It was in the center in the dark where the big ones were, the fat fish hiding out at noon from the heat of the sun. He made a cast and settled down in the willows to let his bobber drift, let his pole hang over his crossed feet.

He saw cousin Ava with Tom Patch, tiny figures skittering down the dirt bluffs. Triple E hid himself. He let his pole go limp underwater. Tom and Ava skirted the pond and found a place at the edge of the field. They smashed the grasses down, Ava doing most of the work, while Tom watched her and shuffled his feet, smoothing the broken stems, then going up behind her and pulling her to him, his hands busy cupping her tiny breasts, cupping her quiver. Triple E watched her eyes close, saw her lips press into a smile. Tom pulled her shorts off, then her panties, then cupped her again. His finger worked in and out. Lips slack, she was breathing loud. Triple E could hear her breathing to the rhythm of the water lapping, then it was himself he heard breathing.

Through the tassels he saw Tom giving it to her good, the muscles of his butt flexing as he plunged in and in and in. Her head rocking. Her lips pressing in a grimace. Her eyes snapped shut as if to see is to know bad things. In a minute Tom was pulling out and shooting up her belly, spurts flying from him, some going as high as her chin and neck. She lay there, open for more, the semen thick and cloudy on her skin.

SHE WIPED HERSELF WITH grass, then they talked, Tom and Ava side by side, she talking mostly, coaxing him to say sweet things to her, coaxing him to kiss and pet her, he doing what she asked, until he thought of an excuse to quit, to sit up and talk about something else.

It was a tooth. He had Chuck Pump's tooth in his pocket. Jasper John had knocked it out. Pump had been giving Jasper a wedgy and got an elbow in the chops, the tooth broke off, and

Pump was running around holding his mouth and bleeding and bawling. The cunt. Jasper could be bone-cool. A quiet guy, watchful, but don't fuck with him. Tom showed the tooth to Ava and they laughed about it, and talked about the tartar on the back of it and said it was no wonder that Pump's breath smelled like caca. "Piece of kid," Tom said, flipping the tooth like a coin in his hand. "Piece of kid. Piece of ass," he said, pinching Ava's quiver and acting like he was going to shove the tooth up it. She knocked it away and grabbed him and kissed on him some more. Desperate kisses.

She was sitting up and she was leaking something clear as airplane glue. He could see it wetting a stem of grass that snagged between her legs. She kept begging Tom to kiss her to love her and he got mad, said he wasn't a machine; but she wouldn't let up on him—"Love me, why can't you love me? There isn't anything I wouldn't do for you, anything I wouldn't give you, Tommy. Love me, kiss me, do me." She took his hand and guided it to her. She placed her fingers around his penis and massaged it back to life.

She was pitiful, she made Triple E ashamed to call her cousin, drooling all over that bastard, when it was obvious he didn't give two cents about her, had planked her and was ready to move on, tired of her already, sick of her groveling. It was disgusting, very. Finally Tom pushed her down and got on top of her again and a minute later he was standing up hitching his pants and walking off and she came after, hiking into her shorts and jogging to catch up.

Triple E waited until they were out of sight, then he went to where they had done the deed, and he found the tooth she had thrown away—*Piece of kid. Piece of ass. C'mon, Tommy, love me, kiss me, do me.* It was true. A piece of this, a piece of that. People all pieces of things to be used. Proof in the pieces.

Till you're all used up and become proof in the bones. A piece of earth, like the woolly mammoths and the sabertooth tigers and Neanderthal man. The dead in their kajillions. Every time he and his dad went by a graveyard, his dad would ask if Triple E knew how many were dead in there, and Triple E would play along like he hadn't heard the joke. How many's dead? All of em, all of em in the graveyard are dead.

He shoved Pump's tooth into the dirt beneath the roots of grass to fossilize. Then he went to where her body had been, her pussy on the stem still glistening with drops of Ava. Bending low, he sniffed the spot and could smell her. His tongue came out as if it had a mind of its own and he licked her from the stems. Tasted unbelievably sweet. Tickled his throat. On his knees, he vomited and moaned and wondered if he was going crazy.

THE FIRE SPITS AT him and he covers his face. "Did I do that?" he says aloud. He licks his lips, remembering. *Hormones,* he has heard. They make you do crazy things. It's not really you, it's the hormones.

He remembers finding Ava on the patio later that day, sitting on the bench beneath the trees, crying, and he put his arm around her, let her blubber maximal heart-sobs on his chest. Life was a sad deal. A big bastard tragedy. She sobbed and said she was stupid. She sobbed about Tommy not loving her. She sobbed that she was a total geekizoid, freaky, ugly girl and too dumb to live. In a dramatic voice she told him she was a whore. She slapped her own face, slapping it until he made her stop.

Ava: Nothing ever went good for her with boys.

The fire is dying down, the cold taking over again. He gets up and breaks more wood. He shoves more into the fire. The fire flares. He turns round and round in front of it, doing a little war dance again, stomping his feet, kicking his knees high, waving his arms up and down. At last he is puffing and hot and ready.

PLUNGING INTO THE SNOW, he goes after Jeanne. He decides he is better than Tom Patch. He decides he is real, that it isn't just cunt with him—it is *her,* the total package, the total Jeanne Windriver head to toe and everything in between. He is going to save her life. He will tell her he has found a home, a warm fire, a place to wait out the weather. He can see her smiling at him, how cheerful she will be at the news. "We got it made now, Jeanne," he will tell her.

Hustling uphill west, out of the valley, toward the road and the way back to Jeanne, he has to shield his eyes. The cold amber wheel of the sun blinds him.

CHAPTER **6**

IT IS UPHILL, NOT steep but tiring, and within minutes Triple E is gasping for air. The air steams from his mouth. His nostrils run, snot freezing to his upper lip. His eyebrows and the stubs of his lashes stiffen and seem to tug at his eyes, twisting them, causing him to see as if through distorted lenses. The cold numbs his cheeks and ears, frostbite gathering. He counsels himself, tells himself to put one foot in front of the other and eventually he will be out of the valley and back to the road. Down the road, south somewhere, is the car, is Jeanne.

"One step at a time, coolbreeze," he whispers.

To take his mind off the endless climb in front of him, he visualizes Stone Garden, how he used to walk down East Colfax, pimping bone-cool, feeling full of life, like if he didn't yell or kick his feet at telephone poles or punch somebody, the pressure would build to a climax and he would take off like a rocket, burst all over the atmosphere. That's how it was when he got out of jail the first time. Being bone-bad, swapping punches with his father at home, then cutting out, heading for the streets, full of himself, full of fire, jailbird boy, bad bones and all.

A WEEK AFTER HIS arrest for car theft and a long list of grim charges, he pimped down the road soul-cool, his chin stiff, his swollen eyes proud, proud of the bandage on his forehead covering a bullet wound, proud of his prizefighter's face, proud of what he had done to his father in the living room.

"You're a monster, Triple E! You're not our son," his mother had cried. Shrieking at him, "Monster! monster! monster!" And then blowing off huge, heartbroken sobs, tears gushing.

"Aw, quit your cryin'," he had told her.

And the punches flew. The old man gone John Paunch from fifty thousand beers. No longer the fearsome one. Not one of his father's punches had hit home. Telegraphed them all. Moved slow as a glacier.

Coming out of the house, slamming the door, Triple E had yelled *Fuck you!* to his parents. He put on a fine limping pimp, dragging his tennies on the icy sidewalk, strutting his stuff. A bad motherfucker. Bitching bad thing.

TRIPLE E PAUSES, HIS ear cocked. He thinks he hears voices calling. But only the wind whistles and hums and snarls. Whimsical wind searching his ears. After a second he crams his mouth with snow and trudges on. There is forever yet to go.

He keeps hearing the judge's voice and he sees the judge's mouth stretched out like a trout being pulled into a boat, thrusting toward him, that moving mouth wanting to bite him: how dare he steal a car, how dare he put a loaded gun in that car, how dare he shoot that young lady in the leg, how dare he try to evade the police and create such havoc and danger. *How dare he! How dare he!*

THE MEMORY OF THE judge's face made Triple E giggle as he sauntered along so bad that day. Old fart, who did he think he was scaring? Triple E had hung his head in front of the judge, but he hadn't been scared. He had explained that he and his friends were just going out prairie hunting, spotlighting rabbits and skunks. They were going to take the car right back when they were done. It was an accident that Jeanne got shot. One of those things. A little joyride.

"Joyriding. I'd like you to tell me the joy in it," the judge had said.

Triple E had kept his head down, like he was real, real sorry. His father and mother apologized to the judge. His mother wept like a tragic figure in a movie. She was good at that, good at looking like the poor, put-upon mother, good at getting people's pity. She kept reminding the judge that it was the boy's first offense. The look on her face, her blubbering—it was disgusting.

HE CLEARS HIS THROAT, blows a wad sizzling into the snow, wipes his nose across the sleeve of his jacket. Wipes his eyes with the back of his fist. The wind is making him teary-eyed, the tears are freezing to his cheeks. Looking up he sees broken clouds and blue sky and darts of light. He wonders where his dead grandparents are. Still hanging around like his mother said they were—*Nana and Papa are always with us*—

shaking ghostly fingers at their bad grandson and saying *God is watching you.*

Or are they like the lights ricocheting off the clouds, heading into stellar space? Where is heaven anyway? He has heard that in the beginning of time, a microsecond after the Big Bang, there were ten dimensions created, maybe more, and that some of those dimensions were still around, except that they were invisible to human eyes. Had Nana and Papa eased into one of those dimensions, found a little crack in the space-time thing?

Maybe if he puts his hand out in just the right way, with just the right concentration and faith, it will go through a seam. He sees himself doing it, fingers first, his wrist, his arm, then stepping through as if through a gap in a fence, and *bam!* he will know everything. All the codes of the universe smashing into him like pellets from a shotgun.

Out of the dark belly and moving toward the light, like a baby being born.

But they might be mad at him. No, they *would* be mad at him. *What have you done to your parents?* they would say.

HE WAS A FIGHTING fool—*biff! bam! boom!* Gave his old man an uppercut to the jaw, a couple of lefts followed by a right. Snapped that head back *bam! bam!* Grabbed the vase by its neck and gave the bastard a crack like thunder on the knee. He had been aiming at his head, but the blow went wild and hit the bastard's knee. Had him hopping—boing, boing, boing, yow, yow, yow.

Triple E chuckled. "Tit for tat!" he said.

He hadn't gone soft, hadn't forgotten a thing the old man had done to him—every busted lip, every welt, every slam upside a wall. The old man's face furious, his words cutting Triple

E's mind to ribbons, calling him *bed pisser,* calling him *Swiss cheese for brains,* calling him *perverted little bastard, stupid little bastard . . . little bastard,* calling him . . . all that hate in his father's eyes! The fists working, raising black eyes, bloody noses for teachers to wonder about at school. Openhanded slaps busting eardrums, like a pencil jammed in there.

"You gonna learn, you little goon! You gonna learn!"

He went into a crouch, feinting with his shoulders and his fists. He had been a kickass sonofabitch in juvie. All the other kids had stayed away from him. He overheard them talking to each other, saying *Got shot. He shot a fuckin girl, man. Watch out for him—soul-bad, baby, he's crazy.*

Jasper and Tom got released the very next day. Their parents had come and gotten them out of jail, but Triple E's folks stayed away three days, leaving him holding off the other little sonsabitches, awed by his head wound and attitude.

And then his father told the judge not to worry, that they would lock the kid in his room if they had to, that it was going to be *tough love.* Tough love. Like, what the hell was that? So the judge let things ride, waiting for recommendations of a probation report.

And then the old man thinks it's time for a *whuppin* on Triple E. Only it wasn't time, not ever again, it wasn't the same punk Triple E made of broomsticks who had to take it and take it. Jailbird, street-trained Triple E knew how to throw punches.

His fists flew through winter light and he said aloud, "Bring em all on, bring on every motherfucker."

While he was whipping the world, pumped up monster-bad, some people came along. It was a sweet little family all bundled up in heavy coats and stocking caps, a woman, a man, a little boy. They looked alarmed as he closed in on them, his fists working. Feeling perverse, he went round the little boy, throwing punches that dented the air six inches away. The kid gawked at first, then put on a big pout.

"Hey!" the man said.

"Stop that, you damn brat!" the woman said.

"Fuck you," said Triple E. He ran off giggling.

He walked by a cool El Camino parked in a loading zone and wanted to steal it, but the tools of his trade had been confiscated by the cops. They had kept the rifle too. Chuck Pump had been lucky that night.

"Terminate you with extreme permanence," whispered Triple E. There was revenge to be had yet. Something special for Chuck Pump.

HE STOPS IN HIS tracks, panting, snorting like a winded horse. He looks up the long gradual grade of the valley, then decides he isn't going to look up anymore. It is discouraging to see how far he has to go. He glances back at the farmhouse.

"This is stupid," he says. "Everything out here is lying to me." His eyes search for some sign that says it is still a solid world and he is still a solid flesh-and-blood boy. His eyes are warped with cold and won't focus. But they were once good eyes. They were eyes that could spot a key in an ignition from thirty feet away. The beauty of his eyes, how keenly they had searched the cars at the curb, looking for something easy, the keys in it. Maybe idling like the Thunderbird with the ski racks had been, its owner gabbing on a porch not ten yards off. The guy was just asking for it!

He raises his coat collar, hunches his shoulders. It is getting beyond nippy as the afternoon comes on and the shadows lengthen. The snow has a glaze on top. It is no longer fluffy. It crunches. The bushes look as fragile as glass, like if he kicks them they will shatter. There is a deep ache in his forehead,

102

where the bullet fragments had been. It amuses him now to think of how he had actually gloried in looking so awful, that lump on his head and two black eyes and a nose he couldn't breathe out of. He had liked the way people looked at him. Startled, apprehensive. Scared. If anybody asked him what happened, he told them he was a prizefighter and had lost a close one to the champ.

"Jesus, what a liar I am," he says.

AFTER THE FIGHT WITH his father and playing Sugar Ray on the street, he went to Graham's Café and had a cup of coffee. Sitting in a booth, he sipped the coffee, warmed his hands on the cup. School let out and in came Tom and Jasper as he knew they would. They got coffee and slid in across from him and looked at his face and asked if he was okay.

"You got shot," said Jasper, shaking his head like he still didn't believe it.

"In the head, man," said Triple E.

Both boys nodded.

"When I heard it was your head, I knew you'd be all right," said Tom, grinning at him.

Triple E laughed. "Fuck you," he said.

Jasper told him how everybody was talking about how he shot Jeanne. The rumor had grown a bit. It was now gospel that Triple E went nuts and shot the fuck out of her in a jealous fit over Tom and her shacking up.

"What a bunch of crap," said Triple E. "What do I care what her and you do?" He hesitated to talk of what had happened to Jeanne. He told them the bullet was meant for Pump, not Jeanne.

"We know," said Jasper.

Tom said Pump was wondering what Triple E was going to

do next. Pump had asked if Triple E had gone so low he would shoot an old pal.

"Old pal, my ass," said Triple E.

Tom and Jasper looked at each other and smiled. "Bad," said one. "Bad bones," said the other. They wanted to know the details, how the cops had caught him, what the judge had said. Triple E said he didn't want to talk about it. Then he talked about it, told how the fuzz chased him and he was trying to blast his way out of the alley and one of them shot him in the head, but he kept going, firing like a motherfucker till his gun was empty.

"I didn't hear your gun," said Jasper.

"Maybe them cops kept you too busy," said Triple E.

Tom told how the cops grabbed him and Jasper and threw them on the ground and pulled their hair, kneed them in the back, cuffed them, threatened them. Those cops were mad.

Tom offered Triple E a cigarette. They all lit up. They all blew smoke.

Triple E said how the cops caught him at the house and how he went duke-city with three or four of them, how he called them all faggot bastards, said it right to their faces.

"Good for you," said Tom.

"Not takin no shit."

"That's right."

"Don't give a fuck who."

"You got it, baby, you got it."

They paused to suck deep on their cigarettes and sip coffee. Enemies fell right and left inside Triple E's mind. Jasper asked if he was going to hang out. The Murphy twins and Ava were coming by.

Triple E said he might, but he had to see Jeanne first, had

to tell her something important. He scowled and said the judge had wanted to put him in Goodpasture but was waiting on a probation report and something from Jeanne's parents, some written thing about how they felt about what he had done to their daughter.

"After we got home my old man tried to beat fuck outta me, but I kicked his ass, man," said Triple E.

"Soul-cool," said Tom.

"Bad bones, I say," said Jasper John.

He told them how he whacked his father's bad knee and how his father said he had no son no more, and his mother told him to get the hell out. Wasn't responsible for him, was going to call the judge and tell him to send a cop to arrest him. And he told her to fucking do it. He didn't give a flying fuck.

"Bad bones," repeated Jasper.

"Soul-cool," said Tom.

Triple E looked at Jasper. Everybody liked Jasper. Especially the girls. They liked him, loved him, shagged him. He was tall and had the hair. Guys like that, they would always slide by. No cop would ever shoot him in the head. No father would ever grab him by the throat, or ever punch his lights out, break his eardrum, put him in diapers and tie his peter with rubber bands so he wouldn't pee the bed at night. Jasper John had a charmed life. Triple E wasn't sure if he liked him all that much.

Tom was talking, telling how it was Jeanne's fault that Triple E got caught. She ratted on him right away. The cops would never have gotten anything from Tom or Jasper. But Jeanne was weak.

Triple E seethed with hatred for Jeanne.

"She's still in the hospital," said Jasper.

Triple E knew where she was. He felt a real bad mood coming on. His head was pounding. He could feel his eyes pulsing. Jeanne had ratted.

"You guys got any money?" he asked.

Jasper John dug some dollar bills from his pocket and Triple E took them. It was three bucks. He stood up and said he had to go tell that bitch Jeanne what was going down. He said he thought the judge would give probation. The judge was soft, lots of bark, no bite. Big wop eyes so sad. The kind of guy that wanted to believe your lies.

Tom agreed. He said a first offense by a kid was always probation. He told Triple E to act meek when he went to court, to cry a little if he could. That's what judges liked to see—tears. Repentance.

When he went to pay his bill at the counter, he saw the girls coming in, cousin Ava leading the way, shaking the cold off her feathery hair, her cheeks rosy, her eyes bright. She saw him and smiled and said, "Triple E, have you gone crazy?"

"Shut yer goddamn stupid face," he told her.

Ava frowned deep at first, then she started to cry. She was standing there lip dripping, little bird of a thing with leaky eyes.

"Dry up," he told her.

The Murphy twins checked him out like he was a centaur or something. They slid by and jumped in the booth with Tom and Jasper. He felt their eyes on his back. He knew they were expecting something, like he should pull a knife and rob Mr. Graham or throw a chair through the window or whatever, just be Triple E. He bought some Camels with the money Jasper had given him. While he was waiting for change, he racked his brain trying to think of what would give the girls a goose. Then Chuck Pump and L.D. walked in.

106

Triple E followed them to a booth. He stood beside them as they sat down, and Pump asked him what he wanted. Pump's brow was pale, his birthmark burned. He was swallowing dry, his Adam's apple rising and falling.

"Lookin for you," said Triple E.

"Don't fuck with me," said Pump, puffing up his chest, trying to raise his sack of guts upward.

L.D. said, "You put Jeanne in the hospital, you bastard."

Calm and cool, Triple E told L.D. she was a syph mouth Colfax floater.

L.D. bared her teeth like she was going to bite him. She glared, but he just smiled at her. He knew everybody was excited now. The Murphy girls were squirming in the next booth. Tom and Jasper were beam-eyed, full of anticipation, ready to get it on. Something coming from wild Triple E, something everybody would tell around school: *Even with his face still busted, a bullet hole in his head, he kicked Pump's fat ass right there in Graham's! Crazy! Insane!*

"I was coming to dance on your face," he told Pump.

Triple E's heart was knocking. He was almost breathless. He knew he would have to shut up and start swinging soon, or his voice would betray him. He reached over and grabbed the sugar jar. Pump started to get up and Triple E raised the jar.

"Put that down, Triple E!" ordered Mr. Graham. "You goddamn kids. What the hell's gotten into you? Put it down I said, Triple E!"

Triple E lowered the sugar jar. He leaned close to Pump's ear and told him that when the hearing was over it would be time to rumble.

"You fuckin come on then," said Pump.

"Will do. Death, taxes, and Triple E. Count on em, Pump."

He was calm again. He knew Pump was gassing, bluffing it

out, no booze to make him brave. Triple E set the sugar jar down, then slid it across the table. He rolled his shoulders and walked out. He could hear the buzz of voices as the door closed behind him.

He felt good, felt he was the insane torturer of dickheads. Exploding with energy, he wanted to do something deranged. "Gonna get you, Chuck-a-Pump!" he yelled back at the café. He gave the air a karate kick and a few chops, going, "Eeeyah! Yah!" Swish, went his hands, swish, swish.

A man stepped out of a bar, an older guy with plastered gray hair and deep lines in his face. He was watching Triple E and grinning at him. Triple E went up to the man and gave him a shove.

The man said, "Hey kid! What the fuck?"

"Kiss my ass," said Triple E.

"What's the deal?" said the man.

Triple E called him a fucking barfly, said he didn't like his fucking face.

The man put up his hands and backed away. His eyes were full of puzzlement and fear.

"Don't be grinning at me!" said Triple E.

The man turned around, went back into the bar.

Triple E saw a BMW pulling away from the curb, its tailpipe breathing a cloud of vapor. It had a bumper sticker: NIP CRIME IN THE BUD! SUPPORT ABORTION! Triple E grabbed an ice ball and threw it at the car, hitting the back window. The car slid to a stop, the driver, beefy in a suit, got out and started yelling. Triple E ran laughing. He turned down an alley, jumped a fence into someone's backyard, and barked his shins on a pile of two-by-fours stacked on cement blocks. He jumped around in pain, holding one shin first, then the other.

Some bearded guy standing on a concrete slab in the back-yard, a two-by-four in one hand, a hammer in the other, asked him what he was doing.

Triple E sneered at the guy and took off hobbling out the back gate, his shins in the grip of eagle claws.

WHEN HE GOT TO the hospital he stopped at the information booth and told the woman at the desk he wanted Jeanne Windriver's room. The woman raised her eyebrows at him, her eyes searching his face like he was a suspect in a lineup.

"Jeanne Windriver," he repeated. He felt like socking the woman, slapping her silly. His fingers itched to get at some-body.

She looked up the room number and told him where to go.

He took the elevator to the fourth floor and got off and followed the numbers and found Jeanne's room.

There she was, lying in bed, a sheet over her, looking like she was cuddled in snow. She was staring at a TV hanging from the wall.

Looking at her, the rage drained out of him, leaving him wondering. He stayed back, leaning on the wall, watching her watching TV. She was looking good, her hair spreading out on the pillows like black wings, her lips parted, smiling, teeth white as piano keys, fine flashing eyes, dark skin. Cheekbones that would make her ancestors proud. And kicking back in a bed that way, one leg cocked at the knee, what could be sex-ier? He would go in there and make up with her, tell her he didn't care that she finked. It was his fault after all. Hey, he was sorry about the leg. Does it hurt? Let me kiss it. Yeah, that would be cool. Kiss her leg, oh yeah. He would go over to the Shift and say, Hey, fellas, I kissed Jeanne's pussy tonight. Put my head under the sheet and kissed it. Tom would shit. He'd say, That Triple E, man, you never know what he's gonna do next.

He would go in, play it cool, like he didn't care. Just stroll in looking pitiful. Tell your folks not to press the judge on me, Jeanne. It was an accident, that's what he'd say. He'd fix his lonesome eyes on her. She'd be sympathetic. She'd look at his bunged-up face and probably cry, and her voice would be so soft it would feel like velvet kissing his ears. Oh, Triple E, oh your poor face. Sweet, brokenhearted Jeanne. Sorrow, all the sorrow. Yeah, I'm a mess, he'd say, Somebody ought to just shoot me. She'd laugh at that. Then he'd tell her how he never meant to shoot her. Does it hurt? he'd say, and she'd say that it hurt a little. And he wouldn't say a word, just lift the sheet and kiss her leg. Soft and kind. Leave it at that. Don't jump her bones yet. Leave her knowing what a sensitive guy is Triple E.

He took some deep breaths and composed himself. He was going in there and make it happen.

Any second now.

She laughed at something on TV. She scratched her nose. Painted fingernails—bright like cherries. She was like an Indian maiden lying on a field of lilies. No-no, white chrysanthemums, that's what. A field of white chrysanthemums. He wondered what she'd say if he told her something like that.

Mrs. Miller had told him one time there was more to him than met the eye. It was when she read a poem in class and asked for an interpretation, and it just blurted out of him that the poem was about a man giving his heart to a woman, but the woman played with him, had fun making him fall in love with her, then she left him to pine away forever, longing for a love that would never come where—*the sedge has withered from the lake* . . .

He knit his brow in thought, trying to come up with the title, but he could only remember the sedge line and something about the birds not singing. The title was something French. A knight is what the guy was, and a woman took him to her elf grove, and the poor bastard thought he had found this great love, but she boogied in the morning. "The knight is longing for love in vain," Triple E told his teacher. "The sedge is withered love, and no birds sing because birds don't sing for losers."

"Why, there's more to you than meets the eye," Mrs. Miller had said. And she told him the poem was also about "the vain pursuit of ideal beauty." Did he see what she meant? Sure, he saw. Clear as her pretty brown eyes.

Ideal beauty, its name was Jeanne Windriver. He turned away and leaned harder on the wall and took deep breaths. He still had a headache. His face was stiff with pain. He looked like a monster, an elephant man. Jeanne wouldn't want to see him, she hated him, he was ugly, he was a freak. He wasn't anything a girl like her would want. Scarecrow hanging on a T-frame, dirty hair, a nose too funky flat, a grim line for a mouth. Only ugly fat girls like L.D. would go for him. Foxes like Jeanne, they went for guys like Jasper John.

"No way, no way," he said, clenching his teeth. He peeked around the edge of the doorjamb and there she was, Princess Pocahontas floating in chrysanthemums.

A nurse walked by and gave him a look. She asked if he needed help. "Y'all wann the margency room?" she said, her voice full of southern comfort.

He shook his head, backed away, turned to catch the elevator.

"It's downstays, hahnee," she said. "Bottom flo, go east." She pointed the way for him to go.

He liked her voice. Soft, sexy. "This is not my real face," he said, pausing, hands in pockets, shoulders hunched. "I been beat up and shot. Underneath I ain't like this like you think. Just need time to heal is all."

"So Ah see," she said. Her eyes were kind. Full of sympathy. He had a notion that if they could sit down over a cup of coffee and a smoke, he could tell her all about it and she would understand, and she would say things she had learned from being a nurse, and her words would calm him down, wisdom would enter his soul, and he would see deep into the heart of Texas, or wherever she was from . . . and things might happen between them, older woman, younger man . . . tangled hearts . . . something might come of it.

"Hello, I love you."

"What's that, hahnee?"

"Gotta go, gotta boogie."

He ran off, his ears burning. He could hear her behind him giggling like a little girl. He loved it, loved her and Jeanne and all women except his mother. He would love her too, if she didn't hate him so much and if she weren't married to his father.

He took the elevator down and went past the information desk and back outside. The cold air stung his face as he stepped through the pneumatic doors. Standing on the sidewalk he looked left and right, wondering where to go. A car was sitting at the curb, the engine running, the door open. Triple E looked behind him and saw a nurse pushing a lady in a wheelchair across the lobby. In the lady's arms was a blue-blanketed bundle. A man with a suitcase walked beside her. They were discharged and going home with a new baby. The woman was looking up at the man saying something. They were both smiling. The nurse was smiling. It was a Kodak moment, something Triple E had seen a hundred times on TV.

Ambling over to the car, he slammed the door shut, went around to the other side, jumped in and drove away. He turned the heater up high as it would go. He searched the radio for rap. He drove slow, kicking back. He wasn't in a hurry to get there, wherever he was going.

CHAPTER 7

HE AND TOM PATCH rolled drunks on the street, knocking them silly and rolling them for their money and jewelry. They dropped a guy one night coming out of a gay bar as he was reaching for his keys. Tom hit him high, Triple E hit him low. And the man's head hit the pavement with a sound like a tomato busting. Triple E snatched the man's watch and his wallet. Tom kicked the man's head to make sure he stayed still. In less than ten seconds they were off and running. They left the man gurgling and twitching.

At the corner, they slowed to a walk, strolled onto Colfax Avenue, then got into their stolen Firebird and drove away. A Saturday night. Payday for flyboys.

On Colfax were lots of cars, lots of people looking for a good time, hitting the bars, hitting the dance halls, the parties.

Cops and taxis cruised. A bus roared in front of them, stinking up the air with diesel. Along the broad salmon-pink sidewalks were some people going by. There was a panhandler shaking a paper cup, trying to mooch.

"Wanna give that poor bastard somethin?" said Triple E.

"Your ass," said Tom.

They were at a red light, the car idling, the pipes rumbling. A group of men stood outside IM BLUE. They were shouting. Cuss words flying back and forth like razors. The men were puffing themselves up, trying to look bigger. Necks thickened. Teeth grimaced. Eyes flashed. A gathering of bodies, like a pack of wolves on some ancient plain. Noise blasted through the open doors—hard metal blues guitar and heavy drum, back-alley sounds that Triple E loved. From Lowry Field a jet plane soared into the air, blowing by overhead, drowning out the music and the sounds of battle. The light turned green.

In the next block Triple E saw a couple kissing on a bus bench. He rolled the window down and shouted, "Suck-face Sue, she likes to screw!" The man and woman broke apart startled, staring at him. He rolled the window up, laughing. He was real funny, was Triple E.

HE SEES HIMSELF BEATING time on the dashboard, his eyes searching the city lights, his heart in love with hell. And Tom is asking how much they got, and it turns out not so good.

"What was it?" says Triple E to himself. He remembers that the name on the driver's license was Peacock. Peee-cock. Duane T. Peacock, a tech-sergeant, married. So what was he doing hanging Tenderloin? One of them AC-DC dudes. Motherfucker deserved to get rolled, gonna bring plague home to the old lady.

The wind blows in Triple E's face, bringing with it seeds of

116

snow that pepper his eyes. He turns away, bending his back like a cow protecting itself.

Once in the ring at Goodpasture, a kid had done that, turned tail on Triple E, exposed his back for beating, and Triple E had been embarrassed for him. He could have given him some shots to the kidney, but he didn't, even though Tozer Douglas was saying to do it, to kill him. But Triple E had stepped away, looked at the ref and the ref waved his arms and said, "TKO" and raised Triple E's arm in triumph. The kid had slunk back to his corner and he said, "I think I gotta blow chunks." And he did. Triple E heard later that the kid had the flu.

"Should'a let me knock you out," says Triple E as the wind paws at him. "That's what I'd have done if I was sick."

What the kid had done was dishonorable. Being knocked out wasn't. Triple E straightens up and faces the wind, the snow lifting from the earth driving at him, and he goes into the teeth of it and he is whispering, "C'mon, c'mon."

THE WIFE OF PEACOCK. There was a picture of her. He held up her picture, a woman with dark hair and a nice smile. He called her Goosegrease and said he was going to get in touch with her, tell her that her husband was in a gay bar and was going to give her the plague. But he never did, he never called her.

He and Tom talked about becoming pimps, having a stable of hoes working for them. It was one of their fantasies, all that pussy making money for them. Women working their asses off. Soul-cool. And Triple E packing heat and wearing gold chains. On the radio the rap got harder. Triple E turned the volume high and pounded on the dash, keeping the beat.

A while later, Tom drove by A&W, cruised through and

Triple E saw her, saw Jeanne, and told Tom to go through again.

HE RESTS AND AFTER a while the wind has slacked off, and he can get up and go on. He takes a step, then breathes, takes another step, then breathes. His lips hurt. They are swollen and cracked. He keeps biting off pieces of peeling lip. His tongue tastes salty blood. He eats the skin of his lips, swallows it with snow. He remembers reading once about a mother in the big war having her arm shot off at the elbow and roasting it and feeding it to her little boy and eating some herself. She lived through the war. Lived through terrible things. The heart won't quit.

"Me too," he says. "I'll eat my own fuck'n arm if I have to," he says.

Hitting rewind in his head, he sees Jeanne with the scar on her leg. Her friends are with her. They are sitting on the patio at A&W having drinks and fries.

She is with Ava and the Murphy twins. He puts his elbow out the window and pretends not to notice her as they cruise by. Tom turns at the corner, then into the lot and they pull a U and stop at the entrance back onto East Colfax. Jeanne is ten yards away. She and the other girls look at him. He can tell they are getting a rush. They are bright-eyed quivery. Their toes are tapping nervously. He lets his eyes drift to Jeanne's eyes and they look at each other. They have been doing a lot of looking at school. They are forbidden to look, so they look. The judge told him at the probation hearing that Jeanne was off limits:

"You so much as look at Jeanne Windriver and I'll revoke your probation on the spot and send you to Goodpasture. Have I made myself clear, young man?"

Triple E looked her over and she looked him over, and what was the judge going to do? Triple E had learned that grownups talked and that was mostly all they did. Jeanne's eyes kept shifting his way, lingering, darting off, then back. Word was out that she called the bullet scar on her leg Triple E's brand.

He's branded me, she told her friends. A crazy thing to say, but very cool too. It was high drama. They were in awe of her for being shot and in awe of Triple E for shooting her. Dangerous duo. It was like the movies, only it was real, it was better.

Tom asked if he was going to do something. The car was rumbling, idling, music blasting.

"Like what?" said Triple E.

"Talk to her."

Triple E thought about going over and sitting by her and saying, How you doin, Jeanne? But he wondered what she was thinking. His mouth went dry thinking about what might be on her mind. See my scar? I'm scarred for life, Triple E! That's you, you done that. He tried to read her face, but it was a mask, a puzzle, it told him nothing.

Tom said Jeanne was goofy in love and everybody knew it. There was no telling why she had picked Triple E, but she had.

"Hard to believe," he said. "What's to love?"

"It's gospel," said Tom. "You make her heart go pitty-pat." Tom snorted. He slugged Triple E's arm.

"Fuckin guy," said Triple E. "Cool it, man."

He kept his eyes on Jeanne. Touching her hair would be heaven. Kissing her would bust a nut.

Tom told him to ask if she wanted a ride home.

Triple E shook his head. Gone shy. Tom had to lean over and shout to the girls. The girls looked at each other as Tom kept coaxing them, saying, "C'mon, we'll give you a ride. It's cool."

Ava came over and talked. They were having a sleep-over at her house. They had just walked down to A&W to get something to eat. They had to go right back home. Tom said the Pontiac had a great radio, four speakers. He cranked it up.

"Totally cool," said one of the girls. They all stood behind Ava. Ava's hip was twitching.

They came closer to the car, a couple feet off, checking it out, listening to the music. The pipes continued to rumble underneath, calling to the girls. They leaned forward, then they leaned back. They wanted to get in, but they didn't want to get in. Triple E and Tom Patch, double trouble. Ava was shying eyes at Tom and kept bumping her hip to the beat. The Murphy dorks were grinning. Jeanne was looking at something interesting in the sky.

Tom nudged Triple E and told him to open the door, which he did, and the girls looked at each other. Jeanne moved first, then the others followed. They all crowded into the backseat. Tom peeled out of the driveway. He said he was taking them past the arsenal to show them what the Pontiac could do. The girls stayed still, breathing, clearing their throats, trying to get their bearings.

Triple E could smell them. He wanted to leap the seat and wallow in them. He slipped his hand over the back of the seat, wishing one of them would put something soft near his fingers. Karen asked if the car was stolen, and Tom said it was his uncle's. He winked at Triple E.

Jeanne said, "It's stolen."

Tom asked her if she wanted out.

Triple E told her he didn't want her getting in trouble anymore because of him. He put on a serious face. He wanted her to know he was a sincere guy. And she said she didn't give a fuck about trouble, and her eyes lingered, her eyes threw signals at Triple E.

When they got way out past the arsenal, Tom took the Pontiac up to eighty on a dirt road. Fence posts and brush flew by. The eyes of animals glowed in the dark. The engine strained and Tom said it was pulling too much weight. He slowed down, came to a skidding stop, and asked who wanted to lighten the load. Triple E and Jeanne volunteered to get out. It was a white night, big moon. Endless prairie. Coyotes and things.

Tom left them standing together on the road. They watched until the lights disappeared over a rise. Triple E looked at heaven. Lots of stars—spangles on a black dress. The moon low and clear, dark seas, craters. Around him the wind moved slow, humming harplike through the brush.

Jeanne said it was a good thing her parents didn't know where she was. She toed the gravel. "Especially if they knew I was with notorious Triple E," she said, chuckling softly. "What a reputation you got," she added.

There it was again. The bad opinion people had of him. People hating him, even his own parents, who had washed their hands of him. Like Pontius Pilate, I'm washing my hands, his dad had said. He was ashamed of Triple E. He said Triple E should go to military school and learn to be a man, and Triple E said that would be the day and he dared his father to try putting him in some fool school. But it was amazing, when he thought of it, how many people hated him, wished him ill, wished him, no doubt, dead. It was hard for him to see himself as worthy of so much hatred.

He asked Jeanne what time she had to get back.

She shrugged.

He smelled dust and sage in the air. He walked away from her, toward where the car had gone. He was trying to figure out what to do with her. He didn't want to seem fast, eager, but Jesus, there she was blue in the moonlight, her hair like ink, lips half-parted. She was watching him. He couldn't read her face. He didn't know what to say to her. He wanted to talk about it, but he didn't want to spoil anything. Coming to a stop close enough to smell the damp orchid aroma of her skin, he asked about the bullet wound. "Is your leg okay?" he whispered.

She said it was no trouble. She pointed to it, lifting it at an angle, her finger touching the scar. The scar was white. It looked vaguely like a lopsided heart.

He said, "Man, I thought I killed you."

They looked at each other. There were more things to say, but neither one of them spoke. He held his palms up in a gesture of helplessness. She gazed toward the moon. "Look how bright," she said.

He licked his lips. Then he murmured in his softest voice that he wouldn't hurt Jeanne Windriver for nothing, not for a million bucks. And he offered to let her shoot him in the leg. He would supply the gun and everything.

She didn't want to shoot him. She put her hand on his arm. "What is it about you?" she said. Her eyes searched his face like she was trying to find a secret code. What made her want him? He couldn't figure it out either. Fine fox like her.

Then he kissed her. Or she kissed him. Somebody moved. Lips met. Her nose was cold against his cheek, but it was the sweetest kiss he had ever had, the sweetest mouth he had ever imagined. When their lips parted, she told him that she had been thinking about him all her life. He told her she was always on his mind too. Every single day, over and over, all winter and spring and summer, she had been on his mind. He had wanted to get in touch with her, but had been afraid to. Not because he was afraid of breaking probation, or afraid of her parents, or anything like that, but because he was afraid she hated him. He wouldn't be able to stand it if she hated him.

"Never hate you," she said, her voice breaking.

They sat on a small boulder at the side of the road. Put their arms around each other and looked at the prairie and the starry heavens, and Triple E knew that what was happening to him was love, the real thing pouring into his heart. He was ready to do whatever she wanted. He was ready to die for her. He would kill her parents if she wanted him to. He would take her away to some far-off place, where they would find happiness in each other's arms and to hell with the world. They leaned their heads together and she told him how she had been watching him at school, and she had almost given him a Valentine in February, and she had called his house probably a dozen times and hung up when his mother answered the phone.

All autumn long at school he had watched her summer-grown hips. That Indian hair falling on her shoulders. His heart aching for her. Aching. And she had been aching for him too? Amazing.

He had no words to express himself. He hoped his lonesome eyes were speaking for him. He kissed her again. Both her arms went around his neck and locked him up. He kept his lips sealed to hers and massaged her hip, her ribs, and finally her pert breast. The kissing went on and on, tongues probing, lips turning inside out. It was like something he couldn't get enough of. It was like a world's record for kissing.

Finally they broke away and sat hugging one another. Then

they talked. The subject of Tom and Ava came up. Jeanne didn't think it was very nice the way he treated her. "He's so mean to her. He just uses her."

"Yeah, and she lets him," said Triple E. "Ava is hard-up for love. It's her mother's fault. She's a fuckin lush, man."

"I heard," said Jeanne.

Triple E sang a ditty, making fun of Ava's mother, he sang: "If the ocean was whisss-key and she was a duck, she'd dive to the bott-tom and never come up . . . drinking whisss-key rye whiskey, she's a wild, wild woman . . . she'll drink that rye whisss-key and live till she dies—"

He got up and paced back and forth, kicking stones into the ditch, mad at himself suddenly for making fun of his aunt.

"You mad?" said Jeanne.

"No I ain't mad, it's just that everything is so fucked up. I don't know what to do sometimes. Sometimes I wanna kill somebody, you know? And sometimes I wanna just get the fuck away from here. Go to Alaska maybe and live off the land. You can still do it up there. I don't know. It's just all these crazy things chasing each other. Sometimes I feel like I'm gonna blow. Detonate like nitro."

"I know," she said. "I feel like that too all the time. I hate this world, don't you?"

"Yeah, it's fucked, everything's fucked."

"I keep thinking I'm gonna die, get shot or something in a drive-by. And there's that AIDS thing now and everything."

"Yeah," he said. He was suddenly very depressed.

"Hard to be happy in such a world," she said. "I wish I'd been born earlier when things were nicer."

"I wish I could've been in World War Two," said Triple E.

"My mother is always on my ass," said Jeanne. "Picking on

me all the time, saying I shouldn't wear short skirts like this. You know what she called me? She called me a Colfax floater, a slut. I almost slugged her."

"I slugged my old man. Him and me duked it out and I kicked his ass. He don't fuck with me no more."

"My brother's gonna turn out just like my dad, a military man. He's already just like him."

Triple E walked in circles. "Goddamn, I'd like to kick some ass," he said.

"I wish I had my own car," said Jeanne. "I'd run away. I'd go to California and live on the beach. My parents hate me."

Triple E put his arms around her to comfort her. It was the two of them—picked on, misunderstood.

Jeanne snuggled in his arms.

He started to say more, then words failed him. He wanted to tell her who he was, but at the moment he didn't have the vaguest idea: just a bad boy, just a boy in love, he told himself, feeling awful tragical.

She leaned her shoulders back, her groin pressing forward, eyes regarding him, her eyes making like magnets. They kissed some more, sloppy and hard, he pressing against her, she pressing back, and he told himself what the hell more is there than this? What else could anybody want? Nothing, certainly not growing up and becoming a big fat zero like his parents, like Jeanne's parents, like anybody old was. Boring, boring, boring.

Being young, young, he wanted young forever.

The headlights pressed down on them, and they watched as the Firebird pulled up and stopped, a cloud of dust boiling over it. Tom rolled the window down and said he had pegged the speedometer. He said they had cruised on after, taking it slow, the lights off, and caught a couple shagging on the trunk of a car, the girl's legs up over the guy's shoulders and him giving it to her, not even stopping when Tom turned the lights on. Ava said it was true, every bit of it. The four of them had watched the couple banging and they wouldn't even stop. They didn't even care that they were in the lights and people watching. It was like a dirty movie. It was like, get your eyes full, get your jollies, who cares?

"That's what we're comin to," said Ava.

"We all kissed Tommy," said Karen Murphy.

"All of us," said her sister Kory.

Tom was grinning. He said he and the ladies had a little orgy of their own.

"You should've seen us!" Kory said.

"Not a real orgy. We just kidded around," said Karen.

Tom said he would know Karen's boobs anywhere now, he could pick them out in the dark with just the tip of his tongue. He looked at Ava and leaned his head closer to her. "And what would I know of yours, puddin pot?" he said. He put his finger under her nose and she knocked it away.

"And what did you guys do, huh?" said Kory, wiggling her eyebrows.

When they got into the car Jeanne sat on Triple E's lap. They ignored the others. There was lots of kissing to do. He wanted to tell her he loved her, but she wouldn't let up enough to even whisper.

THEY DROPPED THE GIRLS off at Ava's house, and Jeanne told Triple E she would find a way to call him and they would meet at places like school and the Shift and the park and the movies. Nothing would keep them apart. She kept kissing him.

It seemed like she wanted to swallow his whole face. The others had to pry her off. She was kissing him through the open window as Tom eased the car away.

"I'll see you later," she said. "Will I ever!"

She was watching him. He waved out the window, then turned to Tom. "What lips!" was the first thing Triple E said.

"Bet you got major wood," said Tom.

Triple E told Tommy he didn't know the half of it. He said he was swallowing Jeanne's spit and coming in his pants, her ass pushing against his joebuck and he couldn't help it. "She got me off, man," he said. "I wonder if she knows."

Tom said he knew some things about Jeanne. He said Jeanne would let you do anything to her but put the wood. Tom had snatched her at the Shift, gave her a monster button massage, but she wouldn't let him put the wood, but yeah she knew how to get a guy off, her ass understood.

Triple E remembered Tom talking that way after the incident at the Shift, but it hadn't bothered him much then. This time it bothered him. Thinking about Tom and Jeanne and how he said she was willing to do anything but put the wood, the thought of that, the image of him and her, their hands, their lips, it pissed Triple E off. He wanted Tom to shut up with that shit. He didn't want to think that Tom had had his hands on Jeanne at all. He hated to think about that goddamn night. That dirty goddamn winter night. Them in the Shift. Hands and mouths. Triple E wished there were some way he could take that night back, toss it out. That whole winter had been fucked. Loser of a winter for sure. He looked out the window at the traffic zipping by, and he wondered what was next, what was the future bringing him?

They were headed toward a place called Bunny's Bar, a

nightspot they had hit before. It was off the main drag, in a residential area, an old, dark part of Denver. Tom wanted to roll one more mungo before calling it quits. Forty-two bucks, a Visa and a Benrus from Duane T. Peacock flyboy, man, that was nothing.

BEFORE THE HIGH-LOW system, they used to walk up to some guy and put a knife to his ribs, take his wallet, and run away. Then one night a guy who didn't look like much almost broke their necks. He went berserk, feet and hands flashing so fast the boys couldn't see what was hitting them. They both ran for their lives. It was afterward that Tom thought up the high-low system. He said it was the way the Brothers did it, the Blacks. They called it double-banking. A single victim, always someone coming out of a bar, and not too big. No words. Hit with no warning. Slam the head on the pavement so to stun the motherfucker. They had practiced on Jasper John in Tom's backyard, hitting him high and low together, getting his wallet and stuff, honing their technique to perfection. Since then, it had worked every time. Jasper John had been invited to join as a getaway driver, but he declined. He wasn't physical in that sort. He stuck to ripping off cars and a little shoplifting here and there. He didn't have a true criminal drive.

Triple E turned to Tom and asked if he had ever thought what they would do if somebody pulled heat on them. Triple E said he was going to get his hands on a gun. He was going to get it from Conroy's Pawnshop. There was this stainless steel revolver, a .38 Ruger "snubby" in the display counter. Triple E coveted it.

"Conroy buys our stuff, we can't rip him off," said Tom.

Triple E got mad. He accused Conroy of ripping *them* off. All pawnshop pricks were rip-off artists, everybody knew that.

They deserved to get ripped off themselves, that was Triple E's opinion.

"Conroy owes us," he said.

"You think everybody owes us," said Tom.

"Everybody does!" said Triple E. He folded his arms across his chest and checked out some houses flitting by. He thought of the people safe and warm in their beds and it pissed him off, he didn't know why. "Christ, my cock is all sticky," he said. He took some tissues from the glove box and wiped himself.

Tom said the problem with Triple E getting a gun was that he could hardly wait to shoot somebody. Triple E wanted to shoot his father, wanted to shoot Chuck Pump, wanted to shoot Conroy. How long did Triple E think he would last out there with heat?

"Longer than without it," said Triple E.

Tom laughed and he told Triple E that he was number one, the best friend Tom had ever had. Tom knew that Triple E would go down with him if he had to. Dependable, that's what he was. And it would hurt Tom to lose him. But the thing was, Triple E would kill somebody just to be killing and then that would be the end of everything.

"We do all right, don't we?" said Tom.

"We make a livin," said Triple E.

"And we can keep doin it till the Second Coming. But if you off somebody, brother, the story changes. The cops will hunt us down like dogs. Use your fuckin brain, Triple E."

Triple E said let the cops come. He would go down guns blazing. "A blaze of glory," he said. "Think of us going out like Butch Cassidy and the Sundance Kid, what a great way to go."

"They're real dead," said Tom.

"Everybody's gotta die," Triple E said. "What matters is how."

Tom didn't answer.

Triple E thought about death, the big *nada* of it, the big vacancy where there used to be a body. A ton of earth on top of him, like his nana and papa in their prairie graves. He knew he was being dramatic, but he wondered if he meant it, would he go down guns blazing? Bodies piled up around him? How could he love Jeanne so much and want to kill everybody? Wasn't love supposed to make the world sunshine and roses or something? What a load.

Bunny's Bar wasn't far from the freeway. It was a small bar next to a laundromat and a gas station. The houses nearby were old. The trees were cottonwoods mostly, tall and gloomy and gnarled. They had angry roots that made the sidewalks roll. The streets were narrow, cars parked along both sides and just barely enough room for two cars to pass each other.

Tom parked the Firebird a block over, and they walked to the bar, peered in, saw it jammed with men and women. There was music on, soothing Frank Sinatra crud, and the din of voices. The boys went across the street and sat on the porch of an abandoned house. It gave a good view of the bar and the street. They perched high on the last step, like gargoyles waiting.

People came and went, but most were in pairs or foursomes, and the ones alone did not look mungo enough, too big, too alert, too steady, too ready. It was well past midnight when a man finally came out who looked doable. He was short and stocky with a beer belly. He was unsteady. He had a heavy round head bristling with silver hair. The boys looked at each other, then went after him. They let him get halfway down the block, under the cottonwoods, before they jumped him. Tom hit high, Triple E went low. They hit him with all they had, but he hardly even budged. It was like tackling a fireplug.

"Fock," he said, and then he laughed and grunted and started kicking the shit out of the boys.

Triple E clung to one of the man's legs and tried to trip him up, lifting the leg at the knee and driving forward like a football player. The man hopped on one foot and clubbed Triple E's back with his fist. At one point a slap caught Triple E on the side of the head. It felt like a spike had been driven into his ear. He yelped and let go of the man's leg. Leaning out of reach, he considered for a second what to do. The man had Tom Patch in a neck lock and was slamming a fist into his belly. Tom was down on his knees and the guy was lifting him again and again, hitting him, dropping him. It was no contest. Triple E wanted to get Tom loose and run. The man wasn't human, he was an ass-kicking ogre is what.

Triple E started punching him in the head. It was like hitting a piece of oak. The blows hurt Triple E's fists. He changed to kicking the man's legs and buttocks, trying to get one into his balls. The man let go of Tom and caught Triple E's foot, jerked him over backwards, slamming him on the side-walk on his back, knocking the wind out of him. For several seconds he lay there waiting to get his breath back. Tom Patch was curled around the man's left foot, biting his ankle and taking hammer blows from above.

"Fockin punks," said the man. He was shaking his foot like he was trying to shake off a puppy, just some nuisance playing with him.

Air rushed into Triple E's lungs, and he knew there was only one way to save himself and Tom. He stood up, pulled his knife, and started slashing. He slashed the man's arms. He slashed his back, he slashed his head. The man turned away, raising his hands to cover himself. He backed off, Tom still clinging to his ankle and being dragged along, while Triple E worked the blade up and down, opening wound after wound. The man was bellowing. Porch lights were coming on. People were yelling.

The man went down. Triple E stabbed him in the side and in the leg, both wounds hitting bone. Standing back and motioning with the knife, Triple E shouted, "C'mon, c'mon, you think you're so fuckin bad!"

The guy wiped his hand over his face, looked at his black palm, looked at his carved arms, and growled.

Tom lurched to his feet, holding his stomach and moving away, gasping. The man got up too. He came after Triple E.

The boys ran. Tom went one way, Triple E another. Past the bar Triple E went, the guy chasing him, looking in the night like a bowlegged ape, arms and hands raised, fingers grasping. He wouldn't let up, he wouldn't quit coming. They ran two blocks and it was like the wrath of God was after Triple E.

He could see nothing for it but to turn and face him. But he didn't want to face him. He didn't want those terrible hands on him again, hands that could tear him apart, tear his heart out.

"*Stop!*" Triple E cried over his shoulder. "Go'way, go'way!"

He was winded from the fight, his ribs hurt, there was a stitch in his side, a pain in his ear, his lungs burning, his mouth feeling like sandpaper. He ran and ran, stumbling and gasping and trying to find his stride. His legs were turning to molasses.

It was just when he couldn't go a foot farther and was ready to fall down and let it happen that Triple E got a reprieve. There was a cross street ahead. A car shrieked to a halt, a door swung open and Triple E could see Tom waving an arm, urging him on.

"Run your ass off, baby!" Tom yelled.

Triple E put on a final burst and threw himself into the Firebird. The tires squealed and he felt a welcome surge of power carrying him out of harm's way. He could hear the man behind them howling. He laid his head back, sucked air, gasped and gasped. Tom was grunting, complaining about his stomach. Said his guts felt like scrambled eggs. "I bet he's busted my ribs," said Tom.

"I thought I was fast, but I couldn't outrun him, he just kept comin and comin!" said Triple E.

They agreed the guy was the baddest muther they had ever met in their lives. A real animal, a bull. And yet he was so old, so gray and dumpy. How could a man so old be so bad?

Triple E said he didn't know. Once upon a time he knew things, but not no more.

Tom said that never again would they try to roll mungo muthers with low centers of gravity. It was like wrestling a bowling ball.

THE ROCK IS LIKE a desert tortoise, huge, smooth, round, its shell made of snow. He brushes the snow off and sits down. His face is turned southwest as he watches the white dime of the sun fall. It is at least two o'clock, maybe three.

Snow dust keeps swirling over his face. Somewhere is the car. Is Jeanne. He wonders if Tom Patch is back. Rescue waiting, everything fine. He wonders if the car has gas, is it still running, is it warm, will it thaw him? He looks at his feet and doesn't recognize them. From the ankles down he is paralyzed. Reaching along his shins, he raps them with his knuckle, sends vibrations into his knees. It is like he is turning into wood. The cold is creeping up. It will deaden his lower body first, then numb his torso. When it reaches his heart he will be ice dead.

Sliding off the rock, he curls up in the snow and closes his eyes. Ice crystals coat what's left of his lashes. He will sleep a moment, get his energy back, go rescue pretty Jeanne.

A MOMENT LATER HE feels it, something wet and raspy running over his forehead. He digs a fist into his eyes and his lashes snap off. He opens his eyes and sees a red and white Hereford standing stupidly in front of him.

What's up, whispers Triple E.

The cow cranes its neck, its long face stretching, its nostrils smoking. Cold, says the cow. Foooood, it says. Fooood, foood, foood, it says.

You think I carry hay in my hip pocket, you dumb ferlie fucker? says Triple E.

The cow lows at him. Snorts. Lowers its horns and paws the snow.

Go'head, says Triple E. I ain't goin nowhere.

The cow's nose is coated in ice. Little picks of ice hang from its nostrils and the corners of its mouth. Its ears are pointy and black with frostbite.

We're dying, the cow says.

Fuckin-A, says Triple E. He looks around for other cows, the herd. Where is the herd and the rancher who owns it? Cow is starving. Ribs like a xylophone. Triple E takes out his knife and makes music on the cow's ribs, *ting, ting, ting.* There was a movie: this guy slaughters a cow, guts it, and crawls inside to get warm and the cold is so cold it freezes the guy inside the cow. Triple E feels along the cow's belly with the blade of the knife. The cow trembles.

Steak, says Triple E.

The cow knocks him down.

But the knife stays in the cow's belly and it bleeds over the snow. The cow goes down, resting on its side. It reaches over its shoulder, licking the wound, its head sagging lower and lower.

Says Triple E: Sorry, there, buddy. Oh gee, looka the blood.

The cow is swallowing, but it can't swallow so much blood. The cow starts coughing. The cow is coughing blood all over the place. The snow turns red, bleeds a tide over Triple E, swimming in a sea of blood, kicking, coughing, swallowing, drowning.

CHAPTER 8

BREAKING INTO CONROY'S PAWNSHOP. He did that on his own. He had all this frustration and energy inside him, making him feel like a cyclone whirling, wanting a path of destruction, wanting everything flattened. He had to have a gun, he had to have heat, because life was risky, it was ominous, and anything could happen out there. A gun leveled things out. With a gun he was as bad as the heavyweight champ of the world, take no shit off him, blow his head off, the sonofabitch.

It was a chunk of concrete he tossed through Conroy's window, and he slipped over the jagged edges, while the alarm was going *woo-woo-woo-woo*. He went right to the glass display case and busted it with his foot, reached in and plucked out the snub-nosed .38. He grabbed a box of bullets and as an afterthought took a saber with a brass handle and a chrome blade. He was in and out in less than a minute.

On the way home, he went through the back alleys and vacant lots and spent some time playing with the saber, slashing weeds and trees and trash cans. Dogs barked at him in the alleys and he tried to reach over fences to cut them, but they always jumped away and kept barking till he left. At one place he chased a cat and almost stabbed it, but it zipped along ahead of him, like a tease wriggling its tail, like the two of them were playing a game.

After an epic battle with overwhelming forces, he took the saber and broke it over his knee, rather than hand it to the general demanding his surrender. He threw the brass hilt in the general's face and was executed on the spot, dying heroically, defiantly, his fist raised.

Afterward he went to Chuck Pump's street and stopped at his house, sizing up the situation. The lights were out. They were all asleep inside. Safe in their beds. Unaware of the danger prowling in the night. Walking around to the side of the house where Pump slept, Triple E got close, his ear to the window. He imagined he could hear Pump jacking off, keeping his willie in practice for the day the pornos called to make him the new John Wadd. Triple E giggled and slammed his hand over his mouth. He walked backwards giggling. Taking out his gun, he loaded it and got some practice. It was a six shot and he blew off five—*Blam!Blam!Blam!Blam!Blam!* Pump's window shattered. Lights came on all over, dogs down the block made a savage racket. Above the noise, Triple E could hear Chuck inside shrieking, "Maaaa!"

Jesus what fun! He was going to shoot Pump's house once or twice a week. Do it at various times, hit the walls right where Pump slept, keep the fat bastard on edge. Just drive by and *blam-blam,* listen to the fat boy squeal. Triple E took off, his easy legs eating up the first block and then another, the gun in hand, no one daring to deny him anything.

In his room the next morning, a Sunday, he lay sprawled on the bed rereading *Mad,* and he heard the doorbell ring. Then he heard his mother saying, "Yes?" and a man's voice said, "We'd like to speak to Elbert Earl Evans."

Triple E peeked. He saw his mother and father standing in the living room, the Sunday funnies hanging from his father's hand, his mother hugging herself, while the man talked, while he told her that Elbert Earl was suspected of firing shots at a house on Ironton Street, the home of Charles Pump. "Do you know Elbert's whereabouts around midnight last night?" asked the man.

"Last night?"

"Last night, yes ma'am."

Triple E didn't wait for her to answer. He slipped on his fatigue jacket and put the gun in his pocket and jumped out the window, hit the ground running. He didn't let up until he passed the Pioneer Cemetery, where his grandmother and grandfather were buried.

He crossed some pasture, where cows were browsing and a windmill pumped water into a huge oval tank, where he rested a moment and played with the water. It was the same spot where years back he had shot a dozen baby rattlesnakes with his BB gun. They had been no bigger than his finger, but curling anyway, striking at him, going down angry and biting his tennies as he pumped BB after BB into them. Snakes were bad. Him too. He was like them.

"Don't tread on me," he said.

Running to the bluffs, he stood in the wind overlooking the trees and the valley. He found the skull of a cow and tossed it like a discus over the edge. Below him, leaves were dying, scattering, turning orange and yellow and fiery red. He remembered the homeless cat parachuting down and down. He thought about jumping himself. He wondered why he shouldn't. He wasn't going to live long anyway. Live fast, die young. No future for the Triple E's of this world. All the gadgets a guy needed to know about, all the education and stuff you had to have to get along. He was a Wild West Billy the Kid type. He was a time-warped misfit mountain man.

Beneath him Herefords moved like lumbering mowers. The wind blew in his face, peppering him with sand. He went down to the creek. He sat at the edge of the water with the gun in his hand, waiting for the crawdads to come out of the reeds, where they were hiding from his shadow.

Flipping the chamber open, he emptied the shells into his palm and looked at them and remembered that he hadn't reloaded. He had forgotten to bring the box of ammo and there was only one live bullet left. He threw the empty casings away, reloaded the one bullet, closed the chamber and gave it a spin. He put the muzzle in his mouth, put it in his ear, put it against his forehead, against his heart.

He pulled the trigger with the muzzle against his heart and felt exhilaration rush through him as the hammer snapped on nothing. He spun it again and aimed at his right foot, the big toe. Again, he pulled the trigger and again the hammer snapped.

Not far away, a cow was grazing, not paying any attention to Triple E. He aimed at the cow. When he pulled the trigger the gun went off. The noise startled him and he dropped the gun in the water and had to fish it out. The cow ran a few feet, kicking its heels, then it stopped and stared at him. All the cows dotting the pasture were also staring at him. After a minute, they resumed clipping grass or chewing cud. He could see blood running from the belly of the one he shot, a steady trail of blood brightening the grass. The cow kept throwing its head back, licking the wound.

"Shot a goddamn cow," murmured Triple E, a bit over-whelmed by it.

An hour passed before the cow went down. Triple E walked to where it rested on its knees and stomach, its head up, its mouth working on a darkened cud. The cow looked at him with bulging, bloodshot eyes. When Triple E bent to stroke its back, the cow shivered. After a few minutes, the head started drooping like a drought-stricken lily, the eyes closed, the cow slept. The air blowing from its nostrils frothed pinkish.

"Goddamn," said Triple E. "Wasn't meaning to kill you, cow. It was just . . ." He shrugged his shoulders, unable to explain. The cow's ears flicked back and forth, sweeping flies away.

WHEN HE OPENS HIS eyes, he is curled beneath the turtle rock and there is no cow or cow blood. "My mind is gettin goofy," he says. He sits up teetering and uncertain. There is nothing to see but the immense vacancy of whiteness before him. He ponders whether or not there ever was a cow he shot, or was that a dream too that day? Dreams and reality seem like the same thing to him now. Just like the past and present, it is all one, laid out like a map inside his head.

Looking at his feet, he sees a black sock with a hole in the toe, the toe poking through purple and swollen. Certainly this can't be *his* toe. He touches it and it's like touching a stone. He searches for his shoe, finds it, knocks the snow out of it, slips it on.

Ahead of him are endlessly curling drifts, like frothy waves frozen on a beach. He turns in a circle, uncertain which way to go. He feels icicles in his groin, ice tentacles reaching for his heart. He turns and turns, recognizing nothing.

"My name is Triple E," he says aloud. His voice is creaky. It is very, very old.

Inside his head is something gooey. He hears noises, metal against metal, clanging doors, feet treading cement floors, voices echoing. A hand falls on his shoulder. A hand guides him upward as he falls.

IN STONE GARDEN THE cops were searching for Triple E, never thinking he could be far-off east in farmland. He chuckled about it, how he was always ahead of the cops. It was dusk, the wind picking up, the clouds racing by as he headed toward some storage silos rising like tombstones out of the earth. The wind tugged at his clothes. He bent forward and walked as fast as he could, but it was rough going until he reached the silos. Rain started flogging him. The wind drove the rain into his face and he could barely see where he was going. Behind him was the dark pasture and the cow with a bullet in its stomach.

An office building stood with its back against the first silo. The office was locked up. He went around to the side and broke a window and climbed in. The weather went crazy. Thunder and lightning and yowling wind, the rain coming down like Noah's flood. It sounded as if steel bolts were hitting the roof. Triple E hunched in the knee space beneath a desk in the middle of the room, where he curled and waited for the storm to end for morning to come for daylight to show him which way to go. He imagined the cops combing the city for him, telling everybody he was armed and dangerous. Grimly he smiled about it and felt a fine sense of accomplishment.

THE NEXT MORNING HE found pretzels and pork rinds in the desk and ate them. He drank water from the cooler, letting some of it run over his face. Out the back door he went, following a narrow hall into a machine shed full of plows and planters, a tractor and a combine. The machine shed leaned its roof against the silo, and the loading booms curved from the silo like a spout from a teapot. On the loading dock was a bobtail truck filled with wheat. The key was in it.

He stole the truck. He drove it onto the dirt road and went east. Kansas was up ahead somewhere. He would go there and cash out the wheat, make a killing and drive on to Minnesota, where some cousins lived.

The truck moved along at a waddling pace. Every time he tried to shift gears, the truck would stall and he would have to start over again. He couldn't figure out the shift pattern. He was in compound low and he thought the next gear should be regular low straight down toward his knee. As he studied the faded pattern inscribed on the shift knob, the truck drifted off the road and almost turned over. He poured the gas to it and ran into some barbed wire fencing. The engine was roaring, the truck was bouncing and jerking and rattling as he tried to pull back out, get back to the road. The fencing got wrapped up somewhere underneath the truck. Posts were popping out of the ground. Before long he was dragging a mess of barbed wire and posts twenty feet long. The engine started clucking, coughing. The truck heaved forward a few yards, then died and wouldn't start again.

"Stupid truck," said Triple E as he held the key down and listened to the battery fade to clicks. He got out and slammed the door and kicked the front tire and fell on his ass, tumbling backwards to the bottom of the ditch. "Goddammit!" he yelled.

Looking up, he saw the truck leaning at a dangerous angle, clinging to the steep side, on the verge of flipping over on top of him. The right front wheel was in the air. Wheat spilled over the wall. Behind the truck was a trail of barbed wire and broken posts and curious cattle already nosing around, sniffing freedom. Some of them got giddy and did a little boogie on the dirt road.

Climbing out of the ditch, he went around to the raised wheel. He pushed upward on the fender, using his legs and shoulders like a weightlifter, grunting and pushing with all his might, and that's all it took, a nudge, and the side lifted, seeming to scream, its metal cracking and creaking, then rolling over, crashing, flipping, spilling its load, and landing upright, its squashed body shivering in a cloud of dust and wheat, the husks looking like gnats lifting in the wind.

He ran away. The cattle ran too. He and the cattle frolicking.

A MILE OR SO farther, he came upon a World War One type of plane. Double-winged and big and real, a fantastic prize sitting right in the middle of the road. Oil dripped under the engine, slow plops making a widening mess in the dirt. He climbed inside the cockpit and played with the buttons and switches. He worked the stick between his legs and the tail flaps went up and down. He had a notion he could fly the plane if he could get it started. He played with all the buttons and toggle switches on the dash. A red light came on.

Now what? he wondered.

Getting out he went to the propeller and tried to figure out which way to spin it. He was pondering the curve of the blade and had decided it would need to go clockwise, when he heard a car behind him. Looking back he saw the car closing fast. He ran. When he got a few yards away, he looked back and saw two men getting out of the car. They walked to the plane, carrying some kind of part. One man raised his hand and waved.

Triple E shouted, "What's wrong with your plane?"

"Fuel pump!" said the man. He shook his fist at heaven. "Almost crashed and burned!" he said.

"Bummer," said Triple E.

The man was laughing. He had gotten away with something and it made him happy. Triple E understood him, admired him, the tough, the brave.

AN HOUR LATER HE was back in town, bopping along East Colfax Avenue. He went past the Chevrolet parking lot—Great Gary's Chevrolet: For a Great Gary Deal—and stopped at the used cars. Front and center was a classic Corvette convertible, maroon with white sculpts in the fenders. It had wire wheels and wide tires. He walked around it, admiring its sleek beauty. The key was in the ignition. There were no salesmen outside. He could see them through the plate-glass window, three of them eating lunch at a table. He eased into the seat, started the engine, and drove calmly over the curb and onto East Colfax. He ran through the gears, turned left at the first corner, and got off the main drag.

To entertain himself, he put the Vette through its paces, blasting up and down the residential streets of Stone Garden, making the engine growl, the tires smoke blue. The Vette was bad. Seemed like it was going to leap out from under him. He laid rubber in every gear. He flew over crossroad dips, hitting the pavement so hard he could hear the frame scraping.

Around corners, he laid the car low enough to take the paint off the rocker panels. Then he punched the rpms, thrilling to the power pulling him out of fishtails and side drift. He started believing he could be a racecar driver, win the Indy 500, get a million dollars and some ten-foot trophies, blond babes kissing him in the Winner's Circle.

HE STOPPED AT MCDONALD'S and bought a hamburger and fries and a chocolate shake. He parked next to the Fox Theater in the shade of a tree and ate his lunch. People strolling by checked him out. "Bitchin Vette," said a cool black guy pimping by in a silky black shirt, gold chains, and a black beret. Triple E nodded but didn't say anything. He was cool too. Too cool to talk.

Later he drove to Stone Garden High. He saw kids on the lawn, soaking up the sun. The boys sloppy, looking like overgrown ten-year-olds. The girls in jeans and skirts, vests and blouses and every color of hair, glittering like tropical birds. Triple E saw mouths moving, hands gesturing, big smiles, some grab-ass going on. He caught their attention with a downshift, the pipes bubbling low notes, growling.

At the end of the block, he pulled a screaming turn into the teachers' parking lot. He spun the Vette cleanly in and out of the lanes, whipping it so close to the parked cars there was hardly room to fit a whisper.

Jeanne, the Murphy twins, and cousin Ava were standing near the curb, a little covey of color watching him. He gave them a show, burning rubber the length of the lot, then swooping a big U that brought him back to where the girls were standing. He arrived in a cloud of smoke.

"You nutso!" said Karen Murphy. But she was grinning, she

was enjoying him. Things happened when Triple E came around. Babes got blood in their cheeks when he showed up and they said to themselves, *What's gonna happen now? Where's the action comin from?*

Kory Murphy was squirming, turning half a hip to him, so he could profile her fine toot-toot in painted-on pants. He knew she wanted him to see what he was missing.

"Where you been?" said Ava. Her eyes were wild, her voice fast and squeaky. "Your mom's certifiable, Triple E. She's crying and crying, I never seen such bawling, hysterical, I swear to God, man, she and my mom and your dad, all of em drunk and fightin and blamin everybody but the pope. You got blamed the most. Man, what they said about you! Your dad says he's done with you. Done with you for good."

"Like I ain't heard that before," said Triple E.

"Did you shoot Pump's house? Pump says it was you."

Triple E spread his palms. "What can I say, Ava? Chuckie ought to know not to mess with Triple E."

She jabbered, she said, "Triple E, you're goin straight to hell! Do not stop at Go, do not collect two hundred dollars! Your folks say somebody switched you with their real son in the hospital. Your dad said your mom was balling a maniac on the side and you're God's punishment for it. What a night, man!" Ava giggled hysterically.

Triple E had a quick flash of his mother—the time he walked in on her and the strange guy, she naked and sprawling over the guy's lap. He was spanking her and she was howling. Triple E had been little, a toddler, a tiny thing reaching up to grab a doorknob, worried about his mother, wondering what was happening to her. She put him outside and locked the door and he sat on the porch steps until late afternoon. When his father came home, Triple E said nothing. It took years to absorb what was going on, and in those years she became his most unfavorite female in the whole world.

"Let her bawl, she oughtta bawl," he told his cousin.

"Walkin chaos, that's what your dad called you."

"The T stands for trouble," said Triple E.

Ava was looking good, all flushed with excitement, her solid titties rubbing against her shirt as she talked and gestured. "So what're you gonna do?" she asked him.

Triple E shrugged. He didn't know one minute to the next what he was going to do. He tossed his hair, lit a cigarette, and gave the girls his best profile. He could hear their hearts tripping. "I'm never goin back there, fuck my parents," he said. He reached in his pocket and pulled out the .38. "Check it out," he said. "Ain't it a beaut? A silver snubby, man."

Ava said, "I knew it! You are truly bone-bad, Triple E. Didn't I say it, Jeanne?"

Jeanne nodded. She had her eyes fixed on the gun, like it was a snake that might chase her. Triple E looked around. He scanned the steps and saw some teachers, three of them, watching him.

Underneath the hood, the engine rumbled. The car was shaking as if it were furious about something. He tried to smooth it out by tapping the accelerator, but it wouldn't quit idling rough. He was about to tell Jeanne to get in the car, when Karen Murphy said, "Uh-oh, man, Triple E, look out." He looked where she was pointing and saw a blue and white nosing into the lot.

"Fuckin fuzz," said Triple E. "Get lost, you guys, vamoose."

The girls walked away quickly. They went back inside the school, while Triple E eased the Vette into gear and drove away. He could see the teachers eyeballing him. They motioned to the cop and went to the curb to talk to him. Everybody was a fink. Nobody could mind his own business.

At the corner he went west and as soon as he was hidden from view by the school itself, he punched the Vette and flew to sixty in about four seconds. At the next corner he went left. He looped the block and came up the alley and waited. A few seconds later the police car swished by. Triple E pulled out and drove behind the cop. He could see the guy looking left and right at every corner, then hurrying to the next and the next.

The freeway entrance came up and Triple E took it. He wound the Vette flat out, roaring by cars like they were going backwards. Wind blew his long hair. He saw himself like a painting entitled *Cool Breeze*. The mountains were ahead of him. All around the freeway were tall buildings and houses and trees, the pavement stretching out in front of him, a path to freedom. Everything was broad and colorful. Colorful Colorado.

When the engine started missing, fluttering, doing quick jerks, he looked at the gas gauge first, but it was all right, had an eighth of a tank. He was doing seventy-five and falling. Seventy-two. Seventy. Sixty-five. He checked the temperature and it was in the red. The car was burning up. He could see a trail of smoke behind him.

"What kind of car is this?" he said. "Stupid Vette!" Corvettes weren't supposed to overheat. Corvettes were too cool to overheat. He slipped into the right-side lane and took the first off-ramp. The car was shuddering. It was getting slower and slower. At East Colfax, he turned east and pulled into the first open parking spot. He turned the engine off and jumped out over the passenger's side onto the sidewalk. Steam poured through the grille. He gave the car a kick and cussed it.

A bus went by and stopped at the corner. Triple E jogged over to the bus. He waited while people got off and people got on, then just as the bus was pulling away, he leaped onto its side, grabbing hold of an open window. He tucked his feet on the side molding. It was wide enough for his toes to grip, and there he rode, clinging like a monkey, putting on an act for pedestrians gaping at him from the sidewalk. The wind made his eyes water. He kept coming perilously close to cars and trucks parked at the curb. He felt the sheer side of a delivery van brush his back. He imagined himself getting peeled off, his body bursting, becoming a bloody spot on the road, a broken egg for a head. Jesus, he was stupid. He wished the bus would pull over and let him off. His fingers were digging into the window frame, the hard aluminum grooves.

Block after block whizzed by. People kept turning to look. They pointed at him. Some yelled, *Hey!* But the bus went on and Triple E drooped more and more, his arms aching, his elbows straightening, his toes slipping from the side molding. He looked ahead, trying to pick a spot to leap off, calculating his chances of making it. He tried to figure how to do it, how did the paratroopers fall? *Fall like a paratrooper,* his dad had told him. Hit the five points—toes, calves, thighs, hips, side. Eyes at tree level. Chin tucked into your chest and your forearms in front of your face. Roll with it, relax, let the momentum take you.

But the pavement was too fast, too hard, and he couldn't make himself let go. *Never again,* he told himself. *Just get me outta this!* With the last of his strength he pulled himself up to the window, stuck his head through and yelled, "Stop the bus, man! Stop the bus before I fall!"

Passengers turned to him, their eyes startled. An awed

child pointed at him like he was a troll climbing in. The child started crying. The bus driver pulled over, and Triple E let go.

The door swung open. "C'mere you!" ordered the bus driver, but Triple E was twenty yards away already. He looked back and saw the passengers jammed against the windows, watching him. He gave them a friendly wave. "It's cool!" he shouted.

AS HE RAN HE calculated he was averaging a six-minute mile, his legs loping easy, his lungs swelling, his heart saying no sweat, baby. It was a mile to school. He would be there in six minutes. It felt good to run so fine, to feel the power in his legs, to know there was extra in them if he needed it. The gun was bouncing around in his jacket. He pulled it out and ran with it clutched in his palm. He could see the school just ahead of him, but before he got there a squad car pulled up and two policemen got out and started yelling at him, telling him to freeze, telling him to drop the gun.

Triple E said, "Hey, she's empty, man."

Both of them yelled at him in command voices, "Drop it now!"

He looked at the .38 and thought about what he and Tom Patch had talked about, how Triple E would go down guns blazing.

"There's no ammo," he said. And he put the gun down.

More cops arrived. He counted two cars, then a third, then a fourth and a fifth.

Geez, all for him.

They ordered him to lie on the ground, then they swarmed over him, one of them taking his wrists roughly behind his back and cuffing him. They picked up his gun.

"We know who you are," said one of them.

"Little bastard," said another, whose voice Triple E recognized.

Faggot bastard, said Triple E, but he didn't say it out loud.

Mrs. Miller, his English teacher, showed up. She bent over from the waist, hands on knees, looking at him trussed up on the sidewalk. "Is that you, Elbert?" she said.

"Hi, Mrs. Miller," he said. "Yeah, it's me, I guess." He raised his brows in a gesture of helplessness.

She turned to one of the officers and asked what Elbert Evans had done. "Breaking and entering. Carrying a stolen weapon. Discharging said weapon at a certain house. He matches the description of the boy who stole a car off a lot this morning. Is that enough for you, ma'am? There's more if you want to hear it."

"Good heavens no," she said.

"Incorrigible as they come, that boy, don't waste your sympathy on him."

"Elbert," she said. "What's gotten into you?"

"Nuthin," he said. "Leave me alone."

Her hand was at her throat. He could see a diamond ring shining on her finger. Probably worth five thousand dollars, he estimated. Get fifty for it at Conroy's. He felt bad about her being there, seeing him at his worst. She was all right, a fine teacher, someone he almost wanted to please. He remembered decoding the poem about the lovesick knight and how excited she got, a poem about beauty. Her big brown eyes so full of hope.

"Go away," he told her.

"Oh, Elbert," she said, and her voice was so sad it made him feel mean.

"Would you just go away?" he said.

The cops pulled him to his feet and shoved him into a car. The sidewalk was loaded with kids from school, everybody getting their eyes full. He looked for Jeanne, but couldn't find her in the crowd. He wanted to say goodbye. He knew he wouldn't be seeing her again for a while.

In the crowd he spotted Chuck Pump. Pump wasn't smiling or giving the finger or looking cocky or nothing. He was just standing there, looking on, looking a little lost even, his face pinched, his eyes worried, his birthmark conspicuous.

Triple E was reminded of the two of them at the bluffs, playing war, shooting BBs at each other, getting stung and seeing who could die best. Old pal Pump, who used to grip Triple E's shoulder like it was a crutch. Followed him around school that way, hanging on, the two of them best buddies for years. Pump had jumped off the roof because Triple E had said it was okay. Chuck Pump . . . before Tom or Jasper or Jeanne, or anybody on the streets. What happened? Time went by and something happened.

The car started to pull away and Triple E turned his head, his eyes holding on to Pump's eyes for as long as they could. And Pump nodded and his mouth formed the words *Triple E*. And that part was over, that part was no more.

HE CLIMBED THE NARROW wooden stairs. He was looking down and noticing how dimpled the stairs were, how lots and lots of feet had shuffled up and down them year after year. At one end of the building adult eyes peeked at him from behind steel doors, faces and eyes showing through slots and six-inch bars, measuring him as he went by. He heard lips smacking. A few wolf whistles. At the other end of the jail was one large cell for juveniles. The door opened and Triple E was nudged inside. The cell had five bunks in it, all of them hugging the walls. In the center were a long steel table and matching benches painted aluminum. The benches and table were bolted to the floor. There was a short partition on one side and behind it were toilets and sinks.

Incorrigible criminal Triple E sat at the table and looked at his hands. He could still see where the bus window frame had cut into them. His mind wandered over the bus ride and backwards to the Vette and to Jeanne, the stolen truck and the down cow. Was it really him doing all those things? He looked at the steel walls and the bars and there was no way out and he wished he could do something dramatic again, find a way to break out and rush back to Jeanne, sweep her away, take her far off to Alaska where nobody could find them.

"Jeanne, Jeanne," he whispered. "I think I done it now."

IN THE MORNING, THE turnkey brought him oatmeal and toast. The toast was done on only one side, like it was heated under a broiler and brushed with butter. It was good and he made a mental note that he would cook his toast the same way after he got out.

When he finished eating, he wanted a smoke, but they had taken his cigarettes and matches. He got the idea to make cigarettes out of mattress stuffing. Which is what he did, digging some stuffing out and rolling it in twists of toilet paper. To light his cigarettes, he unscrewed the cover of the recessed light over the table, using his belt buckle as a screwdriver, then wrapped a bit of tissue around the bulb. The tissue took a long time to get brown, then it caught on fire. He lit his cigarette, inhaled. Coughed and choked. The stuffing tasted like sulfur.

IT WAS A TIME by himself, six weeks in the big cell, and he got very lonely. He also got claustrophobic. It seemed like he was in a coffin, a giant aluminum coffin. He started imagining that when he died he wouldn't be completely dead when they buried him and he would wake up in his coffin, claw the lid, and go crazy. Bloody fingertips. Nails shattered. He didn't want to get buried when he died. He wanted to be burned up. Ashes couldn't wake in the dark.

His fear of live burial got so bad he couldn't sleep. He would catnap and doze now and then, get up and pace, do some situps and pushups. He wished there was something interesting to do to pass the time. He wanted some kid to get in trouble and get put in the cell with him. He would have given his right arm for a TV. It was too quiet. Now and then he could hear iron doors slamming somewhere in the jail. A voice. The yellow light burned constantly. The night oozed through the space outside his bars like cold syrup over a waffle. Morning after morning, the same breakfast, but he ate every morsel, licked the bowl.

WEEKS LATER, A GUARD opened the door and called his name. The guy looked at Triple E like he wanted to fuck him. All cops were faggot bastards. Fingers fat as eels wiggled for Triple E to hustle up this way. They walked down the hall, Triple E boogying ahead, and the cop said, "Where the fuck you going, you little clown?"

Triple E, smiling broadly, trying to be friendly, said, "Feels good to move my dogs after being crammed up so long. These feet are made for walkin," he sang.

The cop shoved him against the wall and started stepping on his feet, his toes, grinding on them. The cop was a big guy and it hurt.

"What's the matter with you?" said Triple E, trying to shove the cop off.

The cop held on to Triple E's neck and guided him downstairs. They went into an office, Triple E limping, his feet burning and bruised.

His father and mother were there with the judge. His mother shook her head at him. Her eyes were horrid. His father looked at the floor. The judge pointed to an empty chair in front of his desk. Triple E slumped in the chair, slouching on his neck and staring out the window, where rain bumped softly against the glass.

The judge shuffled papers. Then turned his eyes on Triple E and gave him the word. "Your parents and I have been talking here, son. We think there's no way to get through to you. You're out of control. Am I right?"

"I guess," said Triple E. "I don't know."

"You don't know?"

"Nope."

"Well, it's over. Enough is enough."

Triple E thought about copping a plea, shed some tears, put on the boo-boo face. But he didn't. He really-really didn't give a shit.

"Six months, then we'll review," said the judge.

"Oh, Triple E," said his mother, sobbing.

"We tried with you," said his father.

His mother was weeping, blubbering, wrecking her eyes.

Triple E hung his lids low. He felt contempt for everything and everybody, especially his parents. He hated their guts. He hated his father's mouth and hands. Triple E wanted to look at him and say, *I can kick your ass now. How you like them apples?* And *her,* cute as a button, *could've been a movie star.* Full of two-bit words and a two-bit fanny, all of her just asking for it. *Seen plenty of your ass,* he felt like telling her. They were talking, explaining to the judge, and he was listening all sympathetic, nodding his head, his big wop eyes dripping with sorrow.

"You raise em and you . . . raise em . . . and then what?" said his mother. "Then they kill you," she said.

"They kill you," echoed his father. He glared at Triple E and he said, "You got a diseased heart, kid, and it's gonna kill you if you don't mend it."

"You should talk," said Triple E.

His father shrugged his shoulders and looked at the judge. "See what I mean?"

They kept up a patter for a while, one picking up where the other left off: love-killing Triple E, the parasite siphoning off love till there's no love left. A taker, not a giver. Take-take-take, until there's nothing but pain and sorrow. If a kid tries hard enough, he can kill your love. Kids are so *me,* a bottomless pit of self-centered me. Sometimes there's nothing you can do when they go wild. Nothing but lock them up and hope they'll grow out of it. Take him away, judge. Get him out of our sight. Triple E is breaking our heart.

WAKE UP, BOY! SAYS Papa. Rise and shine! says Nana.

They are right there, he can see them, it is no dream, no dream. What're you doin here? he says.

God is up, looking down, says Nana. Get your ass off the snow, says Papa.

I'm tired, he tells them.

Listen to Papa, boy. At my wake do you remember your father dancing for me? Do you remember him dancing for me? Round my coffin weeping and dancing. And what did you do? You sat like a log, and he asked you to dance and you wouldn't move. You wouldn't dance for me, Triple E.

I was too sad, Papa.

I told you I was goin to find Nana.

Too sad, Papa.

Bah! Dance for me, boy. Get off your ass and dance for me. That's an order! Now!

Triple E reaches to touch his nana and papa. He feels the leathery texture of their skin on his fingers. He embraces them, but when he opens his eyes they have become the rock. He pulls himself erect and stands swaying in the sun and wind. The sun looks like a vanilla wafer he might pluck from the sky and eat. A pair of birds go by, skimming the sagebrush. He stumbles after them, clumsily stomping and shouting and waving his arms, following their flight out to the road. His shadow stretching in front, he watches it limping along, doing a herky-jerky dance on the snow. Hours or maybe minutes later he finds the car. It looks insignificant, a dark stone on the death-white land, a leaf lost in a measureless cloud.

He clears his throat and tries to talk. His voice croaks out of him, sounding ancient, reminding him of his papa's voice the night in the kitchen when the old man collapsed and got busy dying. "Goin to find Nana now, don't worry." They held hands. The old man's hand was clammy cold. And in seconds he went to Nana, was gone before the sirens died outside.

An angle of light bounces off the windshield. He can hear the engine running as he plows through the snow, half-swimming to the hood, sliding across it, knocking the snow aside. He calls out, but Jeanne doesn't answer.

Rolling off the hood, he looks in the side and sees her asleep. He pounds, he yells, he tries to whistle but can't. She doesn't stir. It takes a while for him to realize that something is wrong, and then he knows what it is. Plunging to the back of the car, he finds a drift covering the exhaust pipe. He kicks it away. Then he digs up a golf club and smashes the back window, clears the glass and climbs through. He turns the engine off, rolls down the window, then pulls Jeanne into a sitting position and slaps her face. Grabbing snow he rubs her face with it, hoping the chill will wake her. But she doesn't respond. Her eyes are partially opened, but she sees nothing. Her mouth is slack. A stale, acidic odor issues from her.

Shaking her shoulders, he cries out, "Jeanne! Jeanne!" His arms are strong again, made potent by a fear so huge it dwarfs anything he has ever known. He would give his life for her. He wants to open his veins and pour his stubborn blood into her. He holds her, his cheek against her cheek as he summons voodoo from his soul. "Live," he commands her. "Live, Jeanne! Live!"

CHAPTER 9

SHE COUGHS AND HE knows she's alive. He tumbles her through the window and onto the snow. He rubs her face with snow. He blows into her mouth. He pushes on her chest and counts to five and blows into her mouth. He pushes on her chest again, counts to five, blows. He pushes on her chest and counts to five and—*I'm doing it!* he tells himself. *Live!* he says to her. He pushes on her chest. He blows. He pushes. He blows.

She vomits. "Pah!" he says. "Yuck!" But he doesn't stop working on her. He rolls her onto her side and she vomits liquid Oreos over the snow.

"Get it all out, Jeanne," he tells her.

Nothing more comes up. A dribbling, brownish stain eases over her jaw. He rubs her lips with snow. Her lips move like toggle switches back and forth. He shakes her, orders her to open her eyes, but she doesn't. She won't wake up. She whimpers in her sleep, shrinks from him as if his touch causes pain.

The sun is seeping away, the bottom edge scarcely three or four feet above the horizon. Triple E decides what to do. He gets the toolbox from the trunk and hurriedly dismantles the hood. He snips the washer hose and the thin wires for the washer motor and the nightlight. Four half-inch bolts whirled with a ratchet and the main brackets are loose and the hood is off. The hood is lighter than he thought it would be, made of thin, gas-saving metal. He turns it over, gives it a shove over the snow and it flies like a hockey puck. He tears the plastic-coated wires out of the trunk and weaves them together, makes himself a rainbow-colored rope. He ties one end to the hood latch. He rolls Jeanne onto the hood, then fashions a loop of wire, creating a harness for his shoulder. He sets out for the farmhouse. He pulls her up each hill by heaves and jerks, then sleds with her downhill. It would be fun, just play, if things were different, if she weren't dying, if he weren't dying too. Even so he still gets a rush out of each ride.

It goes that way, slowly upward, quickly down, the sled zooming, the painful wind freezing his cheeks. His nose is frozen too. When he squeezes his nostrils together, it feels as if the hairs inside break off. The frigid air makes his throat raw. The air smells like a cave. Smells like old, frozen rock.

Beneath her furry jacket, Jeanne is in a ball, knees drawn to her chest, head tucked in the crook of her arm, hair over her face half-hiding her. She is not his warm Jeanne now. She is his sick Jeanne. Deadweight. He tugs and tugs and it seems odd to think of her lying on her back, all aquiver with passion, her hair a rich obsidian mane, her body a wetdream fantasy.

162

He thinks of her at the Shift, on the mattress, the two of them. Himself a horny boy trying to get in her pants. Everything was different then. The half-shadows of the room. The slow music. The warmth. The sound of her quick breath panting.

He tugs on the sled. Moves her along foot by foot. Miles to go. Night is coming. The snow glitters like a crop of minerals sown by a giant hand.

THE GLOSSY MODELS FROM *Playboy, Penthouse, Hustler* shimmered on the walls above them. The radio played music to seduce by. His lips were numb from marathon kissing. He wore a scent called Sure Thing: Sex Appeal for Men. She said she liked his smell. She sniffed and licked the area beneath his jaw. They smoked pot together. Her pupils were dilated.

She told him it was weird the weird things you did when your blood was up. His blood was up. He went for her buttons and got them undone, then slipped his hand inside over her panties, his fingers wedging over the edge of pubic bone and finding the soft spot beneath. This was very nice. "Oh Jeanne, baby, you feel so good," he told her.

"Oh, Triple E," she said. "Do you love me, Triple E? Do you love me?"

"What do you think? Geez, baby, you got to let me in there. I can't take this messin around. It's too painful. I'd kill for you, I'd die for you," he told her.

"Oh, Triple E."

He kissed her hard to punctuate his feelings for her. And then he said, "Do you want to do it, Jeanne?"

"I do," she said. "But I can't. Not all the way. We can do everything but that, okay, honey?"

"Geez, Jeanne, c'mon. What's the point?"

"I can make you feel good," she said. "Let me—" She reached for him, but it wasn't what he wanted and he had a time hanging on to his temper, the anger rising, his fists wanting to clench. What was the big deal? There were no more virgins her age and that was a fact. Virgins were freaks. But she had this thing—this stupid promise made on the frigging Bible and with a cross of Jesus in one hand, vowing before the Lord and her parents that she would stay a virgin until she married. Her father had made her take the oath. Therefore it seemed to Triple E that the whole thing was invalid. Was coercion. It was a vow made under duress, forced upon her, and so it couldn't be legitimate.

He told her what he thought, but she didn't agree. "The Bible," she said. "Jesus-God and all, and I held the cross to my lips, Triple E."

"Fuck, who cares?" he said.

He wanted to raise her ass, so he could get her pants down, but she stayed solid against the mattress. She wanted it bad, he was sure she did. Getting on his knees, he put both hands in her waistband and forced the jeans over her hips. He rolled her panties down and took a look. Her bush came into the light, the hairs glistening in a tight, crinkly triangle. "Oh baby," he said.

"Please," she said, her voice tiny, meek, submissive.

"Oh man, you're gorgeous," he said.

"Oh God," she said.

She told him she loved him more than anything-ever, but if she broke her solemn vow, the Lord would get her. She feared the Lord. If Triple E loved her, he would wait until they were old enough to marry. When they got married, they would do it every day, fifty times a week, whatever he wanted. He was rubbing his cheek over her thighs and hairs and she told him to keep doing it. "That's what love feels like," she said.

She was making him mad, making him crazy. He started thinking he didn't give a rat's ass if God got her. He was thinking he would force her legs wide and lay some pipe, that's what. It flashed through his mind that he ought to slug her and that would make her shut up, make her quit teasing him. He wanted to choke her, beat her. Angrily he forced her legs open and got on his knees between them.

"Nuh-uh," she said and sat up, grabbing him around the neck. "No, honey, no."

"Fuck vows to God," he said. "Fuck the stupid Bible. Fuck your fuckin sly-ass parents."

He kissed her, he licked her lips, he told her he was doing it for her, and he pushed her down and he placed his joebuck just so, ready to drill her like a bullet, make her howl, make her teeth shine.

"Got to," he said.

"Oh God, oh God," she said.

"You know you want it, Jeanne."

"Don't make me break my vow!" she cried. She made a pitiful, whining sound and Triple E's passion evaporated.

"Awww, man," he said. He rolled off her and stared at the ceiling. "You don't want me, I don't want you," he told her.

"It's not that," she said. "Not at all. I do want you, but I can't break a vow to God. A vow is a sacred thing, Triple E. You break that and you break yourself."

"That's your fuckin dad talkin, that's not you."

HE CHUCKLES TO HIMSELF and sits in the snow to rest a moment, his eyes on Jeanne. She looks like a fudge cake sprinkled with powdered sugar. And so what the hell, she broke her vow to God after all, broke it in the front seat of an Oldsmobile on a high plateau in the middle of a blizzard and with no way out, and with God in full command of His forces. And she opened up without a word of protest. Funny girl.

Maybe she knew how deep in trouble she was and maybe she knew she wasn't going to survive—and so had made up her mind not to go to her grave a virgin. She was going to know at least once what it was all about, what the feelings were that had to be attended to. Does she know something? he wonders. Did some instinct tell her this would happen to her? Is she one of those who know when they're going to die? Her Indian blood talking to her? Indians are close to the earth, nature-close, and have a special sense about such things, he tells himself.

IT IS DARK BY the time they get to the house. The stars and a rising moon and the snow hang a spooky blue light over the landscape. The house inside is like a gray womb. Triple E has to creep around and gather fire-makings by feel—papers off the wall, splinters of wood. He builds a fire, and shimmers of heat start rising in front of the hearth.

He drags Jeanne inside and lays her in front of the fire, then he goes to the barn and gathers up old hay, which he carries to the house to use as bedding and insulation. He rummages through the mound of trash in the machine shed and finds an empty can. This he packs with snow which he melts in front of the fire. He makes Jeanne drink water. She will drink water, but she won't look at him, she doesn't seem to know who he is or where she is or nothing. It is like she is conscious, but not quite. She still whimpers when he touches her. He knows something has happened to her brain, a short circuit in the wiring. A stroke maybe.

"Jeanne, oh Jeanne," he whispers, feeling lost. There is a tightness in his throat, a lumpy feeling when he swallows. He bathes her face and brushes out her hair with his fingers and folds it over her shoulders in a neat pile, where it rests like a little animal warming her neck. Then he discovers she has wet herself, so he takes off her underwear and skirt and hangs them on some wood beside the fireplace. With hay, he dries her groin, wiping her down. He blows on her thighs and pubic hairs to dry the last smears of piss. She is unresponsive. Pliable as a raggedy doll.

Making a torch of rolled newspapers and cardboard and bits of beeswax torn from the wall, he goes to the barn, searches around, hoping he will find something useful. He finds a broken pitchfork and pieces of a bridle and a mildewed hunk of horse blanket. Inside a crumbling feed box he discovers a layer of frozen oats. He breaks it up, stuffs chunks of oats into his pockets. When he gets back to the house, he tries to be bright, tries to sound confident. He talks to Jeanne as if she understands him. He has heard that the last sense to go is a person's hearing, that after everything shuts down and death is getting its last lick, the person can still hear, can still understand what's being said. He tells her they have it made now, look what treasures: broken pitchfork, a hunk of horse blanket, a piece of leather bridle, pockets of oats. He puts the blanket under her head.

"Cushy, huh?" he says. "We know how to live," he says.

Filling the can with snow, he melts it over the fire, holding it there between two tines of the pitchfork. When the water is boiling, he throws in oats and bits of the wax still in his pocket and carved up bits of bridle. He thinks the leather is just what they need. Protein. He knows they need protein. He boils and boils the concoction. It gives off a sweaty, sulfurous smell, noxious like the cow gutters at Goodpasture. They were too-pee-you, he remembers. The cows would crap and pee in them and in the morning when he got there with his shovel the stench would sting his eyes, and the cows, their tails wet with gutter shit, would slap him as he worked. It was a cruddy job, but he got used to it. His muscles got strong from barn work, which was what the coach wanted, his fighters to have hard, lean muscle. None of this bulky, weightlifter muscle that burns out in five minutes of fighting. Coach Tozer knew about the body. He was a body man, pure and simple.

AFTER A FEW MINUTES of cooking bridled oats, Triple E tries some and makes a face. "Tastes like shit!" he says, heaving it against the wall.

He starts over, minus the wax and leather, and quickly has a can of oatmeal that is tolerable and thin enough to drink. A texture like sawdust, it leaves bits of oat in his mouth to chew on.

"Yum, yum," he says, snickering, feeling lightheaded and giddy.

He cooks some oatmeal for Jeanne, but when he tries to feed her, she turns her head away and groans. Finally he gives up and eats her share himself. Afterward he goes to the bee-hive in the corner and tears the last of the wax out of the wall. He sucks some of it, gets the lingering rush of sugar on his tongue. He tries to put wax into Jeanne's mouth, but she won't have it. So he sits by her, chewing wax, savoring its essence. Gentle as marijuana, its sweetness swimming through his blood.

When Jeanne's clothes are dry, he puts them on her, then rearranges the hay to insulate her from the cold again. Then he builds the fire up, stacking wood high inside. Flames roar up the chimney. Heat breathes into his face like a benign wind. He scoots back and cuddles Jeanne, listening to her lungs laboring. Her eyes are half-open, tacky, not seeing anything. When he waves his hand in front of her eyes, she doesn't blink. He can touch her eyeball and nothing happens. He keeps whispering to her, promising to make it all better. But he knows he is lying. He knows the end of the line is only hours away if help doesn't come.

"I was better off in Goodpasture, definitely," he mutters. "None of this would'a happened if I'd just stayed put."

Goodpasture doesn't look so bad now. It looked bad at first when he first got there, but that really was the worst time, getting used to things, Tozer Douglas especially. Wanting to please him, and wanting to please Mrs. Bridgewater too, wanting her to think she had tapped into his head and really knew him. But she didn't know him. He didn't know himself, so how could she know him?

"Jesus, you paid for it, Bridgewater," he says, remembering the infamous day and the snow coming down outside the window and Mrs. Bridgewater on the floor with her snatch showing and the blood trailing from her nose. "Fuckin cunt-fool," he says. He darts a look at Jeanne and he says, "Everywhere, nuthin but sufferin fools."

THE DAY THEY TOOK him to reform school, Triple E shit his pants. He knew things were going to happen to him. There were bad cats waiting to shiv him. There were plastic blades made of toothbrushes waiting to puncture his lungs. There were sodom-loving homos waiting to cornhole him. These were the prophecies of Goodpasture: sadistic guards beat boys with rubber hoses. There was a black hole filled with spiders and fire ants and ear-drilling centipedes. There was the sweatbox that boiled you, the cold box that froze you. There was the rack that stretched young bones. The penis gobbler filled with straight pins. Bamboo shoots up the fingernails. The water torture drip, drip, dripping on your forehead till you went mad. That was the word, was gospel—was what every kid knew.

He was transported in a van with six other delinquents, all in waist chains, everybody staring out the windows, eyes glum. Denver was left far behind. Twists and rises along two-lane roads were followed by steep lands, frostbitten pastures, interlocking wooden fences, evergreens and boulders, patches of snow in the shade, patches of meadow giving way to great bluffs of shrimp-colored rocks. Farther away, higher still, snow and mist shrouded the mountain peaks.

Two hours later, the van turned onto a dirt road that wound through thick woods. Then came a stone wall and an open archway. A sign hanging from the archway said:

GOODPASTURE CORRECTIONAL FACILITY
ESTABLISHED 1957 ALTA COLORADO

On the other side of the wall, the road led toward three granite buildings that formed a wide U around a grassy slope and a parking lot. The van stopped in front of the middle building, next to a flagpole. The door slid open and the boys were ordered out. The driver went down the line, removing the chains from each boy. The chains made a harsh, slapping sound as the driver threw them onto the metal floor of the van.

"Line up," said the driver.

The air was cold, a sharper cold than city air. It cut

through Triple E's fatigue jacket. It burned his cheeks and ears. Smelled of pine and snow. In front of him was the parking lot, and then a flat space, a sort of miniature parade ground that ran toward the stone fence. Yellowed grass shriveling. The metal pole was at the head of the parking lot, the Stars and Stripes stirring in the gray mist at the top of the pole, the blue and white Colorado flag with its red C and yellow bull's-eye hanging underneath in listless glory.

Fronting the edge of the gravel road, the stone buildings loomed, all of them with multipaned windows, behind which Triple E saw eyes watching. The arms of ancient trees rose behind the buildings, reaching out like giant sorcerers casting a spell. Through a gap to the south, Triple E could see a spire and a rooster weathervane on top of a barn.

As he stood anxious and freezing, kicking his legs to keep warm, miserably depressed and loose of bowel, he tried to ease a fart and a watery blip shot into his skivvies. It was appalling. He looked toward the woods, wondering if he could slip away, make it behind some trees, and take a dump before the guard missed him. He felt a trickle of something warm along the inside of his thigh. He was thankful for the cold now. He prayed it would chill the shit and keep it from stinking.

A black man in a watchcap and ski jacket came out of the center building and descended the steps, clipboard in hand. He called the boys to attention. He looked them up and down. He had purple pouches beneath his eyes. His nose looked swollen, the nostrils wide as almonds. There were bristling gray hairs on his chin. Triple E imagined a rubber hose under the man's jacket. Who fucked up would get it good. Triple E locked his spine in a military posture. He kept a tight asshole. The man went down the line, asking each boy his name. Each name was checked against the paper on the clipboard.

Triple E said, "Yo," when the man got to his name.

The man looked at the clipboard, then at him. "Yo?" he said. He tapped the paper impatiently with his finger. Black against white, division between the back of the hand, dark as fudge, and the palm pinkish, like someone had drawn a line the length of the forefinger. The fingernails half-moons blue. *How does it feel?* wondered Triple E.

"Yeah," he said, mumbling it.

"Yeah?" said the man. His nostrils flared. He narrowed his eyes at Triple E. "I'm *sir* to you, young man."

"Yezzir."

The man wrote something down, then moved on. Triple E looked at the wall and noticed that it wasn't much, only six feet high, maybe less. He could scale it no trouble and be gone. He strained his eyes to see if there was broken glass or something electric running along the top, but all he saw was smooth capstone. The archway through which they had entered had no gates. It was wide open, just inviting him to boogie. There were no bars on the windows, no guards patrolling, no vicious dogs sniffing around. He couldn't figure out what the deal was. How did they keep the boys from running off? He would have to find out everything before he made his getaway.

The man with the clipboard came to the end of the line and said to the driver, "Seven and seven." He signed a piece of paper and handed it to the driver, then he turned to the boys, his voice booming: "I am Mr. Shackly-sir. Not Shack, not Shackly, not man, not dude, not bro, not hey. Mr. Shackly-sir. Is that clear, boys?"

"Yezzir," they all muttered into their collars.

Mr. Shackly-sir sniffed the air. He made a face. "Who keeps cuttin the cheese?" he said.

Triple E's asshole got tighter. He tittered nervously. Mr. Shackly-sir got in his face. "What's so funny, fart-blossom?"

"Nothin," said Triple E. He tried to cool it, keep the anxiety off his face as the man looked him over.

"Nothing what?" said Mr. Shackly-sir.

"Nothin's funny," said Triple E. His shoulders tightened. He got ready.

Mr. Shackly-sir shook his head. He sighed. He told Triple E to assume the duckwalk position.

"The duckwalk position?"

"Squat!"

Triple E dropped down so his heels were touching his butt. He waited for the hose, hunching his neck and back muscles. He tilted his face upward, sneering, contemptuous. He knew he was looking good for the other boys. They would talk about him. They would say, Yeah, Triple E, Shackly-sir beat him and Triple E he didn't bat an eye.

"Go'head," said Triple E. "I don't give a fuck."

"Go'head what?" said Mr. Shackly-sir.

"I'm not fuckin beggin. Don't expect me to give a fuck what you do."

The man's eyes looked puzzled. "Jesus, what I got here, Marlon Brando?"

"I'm Triple E."

"Just shut up, kid, will you? Before your mouth overloads your ass." Mr. Shackly-sir looked up and down the line. "What is my name, men?" he said.

"Mr. Shackly-zir," they all mumbled.

"What is my name?" He cupped his ear.

They shouted unenthusiastically, "Mr. Shackly-sir!"

Triple E didn't shout anything. He saw himself looking like

a monkey squatting at the end of the line. It was humiliating. Mr. Shackly-sir didn't have the decency to take out the hose and beat him.

Looking down at Triple E, Mr. Shackly-sir told him to hold on to his ankles and duckwalk behind the column and quack. He said he wanted to hear it loud and clear, lots of quacking.

"Move out, men!" commanded Mr. Shackly-sir.

Triple E hesitated, then followed along, waddling like a duck and quacking softly, dispiritedly, "Quack, quack, quack—"

By the time the group got to the door, he was far behind. His thighs burning like hot lead. Mr. Shackly-sir watched him struggling, then yelled at him to hustle up. He tried to move faster but collapsed on his knees.

"Quack, quack—"

"What's my name?" said Mr. Shackly-sir.

"Mr. Shackly-sir!" said Triple E.

"On your feet, get your bony ass over here!"

In the basement was a row of showers. At a counter, a man wearing a white turtleneck sweater, head bald as a worm, handed each boy a towel and a tiny bar of soap and said, "Use it up, soap yourself til the whole bar's gone. Scrub your skin off." There were piles of towels on shelves behind him. Overhead were miles of curving pipe wrapped in insulation, the insulation sweating, droplets falling here and there on the cement floor. Over the entrance to the showers was a sign saying:

C-L-E-A-N, CLEAN, VERB ACTIVE,
TO MAKE BRIGHT, TO SCOUR

Mr. Shackly-sir told the boys to kill all their cooties and then come back to the counter with their clothes neatly folded in hand, their shoes on top. The boys started stripping. Triple E slid up next to Mr. Shackly-sir and pointed to the latrine door nearby. "Can I go to the head before I shower?" he said.

Mr. Shackly-sir looked at him and sniffed suspiciously. "Bowel movement?" he said.

"Yezzir."

Mr. Shackly-sir nodded. "Go on," he said. "Six-minute shit," he said. "I'm looking at my watch."

Triple E hurried inside and did his business. Then he took his skivvies off, wrapped them in paper towels and stashed them in a trash can. He went back to the shower area, peeled down, and jumped under the water. The water was scalding at first, then he got used to it. He lathered his body over and over. It soothed him, sterilized him, made him smell new.

After the shower, the boys were marched to the supply room, where there was yet another sign over the entrance:

FOR CLOTHING DOTH DEPICT THE MAN.

Their clothes were tagged and put away, and they were issued four pairs of underwear, four pairs of black socks, a tan shirt, long-sleeved, with pockets and button-down lapels, very military-looking, with a tan tie and tan pants, black shoes, Siberian side-zip boots (rubbery green), and a pair of heavy denim overalls that buttoned up the front. Plus a flannel shirt patterned with brown squares. They were given a cap with adjustable earflaps and a nylon-polyester ski jacket, all in tan.

They were marched upstairs to the barbershop. On the wall above the mirror was another sign, this one telling them:

A CHILD IS A CURLY HEADED,
DIMPLED LUNATIC.

A heavy-jawed kid named Molnar got in the chair and said he wanted just a little off the top. "Leave it long in back," he said, smirking, making eyes at the other boys. "I want to grow a ponytail."

Some boys laughed. Triple E stayed by himself in the doorway. His skin was itching from the shower. He scratched himself and glowered at Molnar. For two cents he would have punched Molnar's stupid mouth. He would have done it for nothing. If Molnar would have just looked at him, he would have done it. Or any of the other boys. All of them shitheads. Everyone a fucking punk.

He didn't mind the barber, though, a quiet guy with bored eyes, a face rumpled as a dry chamois. A cigarette dangled from his mouth. He had big Popeye forearms. A no-nonsense guy. The razor droned and seconds later Molnar was bald.

All the boys were buzzed. Then they were marched into a dormitory, where yet another sign told them:

THE DIFFERENCE BETWEEN GENIUS
AND STUPIDITY
IS THAT GENIUS HAS ITS LIMITS.

They were assigned a bed and locker. They were shown how to hang their clothes and how their shoes and boots should look and how their extra underwear and socks should be folded just so, rounded edges at the rim of the shelf in their locker. They were issued bedding and Mr. Shackly-sir showed them how to make hospital corners. They practiced making their beds until he was satisfied, then they dressed in their tans and ties, put their black socks and black shoes on, and were taken to a first-floor room, where above the door it said:

HATRED IS THE SPHINCTER OF THE HEART.

Inside the room were school desks and a green chalkboard. A placard on the wall declared:

WHO BELIEVES IN THE FUTURE BELIEVES
IN YOUTH.
WHO BELIEVES IN YOUTH BELIEVES
IN EDUCATION.

They slid into the desks and waited. Triple E sat near a window. He saw bare trees, and beneath them were some boys in Goodpasture overalls and boots. They were raking leaves into piles. The boys were laughing about something. Their laughter tinkled faintly against the glass. He wondered how bad things could be if boys were raking leaves and laughing.

A man marched into the room and stood in front, hands on hips. He looked them over. He wore a military-style uniform, with a baseball cap squared perfectly on his head. He had a florid complexion, heavy jowls and pale-gray, bloodshot eyes. He stared from boy to boy as if he might grab a plump one and eat him. The boys looked at their very interesting desktops.

"Crawlin ferlies," said the man, a faint burr in his voice. "No a likely looking bunch." He took the clipboard from Mr. Shackly-sir and read off the names. Then he said, "I'm Tozer Douglas. Fuck with me, and I'll tear you a new asshole! Tell em, Mr. Shackly."

"Tear you a new asshole," said Mr. Shackly-sir, rounding his thumb and forefinger.

Tozer Douglas paced the floor, going boy to boy and shaking his head in disgust. "Look at yew sorry excuse of a heathen," he said. "Look at the goddamn mess yew made of your lives. Turned yourself into a goddamn j.d., a *juvenile delin-quent*. Ain't mama proud!"

He stopped in front of Triple E. "What rock yew crawl out from unter?" said Tozer Douglas. The Scottish ornaments came and went in his voice.

Triple E hunched down. He looked at his knuckles. The cold had caused one of his knuckles to split and there were bits of blanket fuzz clinging to it.

The man's voice whined: "Anoother victim are yew? Wha hoppened? Did your da beat your rotten litul ass? Boo-hoo. Bah! Crawlin ferlies, all of yew! Every motherfucker here's got some goddamn excuses or anoother. Well, I'm sick of it, an I wunt lissen to no bollocks bullshit!" He wagged a fist at them. "That heathen horseshit don't wash at Goodpasture, unter-stand? We got no victims here. What we got is perpetrators and litul sonsabitches."

Tozer Douglas's eyes were like chips of ice. He used his voice to hammer the boys. He said their asses belonged to him now. He was the B for Bravo honcho responsible for their behavior and whether or not they got rehabilitated during their stay at Goodpasture. He said if they were perverse little *bas-trrrds,* refusing rehab, then certain things would happen to them, certain awful bad things that he would spell out as the need arose. Goodpasture was an enlightened school. Its sole job was to turn the dregs of juvenilia into good citizens. He had been turning out good citizens for thirteen years. But now and then there came a heathen who could not be reached, a hea-then who did not appreciate his efforts and the efforts of the staff. That boy who insisted on perverted ways would be sent to more unyielding institutions, where the emphasis was on punishment, not rehabilitation. Goodpasture salvaged the salvageable and to hell with the rest. There were no bars or

guards or razor-wire fences. Any boy who didn't want to cooperate could walk right out the gate anytime he wished. If the
mountains and the cougars or coyotes didn't get him, the sheer
miles of wilderness would. And if through some miracle he
survived, he would still be caught eventually anyway, and there
were no second chances. That boy who ran away and was
caught would be sent to try his luck in a tougher school, where
they knew what to do with knotheads and sociopaths.

"But escape, yew know, it's not a good idea if yew plan on
livin," he said, grinning at them. "Tell these heathens what
happened to the last one who thought he had to escape, Mr.
Shackly."

Mr. Shackly-sir adjusted his watchcap low over his brows
and in a barking voice said, "Dead!"

"Dead, sir?" said Tozer Douglas, as if the news astonished
him.

"Like a block of ice."

"Ice-dead! It's a dangerous world out there," said Tozer
Douglas, looking from boy to boy. He turned to the board and
wrote in huge letters, TOO FAR TIM. "It's what we call him now,"
he said, tapping the words with the chalk. "His name was
Timothy Debee, but now he's just Too Far Tim! Animals got at
him. It was sickening. Scattered Tim Debee all over the place,
so's we only got him back in bits and pieces."

That first night, Triple E lay in his bunk biting his cheeks
and thinking about Too Far Tim sprinkled all over creation, his
bones gnawed by meateaters. Food for wolves and worms and
every microscopic thing turning him into fertilizer. It made
Triple E feel measly, like a dried-out maggot.

A drone of voices hung in the bay. Boys whispering in the
dark, making friends. Here and there he could hear a loner, a
mama's boy, stifling a sob. He stayed alone and hateful, won-

dering how he would ever stand six months of it, the likes of Molnar and Mr. Shackly-sir and a bully like Tozer Douglas. And buzzed heads. Jesus, everybody was ugly without hair. And taking orders and having to snap-to and live by someone else's clock. He didn't think he could take it. If they pushed him, he would kill someone, he was sure of it. Take a knife to Tozer Douglas.

"TOZER DOUGLAS," MUTTERS TRIPLE E.

He gets up and crams more wood into the fire. Going to the back of the house, he tears at the walls, ripping boards and pieces of boards off, hauling them to the front, piling them up. "At least we won't freeze to death," he tells Jeanne. "Enough wood here to last a week," he indicates the room they're in, "not even counting what I can bring in from outside. And we've got lots of oats. Hell, we're not so bad off. Not if you'd just wake up and get with the program. Hey, Jeanne, wiggle your finger if you hear me in there. Are you in there, Jeanne? Jesus, c'mon, baby, wiggle your finger."

Jeanne doesn't stir. Her eyes remain at half-mast, seeing nothing, feeling nothing. "Givin me the creeps," he tells her. He tries to push her eyelids shut, but they keep springing open, and finally he can't stand to look at her. She used to be prettier than Mrs. Bridgewater, but not anymore, not this corpsy-looking thing with its ashen skin and acid-smelling mouth.

He stares at shadows capering over the walls and calls up Mrs. Bridgewater, her heavy breasts, her aqua eyes behind thick lenses. She had a graceful neck. She was wide in the beam, narrow in the waist, sexy. And it seemed to him there was a look in her eyes that wasn't quite what a professional psychologist should have. When she looked at him her eyes said things, her eyes talked of needs. Hard for a woman to fool a man when she's got certain sort of eyes.

"She was asking for it," he says aloud. He paces about, hits his fist into his palm. *"They* were askin for it, both of em . . . fuckin Tozer, fuckin Bridgewater. I give it to em, by fucking God. They won't forget Triple E. Don't fuck with Triple E!" he shouts, hearing it bounce off the walls, coming back at him like a whir of punches, hooks, and jabs, her voice, her kiss, soft-forgiving breasts, very hairy quiver, her elemental lure.

UP AT FIVE, EVERYONE did calisthenics in the bay, push-ups, situps, deep knee bends, jumping jacks, running in place. Then they showered and went down to breakfast and waited for Mrs. Bridgewater to do her thing on the intercom. It made him laugh at first, but then it got old and irritating:

> The more stupid you are, the more delight you take in yourself.
> Losing an illusion makes you wiser than finding a truth.
> He only profits from praise who values criticism.
> A child's behavior is but a symptom.
> The best educational method is to give a child a good mother. . . .

He didn't like quotes. It was like being in church listening to the Bible. It amazed him that people could live their lives by the Bible, take its nonsense seriously. Mrs. Bridgewater sounded like it, chapter and verse, her cadences rolling from the sky, raining word pearls, the words floating like fairy dust over the mess hall, settling on the food, the voice full of faith, believing the words alone would cleanse the boys, get inside and scrub their souls.

ON THE BASIS OF some tests he took, he was assigned a typewriter near Mrs. Bridgewater's office and taught how to hunt and peck well enough to fill out forms.

One day she interrupted his typing and told him to come to her office. When he entered, she had him close the door. She sat at a desk, a window behind her. Plants in pots covered the windowsill, sending out heart-shaped leaves along arms that ran in all directions, some of them climbing the glass as if searching for a way out. The office was small. There was a closet, a clothes tree, and a braided rug. The air smelled of hair spray and book dust. There were books everywhere, shelves and shelves of them. On the walls were embossed papers in wooden frames. He looked them over. Renee Bridgewater had graduated from Boston College and Old Dominion University. Her name was sealed in clear plastic, together with official stamps and signatures and flowery words, most of it written in a language he couldn't understand.

"Sit down, Elbert Earl," she told him, indicating a chair.

On the shelf next to her, running the length of the wall, the books leaned against each other, pieces of paper sticking out of pages here and there. On the spine of one book it said:

Primordial Vision:
Relevance in Jung's
Spiritual Psychology
Dr. Renee Bridgewater

He learned later that her second book, *Art and Soul: A Search for Spirituality in a Technocratic World,* was coming out soon.

"Are you incorrigible?" she asked.

He looked at her.

"In your records here, the probation officer says you're incorrigible."

"Been called worse," said Triple E.

"Is that how you see yourself?"

Jesus, what's this? What the fuck you want? he wanted to say. But he kept quiet. He stared out the window, at the ugly bare trees, the dead-white peaks.

"I'd like to go over your test scores and show you something," she said. She sat behind her desk, leaning toward him, hands folded. The window was behind her, the sun's rays running the length of her forearms and lighting the fringes of her hair. Her eyes regarded him through thick lenses. Protruding, optimistic, magnified eyes that knew the reasons why the world turned. "You did very well, especially your verbal scores," she said.

"Hah!" he said.

"High reading comprehension." She showed him a paper, some scores. Her finger tapped the number 148. "Why is that?" she said.

"That's my score?" he said.

"Does your family read?"

He thought about it. "I guess my mom reads."

Mrs. Bridgewater licked her lips. He could see her tongue, moist. "Yes, well. Maybe you're smarter than people think."

"Well, hell yeah," he said.

She laughed. She was getting a kick out of him. He liked making her laugh. He tried to think of something funny to say. He checked out her blouse where it broke in a V above her breasts. When she laughed, the tops of her breasts jiggled. Guessing her age, he figured she was late thirty-something, maybe forty. Hair dusted with gray if you looked closely.

"Can't cope with a dope," he said, grinning back at her, the words rolling glib cool.

She hesitated a moment, then said, "Yes. Well." She shuffled the papers. "I have your school record here too. It's, ah, hmmm, it's difficult to equate this with this." She tapped his test scores and then his school record. "Mostly D's and F's throughout your career, Elbert Earl. Teacher comments are uniformly negative. Do you know why that is? Why you would get such poor grades?"

"Who cares?"

"Give me a better answer."

"School and me don't get along," he told her.

"School and me?"

He frowned. "Me and school," he said, then winced. "School and I. English grammar sucks, man."

"Yes, well, our spelling is atrocious too. People have been trying to reform it for years, but it stays the same. What can you do?"

Leaning back, she shifted sideways and crossed her legs. Her elbow remained on the desk, while her fingers tugged at a delicate earring. She regarded him with eyes half-closed in thought. Reaching over suddenly, she pulled a book off the shelf. Its title was *Modern Man in Search of a Soul*. She handed it to him, her finger pointing to a passage at the bottom of page 171. "Would you read this," she said.

"Out loud?"

"Yes, out loud."

He looked at the words stretching across the page, small and mysterious. Slowly he read, " '*A great work of art is like a dream; for all its apparent obviousness it does not explain itself and is never equivocal. A dream never says: You ought, or: This is the truth. It presents an image in much the same way as nature allows a plant to grow.*' "

"That's very good," she said. "Who taught you to read? Do you remember?"

He shrugged. "I don't know. Maybe Nana. She was a constant reader. Books in her room. When I was a kid, me and her used to lay in bed and read and we'd do the characters. Do their voices. She was good at it. Cancer got her."

Mrs. Bridgewater nodded as if to say it was all clear to her now. "Can you tell me what it means, the passage?" Painted nail pointing at the book. Nail dark, like a drop of wine. He wanted her to put it in her mouth, suck the drop off.

"Do you know?" she said.

"What?" he said.

"What the passage means."

Triple E looked at the page again. A bad feeling came over him. Here he had this big score and she was testing him to see if he had cheated somehow. But he hadn't cheated. He had read the paragraphs and circled the answers on his own. Why didn't she believe it? Why was she checking up on him? He looked at the words again and tried to concentrate. "This guy says . . . he says art is a dream, sort of."

"Yes?"

"And dreams don't explain theirselves and neither does art."

"Yes?"

"You get what you get and that's that. Every eye sees it differently. It all depends on what's happening in you. Art grows out of you like your plants growing in the window there, from a center root. Look here, lady, you sayin I cheated? I didn't cheat, I swear to God, I didn't look at nobody's answers."

Mrs. Bridgewater threw her hands up. "Heavens, no. For goodness' sake, no. I'm not saying that. I know you didn't cheat. No, no, I just wanted a demonstration. I just wanted to see how quick you are. Look, this isn't punishment. I'm not out to get you. On the contrary, Elbert Earl, I want to help you." Her face was very sincere. "Are you listening?" she said.

He kept his eyes on her.

"I've got this theory." She paused, she smiled. Her teeth looked capable of biting his nose off. "You know what I really want?"

Here it comes, he thought.

"What I really want is to make a reading plan for you, some books other than what you're doing in your classes. I've been trying to tell them they're not teaching enough literature."

"Civics," said Triple E, "it's all they do."

"Yes, that's what I mean. There are some wonderful books, just up your alley, books that can give you a bigger picture of life, push your horizons back. You understand what I'm saying? I want to direct your reading a little, okay?" Her big eyes got bigger, floating like pale blue fish behind her lenses. "Where there is this kind of aptitude, anything is possible." She tapped his scores. "It excites me to think what I can do for boys like you, Elbert Earl."

"Yeah?"

"Yeah," she said, chuckling.

Then she gave him a lecture. Said the world had one wide soul, a collective memory that ran like an invisible river all over the earth and through all human beings, and she believed that art, and especially great literature, taught people how to tap into it, "the universal river of collective memory," and that's what made some people so creative, because it, the river, fed them universal, archetypal visions. Yes, and the river expanded your spirit . . .

. . . and . . . and . . . and . . .

He wondered how it felt carrying around breasts so big. How could she not be preoccupied with them all the time, just wanting to give them a nice appreciative squeeze? He bet she could easily suck her own nipples.

She was sideways to him, rocking in her chair, elbows on the armrests, fingers tapping together, her eyes fixed on visionary things, talking . . . talking.

Triple E slid over by the window and started fingering the plants and looking out toward the parking lot, the sun glinting off the car windows, and the parade ground, the wall beyond, short and inviting. He kept glancing at Mrs. Bridgewater's legs, the knees crossed, the muscular calf curving from beneath the hem of her dress. He wondered if she ever wore mini-skirts.

Her voice droned on and on. "I'll take you as one of my special boys, Elbert Earl. I want to see just how far you can go. I believe when I turn you loose, you'll be a Goodpasture success story. I'll give you the education you should have had. I'll give you books to grow on. I'll change your life. You'll see. I'll . . ."

I . . . I'll, it was getting on Triple E's nerves, all her *I-I-I,* so full of herself. She reminded him of his mama, self-absorbed, all-knowing, flirty-eyed, those mother breasts poking at him like fists. He didn't trust her. He wanted her to shut up.

"Literature is an ax for breaking the frozen sea within us," she said, smiling blissfully. "What do you say, Elbert Earl? Do you want to give it a go?"

"I guess."

"Wonderful."

"So what's the deal?"

"After every book you read, you make an appointment and we'll analyze what you got out of it. How's that sound?"

"Okee-dokee." He checked out her calves again. She had uncrossed her legs and was scratching her knee. The skirt was fluffing. If he dropped something and bent down to pick it up, he might be able to see up her. He looked around and saw a paper clip on the floor near her feet. Bending down, he reached for the clip, his eyes on her legs.

The hem fell back in place. She brushed her lap. Smoothed her skirt. He retrieved the paper clip and handed it to her.

"Thank you," she said, her lips opening like a flower.

Close up he had spotted a varicose vein rippling down her ankle and into her shoe. It was very disappointing. "So what books?" he said. Then mimicking Tozer Douglas's brogue he added, "Don't gimme nothin borrring."

She giggled, delighted with him again. Going to the shelves she perused the books, her neck sloping forward, her pointed nose like a fox sniffing at a hole. "Let's see, let's see," she said. "Nothing borrring." Her fingers perched on the edges of the books, fingering the bindings. "Do you like your father?" she said. "Do you get along with your father? Do you handle his authority?"

"Not much," said Triple E.

She snatched a volume out and handed it to him. "Read these stories," she said. "It's for young men who have trouble with authority figures. I just gave you a clue, you see. When you read these stories, think about what I said."

Yeah, you know everything, he felt like telling her.

On the cover was a picture: a dark-haired, low-browed fellow with a piercing yet sorrowful gaze.

"Nice-looking, isn't he," said Mrs. Bridgewater.

"Got funny ears," said Triple E.

"His eyes are like yours," she said. She held the picture up next to Triple E. "Why yes, those are almost exactly your eyes. How about that."

Triple E looked at the man's mouth—thin, wide, the lips pressed together. "Yeah?" he said.

"Just about," she said.

He read the title of the book: *The Complete Short Stories of Franz Kafka.* He liked the last name. "Kafka," he said, savoring the sound. *"Kaf-ka."*

"He's the one for you," she said.

HE GOES TO THE window, the broken panes crusted with frost, and he looks at the snow glittering beneath the moon. Here and there miserable, frozen reeds reach toward the light. He sees a shadow of something moving. It is twenty yards away, slinking and stopping, slinking some more. He watches it until it goes out of sight. Living in this empty land, this thing. Something that slinks and searches. It might have been a coyote or a bobcat, or maybe even a dog or just a big cat. He wonders if it will be the thing that comes for him and Jeanne when they are dead.

He remembers how, when the boys were all asleep at

Goodpasture, he would get out of bed and go to the window and look at the bare trees rattling their fingers, and he would think about Renee Bridgewater and the way she looked at him, the way she told him that he and Kafka had a lot in common. The look in her eyes had been his reward for being what she wanted, a troubled boy with a brain she could improve. He never saw her look at anyone else that way, not with the same intensity.

"She wanted me," he says. He watches his breath, the little puffs fogging the glass. "I was gonna play it cool," he says. "Play it soul-cool, let her make her move. Then look out!" He guffaws, then wonders why. Wonders what's so funny.

He tells himself that older women are nasty, older women know they are running out of time and so they have no inhibitions about nothing. "She would teach me some fine moves, I'm sure. Porno prime stuff," he says. He is living, moving through what he sees, but seeing only what he dreams.

The wind whispers. The wind moans. Jeanne's quickening breath in his ear, the slippery sliding of her body, the smell of poon rising. Her mouth swollen from kisses, her hand reaching. Mrs. Bridgewater takes her place, wrapping round him. She and Mrs. Bridgewater keep swapping, until he turns from the window, goes back to Jeanne.

He talks to her, he says, "She was just a old fool full of two-bit words and an unsatisfied ass. She thought she knew somethin, but she didn't know nothin. I never loved her. I never really wanted her. Just wanted to teach her a lesson. Wanted to teach her she wasn't all brain as she thought. Her diplomas meant nothin." He shakes his finger at Jeanne, as if she is watching him and he needs to punctuate his words. "Same as Tozer Douglas: *had* to show him too. Nobody fucks with Triple E. Nobody. I'll fuck you up!"

He scans the fire, crackling, dancing like his brain, and he decides he likes being what they call him, he likes being incorrigible. At least they didn't say he was dull or stupid. At least he wasn't like those crybaby punks at Goodpasture with their pussy mouths. Take incorrigible any day. Incorrigible is a cool word to be. And bastard too. The queer cop called him a bastard. Tozer called him a bastard before the toots thing. *Toots,* what the hell is that? Incorrigible *bastrrrd,* incorrigible, litul, *bastrrrd!*

"Damn straight," he says. He feels his heart filling the mouth of the nasty thing slinking over the fish-scale snow. The nasty thing will make a bitter face. Can't eat Triple E, too barracuda, too tough, too buff, a stinkfish boy, *incorrigible,* spit him out, phooey-sputtooy. Chow-down Jeanne instead. Soft and sweet sugar meat.

"Maybe you'll die and I'll have to eat you," he says. "One way or another . . . one way or another it's what us incorrigible bastards do."

CHAPTER 11

THE BARN GUTTER WAS two hundred and fifty-four feet long, sixteen inches wide, and twelve inches deep. There were six gutters in parallel rows, the stanchions, the feed troughs and the cows taking up space in between. Triple E had a scoop shovel and a wheelbarrow. He was in charge of the first fifty feet of gutter. Other boys were in charge of the other gutters. They all had to currycomb the cows too, keep the crap balls off their tails, keep hay in front of their faces, put fresh straw down for them to sleep on. The boys had to lime the walls and the floors. Sterilize the milk machines. And they had to milk the cows twice a day. They went from cow to cow with automatic milkers, and when the bucket was full they would carry it to the bulk tank in the milkhouse and run the milk through a filter into the tank. It was heavy work, and it built muscle, tireless, work-forged muscle.

The first few days at the barn, Triple E missed his typewriter. He thought Tozer Douglas was picking on him and being a jerk; but then he got used to the work and the cows, and it wasn't long before he didn't mind the barn, and in the end he even liked it. He got attached to his cows. He was given ten of them to milk, and he scoured the loft for luscious hay, the darker green bales with lots of leaf and a humid-hot smell. These he kept hauling aside for his ten cows. When he would bring a steaming armful to them, their eyes would bulge, their nostrils flare and snort. They would tear into the soft hay like toddlers into cake. It made Triple E happy to make his cows happy. Heavy prime, he would call them. Milkers extraordinaire, he would say, pumping up their egos. He would wash them every morning. He would currycomb them every night. He would trim their hooves with a chisel. He would rub Bag Balm on their teats to soothe them after every milking.

"A born ferlie farmer," Tozer Douglas told him. "Yew don't belong behind a goddamn desk punchin keys. Yew're not like them other pansies."

He was one of Tozer Douglas's fighters now. All the boys in the gutters were Tozer Douglas fighters.

IT HAPPENED THE NIGHT Triple E defended a kid named Little Ray, stepping in when Bob Molnar said *Fuck you!* to Triple E. Spongy kids like Little Ray got smacked all over the place. The other boys picked on him, called him Snivelzit, and Little Ray had to take it because he pitied himself and he was weak and he had a face full of acne and arms the size of pipe cleaners.

One night after lights-out, Molnar was hanging over Little

Ray's bunk, pointing out all his defects, and finally Triple E had had enough. He was lying in bed, listening to Molnar mouth off, and he raised himself on one elbow and said, "Whyn't you pick on someone your own size, Molnar?"

"You want some of me?" said Molnar.

"I might, if you don't shut your ugly face." Triple E felt his heart speed up. He knew something was coming.

"Fuck you, punk!" shrieked Molnar.

Triple E sprang out of bed, shouting, "You say 'fuck you'? You say 'fuck you' to me? Step out here, I'll kick your ass!" He was standing in the middle of the floor, moonlight roaming through the windows. He could see a handful of silhouettes, the boys sitting up, staring at him, their shaven heads, their sloped shoulders—like bowling pins lined up. He wanted to fight. It was what he needed—to pound on somebody, to feel his fists connecting with boy flesh. He wanted to hit and get hit. Little Ray leaped out of bed, scurried over to Triple E's side and stood behind him.

"Fuck*on*-A, I said fuck you, Evans," said Molnar.

Triple E walked down the aisle, and the boys were pointing toward Bob Molnar. Everybody in the bay started sliding in behind Triple E, not wanting to miss a thing.

Molnar stood there in his skivvies. "I know kwan-do-shee, man. C'mon, fuck with me, I dare you. What the fuck you want, Evans? Fuck*on*-A, c'mon. You lookin for trouble? C'mon. You wanna get hurt? C'mon." Molnar had his hands up, making dancing motions in front of his face, his legs lifting carefully, one then the other, like a flamingo stepping through water. "Waaa," he said, intoning it through his nose. *"Eee-waaa-yo—"*

Triple E rushed him. Molnar was half a head taller, but with slow shoulders and stubby arms, muscular in the chest, but not a real fighter. Triple E went right through his defenses, brushing his karate chops aside and throwing roundhouse punches with both fists, windmilling Molnar back into some lockers. Molnar pawed at him, his blows flicking off Triple E's whirling arms. Molnar put his head down and rushed, tried to tackle him and use his superior weight, but Triple E was too fast. He danced aside, turned, twisted his upper body and shot solid rights and lefts from all angles, his fists working like hammers over Molnar's ribs, turning him, pounding the soft spots, his kidneys.

Molnar went down and curled up. "Okay, man, okay!" he said. "Goddamn, you killin my back! No fuckin fair, man!"

Triple E stood above him, panting. "Anybody else want to say 'fuck you' to me?" he said.

The overhead lights went on.

"Yeah, yew ferlie bastrrrd," said Tozer Douglas. "Fuck yew!" Tozer looked elated, eyes bright as ornaments, hands rubbing together, like it was his birthday and he had just opened a present. He ordered the rest of the boys back to bed.

Behind him Triple E could hear the rumble of bare feet, the squeal of bedsprings.

Tozer Douglas tapped his toe on Molnar's butt. "Go wash your face, big mouth," he ordered. "And next time yew say 'fuck yew,' make sure yew can back it up." Molnar, smearing nose-blood with his hand, hobbled toward the head, mumbling about what a dirty fighter Triple E was. Tozer Douglas took Triple E by the elbow and marched him out the door.

"Badass, huh?" he said. "Ass-kicker are yew?"

Said Triple E: "Molnar, he—"

"Hah!"

They went to the basement, to the gym, and Tozer Douglas had Triple E put on gloves and headgear. "Let's see if yew any damn good," he said. He circled and jabbed, tapping Triple E's forehead over and over. In a minute or so, Triple E had a killer headache from Tozer's jabs. He pulled back, feinting and dodging, but Tozer Douglas hit him at will. "C'mon. Come get me, yew ferlie. Don't lose your nerve now. C'mon, c'mon, yew litul bastrrrd."

All Triple E could see behind Tozer's gloves was his close-cropped hair bristling like silver tinsel in the light. Triple E threw several roundhouses at the man's head, but he picked them off easily and leered and snorted and said insulting things, then went to beating Triple E some more, throwing punches that ticked off his face, his body.

The man was fast. He didn't look fast, with his paunch and his seam-busting thighs, but he was. Triple E was reminded of the guy outside Bunny's Bar, his low center of gravity and his thick fists withstanding everything that Tom Patch and himself dished out. Tozer's eyes burned happily inside their scarred sockets. His jaw looked tough as cactus. It was clear that plenty of punches had gotten to his face in the past. His nose was saddle-smooth from numerous blows, and there were nicks in his skin, gouges and scars on his forehead. He had cauliflower ears.

"Yew think yew a fighter?" he said, sneering. "C'mon, fairy-fucker, prove it."

"You were a pro," said Triple E, hanging out of arm range.

"Twenty-two years in the ring. Ask Emile Griffith, ask Joey Giardello who Tozer Douglas is. Carlos Monzon took ten rounds to beat me in 1971 and I was forty fuckin years old. In my prime I was ranked in the top five. I can clean your clock with one hand tied behind me, boyo."

"I guess so," said Triple E. He backed farther away and let his arms hang, relaxing his biceps, the burning.

"So yew like to fight, do yew?"

"I do all right."

"C'mon then."

Triple E wanted to do it, but his head was splitting, and Tozer Douglas was just playing with him anyway, making him feel like an idiot. Every blow was parried off the man's gloves, or he would sidestep and leave Triple E hanging in midair, open for a right hook. "Need work," said Tozer Douglas. "But *maybe* yew'd make a fighter, we'll see."

"MAYBE I'D MAKE A fighter," says Triple E, and he chuckles to himself, at the memory of that night which changed his life.

The fire seems to catch his mood. It snaps at him, throwing embers at him, the embers doing somersaults. "I kicked ass, Tozer, yeah, and you sayin I'm born so bad! Sayin it to Bridgewater when she goes freakin out cuz you takin me off the typewriter sendin me to the barn to shovel shit and haul buckets . . . and buck hay! Buck that hay, Triple E! You fuckin-A, man! You two dipshits. Jesus, you somethin else! Pair of shitsniffers! . . . After somethin. After somethin, but not got what you wanted from this boy. Cuz this boy, he be loaded with wonders, look out! Look out now!"

Sliding across the room, he throws punches at his shadow. "Whiff-whiff! boom-boom!" he yells. "I knew I would be good, but not *that* good. Jesus, I was *it*. Nobody beat me. Triple E's a mean motherfucker, oh so bad." He glides backwards, turns on his toes, throws a riff of punches, bends, feints, picks off blows with his open hands, gives some shots to the belly, to the liver, to the heart. The fire flickers behind him and his shadow dances gigantic on the wall. He can feel wind coming through the broken glass. The wind seeking out weakness. It cools the back of his head, it runs like a kiss along his fevered cheek.

Jeanne makes a noise and he turns and she is sitting up.

"Hi!" he says. "Hi, baby, good to see you!"

She doesn't answer. She is panting, grunting, looking past him at something. His shadow maybe.

"Jeanne?" he says.

She flops backwards, her mouth grimacing, showing teeth, and it takes him a second to realize she is having some sort of fit. Mucus bubbles on her lips, her back arches into a rigid bow, the tendons in her neck grow taut. Then she is shaking. Her heels drumming the floor, her fingers tearing at the hay. She fights for air, nostrils flaring, her breath blasting in and out.

He has heard that people having fits will bite off their tongues. He searches for something to jam between her teeth. He spots the piece of bridle, grabs it, sits on Jeanne and jams the bridle into her mouth, holds it there as she puffs and snorts and trembles beneath him. More mucus blows from her nostrils. He wonders if he is witnessing her death throes.

It is over in two minutes, maybe less, and her muscles relax, her breathing returns to normal. He watches as peace settles over her face. Her skin has a silver-yellow tint, its texture makes him think of wax, of candles. She is asleep again, making little puff-puff noises through her lips.

"I don't know if I can take more of this," he whispers. "I don't know. I don't know." He wipes his palm across her face, cleaning the foulness off, wiping it on her coat. He looks toward the window. Out there, the far-far world—escape. He is shivering. His legs twitch. There's a tic in his left eyebrow. He feels a compulsion to run. To save himself.

And he says, "I wish you'd wake up and talk to me. I need some help here, baby. I can't do this all by myself. I want to, but . . . but I don't know if I can." He clucks to her, murmurs, makes love motions with his hands, caressing her cheeks, her hair. Bending low he kisses her forehead, and then her lips, and his mouth stays on her mouth a moment, its deadness whispering zero-nada-nothing, causing his throat to constrict, and his lips flatten against her lips, and tears well in his eyes. He is crying, and he hasn't cried in such a long time, not since he was a very little boy, that it astonishes him, he can't believe it. But he can't stop. Real tears are falling, his nose is running. His mouth slips from her mouth and he burrows into her neck and he says, "Oh, Jeanne, oh, Jeanne, please!" Sobs break from his throat. Grief, a reservoir of tears, his courage flickering, his cries loud, resonating with hopelessness and self-pity and a frightened heart.

She moves beneath him, a faint rustling of her arm over the hay. He catches his breath, waits. He feels her arm rising behind him, stuttering upward, sort of spastic, the arm, the hand, hesitating, trembling, tentatively fingering his back as if checking to make sure it is him, and then she is patting him, soothing him, giving him little taps of comfort just below his wingbone. It feels like a tiny bird pecking.

Gasping, pulling away, he looks at her and he says her name again, "Jeanne?" But her eyes are closed and she still sleeps somewhere—but maybe not too far away. He knows his cries got through to her. His cries touched something alive in her head. Some little spark of life hears him. She wants to come back but can't quite make it.

He stares at her, willing her eyes open. Waiting. Watching for signs. Her arm has fallen to her side again, resting there in its fur sleeve like a smooth, sleepy weasel. Her breathing is steady. He knows she is in there. She has not parted to the judgment yet.

Wiping his eyes with the heel of his hand, he smiles at her

and says, "We're gonna make it. Don't you worry, baby. Triple E is here."

Getting up he clears his throat, spits into the fire, and takes a minute to regain his composure. "Boy, what a bawl baby I am," he says. He adds more wood to the fire. He stands in front of Jeanne, searching her face.

"I know you hear me now," he says. "I know somewhere in there I'm comin through."

He thinks again about the kids at Goodpasture, the weak ones like Little Ray, their cries at night, how they tried to stifle their sobs, and guys like Molnar calling them tapioca heart, mama's little pisser, and those kids were doomed. Doomed. There was no pity but self-pity in Goodpasture, and the ones who gave in to it had the toughest time. The survivors had attitude. They put meanness on like a poisoned cape and it kept them from going under.

"No feelin sorry for your goddamn self," he says, saying it through his teeth angrily. He slaps fist to palm. Then rubs his hands like a man with a scheme. "Listen up now," he says, as though Jeanne can hear him. "Tomorrow, I'll patch this place and make it warm and cozy for you. I'll get us somethin to eat. I'll do what I have to do. Cut my arm off at the elbow and roast it, if I have to. I'll feed you my arm. How'd you like some roasted Triple E, huh?" He smiles at her, he laughs. "Protein is what you need. Protein, everybody says. I'll find mice or a rabbit or somethin . . . a rat . . . whatever it takes, by God, if I fuckin have to chase a deer down and kill it with my bare hands. That thing out there I saw slinkin along, I'll murder that motherfucker! Got it all worked out in my mind, Jeanne. Got it all worked out! All worked out!"

Murmurs filter into the room, pouring in, voices out of time, voices from the immovable spot, voices trying to tell him secrets from the measureless pool. He follows their sound into the other room, the one with newspapers on the walls, headlines from outer space, the man walking on the moon *up there, up there.* "Where? What?" he says. "Tell me!" His hand tests the ocean of darkness in front of him. His finger pokes it here and here, infinite fathoms deep—the night sea, moist, impervious, cool.

AT FIVE EVERY MORNING, Tozer Douglas would get him up and have him run with the rest of the team. They would run five miles every day and do wind sprints. Triple E's speed served him well. When it came to distance running, he could beat anybody. He was made for the long haul. He gloried in it, the long lope down the gravel road two and a half miles and back, his legs reaching, his lungs expanding in the mountain air, the steam blowing from his mouth, his arms pumping strong, the sensation of his muscles and organs working in harmony. He would burst ahead and leave the other boxers behind, and Tozer Douglas waiting at the gate would say that he had wind and legs and they were ninety percent of boxing. But did he have heart? Could he fight on when his nose was broke and his ribs cracked and his eyes so swollen he could see nothing but shadows? Could he do that? Tozer Douglas had. Tozer Douglas had stood in there and beat the odds over and over again, because he wouldn't quit, driving and driving and wearing the other man out, wearing him down, and then saving just enough wallop to go in for the kill. Could Elbert Earl Evans do that? Was he man enough for the ring?

After the morning milking and a workout, Triple E would eat breakfast, getting seconds if he wanted them. Then he would go to school for four and a half hours, with a half-hour break for lunch, and then work till six in the barn, then in the evening go to the gym and learn the sweet science from Tozer Douglas and the other boys.

The routine became an agreeable part of his life and he hardly noticed the time passing away. He spent the evening of his sixteenth birthday working out in the gym. Didn't realize he was a year older until he lay in bed that night and it hit him—it was his birthday. He was sixteen! Jesus, he was getting old. He felt for whiskers on his chin, but there wasn't anything, just a bit of down. He wanted whiskers like Tozer's whiskers, like black thorns bristling on his face. He wanted eyes surrounded with scars, like Tozer's eyes. He already had a start on Tozer's nose, that part was easy, a little hook to the left from when it was busted, but the rest of the look would take some work. Lots of banging. Lots of boom-boom. Lots of rinsing his face in brine water like Tozer told him to. Toughens the skin. Makes it like leather, son.

And so the boxing kept him busy and time flew and there were moments of clarity, moments when he felt as if he were going somewhere, that he was finding his true self, finding what he was put on earth to do.

Tozer Douglas had dreams of finding a prospect. He had dreams of going to the top, of being like Cus d'Amato, Angelo Dundee, Eddie Futch, major managers, everybody knowing his name, everybody knowing what a great handler he was.

His boys always did so-so in the tournament held every year in downtown Denver, but in thirteen years of trying, none of his boys had won a title or a trophy. Lots of second-, third-, and fourth-place ribbons and plaques, but no shiny golden trophies, no champion. It ate at Tozer's heart.

He especially wanted to beat Bennie Bogs from Buena Vista Correctional. Bogs had the reputation as a first-round knockout artist. He was *the* Bogs, only seventeen, but already noted in boxing circles. The year before Triple E had gone to Goodpasture, Bogs had taken the lightweight crown and was written up in the paper, his face splattered over the front page and shown on TV news. Triple E remembered seeing it, remembered the article saying that Bogs had nearly killed a boy in a knife fight and was serving three years at Buena Vista's hard-time for juveniles, but was turning his life around and finding a future for himself in boxing.

"The dirty litul bastrrrd," Tozer Douglas would say. "Yew put him away, son, and I'll put your picture on the wall—I'll immortalize yew! I'll goddamn marry yew!"

Triple E was willing to do the coup de coup on Bennie Bogs if it were possible. He had to admit he liked the idea a lot. And he liked boxing a lot. He liked hitting the other boys, giving them good stiff shots that rattled their brains, and he didn't mind getting hit himself as long as it wasn't on the temple or the back of the head. He protected himself in those places as best he could. Those were the places that gave him headaches.

What he really liked was when his opponent tried to tag him and couldn't. Fast Triple E, zoom, zoom. He liked it. He liked being judged physically, the purity of his speed, his savvy, his ability to take a punch and counter. It was the life of a body in tune, working at what it was meant to do, and he took to it with a fanaticism that awed the others and surprised himself. He worked harder than anyone on the team. When he did roadwork, he never dogged. When he worked the speed bag, he did so until his arms were ready to fall off. When he punched the heavy bag or threw punches at Tozer's hands or jumped rope or did situps or sparred with another kid, he did it with a single-minded focus that left him drained afterward but feeling sweet, his body tight and strong, like armor around him.

HE MOVES IN A silent boxer's ballet across the warped floor, moving with his chin tucked, his shoulders slightly forward, his feet balanced, his torso bent, his fists working in short bursts.

Tozer had said everything was horseshit on a hot rock except fighting. Men were made for fighting. It's how they proved their worth. "Lemme see yew move, son, lemme see you glide by and wink the bastrrrds. You're my main man. Sic em!"

"I was his main man," says Triple E.

He is panting. He flops down next to Jeanne, resting his head in her lap. Sweat has beaded on his forehead. His brain is hot, but very clear. He can see himself as if from a parallel plain. "I was good, I was good," he reminds himself over and over. And he tells Jeanne she should have seen him at his best in the ring. If only she could have come to Goodpasture and the other places he went to fight, then she would have seen a Triple E she could be proud of. "I was so good, so fast, and hit so hard, nobody could believe it, Jeanne. It was like it was waitin in me to come out, and when Tozer started trainin me, all this talent showed up and took me over. I felt beautiful out there. Like those gymnasts must feel when they fly a hundred feet and stick it."

Moving, slip, slip, slide and glide, the boy in front of Triple E throwing jabs and the joy of slipping them, of slipping everything, not even throwing a jab of his own, nothing, just moving and slipping and daring the other boy to hit him, taunting him with a nice, juicy chin, and the boy trying hard to nail him, but always missing. Hung out to dry, flailing at space, confused, frustrated. Had anyone ever been so fast as Trouble with a capital *T*?

The fire is dying again. The wood burns too fast. It is decrepit wood. He needs some logs, something filled with knots that will battle it out before being consumed. He stuffs in more wood and feels the heat, the life coming. He stands close to it, soaking it up.

He goes back to his first real fight, when Tozer had taken the team to the Fort Morgan Boys Club, and Triple E had watched the bouts from the doorway of the locker rooms, the boys fighting awkwardly, throwing punches that caught nothing but air. They had been like sissy girls pawing each other.

"That was no way to look in the ring," he says.

Sweat is pouring off his forehead, dripping from the end of his nose. He feels like he is burning up. And yet his back is cold. His front is warm from the fire, but his back is freezing. He knows he is sick. He knows he is on the verge of more hallucinations like the ones with the cow and with his grandparents. He hopes he doesn't break down and cry anymore. He needs to stay strong. Crying doesn't get a guy anywhere, he tells himself. The crying made him weak, made him feel like he was done for.

He slashes his fist through the air. He wishes one of his opponents would show up and start whaling on him. Punch him a few times, wake him from the weird, otherworldly feeling echoing in his head.

"I'd kick his ass," he says. He pictures himself stylish, a real pro. That's the way he wants to be. He hears Tozer Douglas calling him a dumb-shit.

"What you hollerin about now?" says Triple E.

It was those boys, those incompetent jerks in the ring, and they needed to get hollered at, not Triple E. He goes inside the locker room. He stretches out on a bench. Closes his eyes. Practices the moves inside his head.

———

TOZER DOUGLAS HAD TAUGHT him to visualize his moves, going over and over in his mind what he was going to do, going over his punches and seeing himself dominating the other boy, taking him apart.

But what if it didn't happen? What if cottonball punches were all he had? No stone fists. What if? What if?

Stomach churning. Butterflies floating. He had to sit up and burp and burp. He knew that boxing was the last thing he wanted to do. What the hell, the whole thing was crazy, it was barbaric! Mrs. Bridgewater was right, people shouldn't be such animals. People should rise above it all. They should read books and discuss things and develop their minds, instead of running around acting like savages.

What would Kafka do? Kafka would write a story, make it like this carving machine carving I.Q. numbers all over this kid's body, *low* I.Q. numbers, 75, 60, 52—can't read nothing but comic books. Kafka would put the kid in the ring and have him beat at a door that would never open, and the kid would grow up and get old and die, having learned nothing but the sound of knocking. Call the story: "Knock and the Door Won't Fucking Open." Kafka had a barbed brain. Very keen. Saw into the heart of things. Told it like it was. Told what bugs. Everybody was a bug.

"I'm not fightin," said Triple E.

He jumped up and started pacing, banging his taped fists together. He knew he was thinking too much. Thought. Thinking. It killed a fighter, filled him with fear. Not of being hurt, but of being beat.

Jesus, he was nervous. He didn't expect to be so nervous. He whirled and punched the lockers. He banged them all over, made them ring like tin bells.

IN THE RING TRIPLE E forgot all he had been taught and reverted to his street way of rushing an opponent and flailing at him like a threshing machine. The opponent's name was Mason. Mason backed off, covered up, let Triple E pound away. Though Triple E had been jittery, almost trembling as he and the other boy stood nose to nose getting instructions, once the battle was joined, he was okay. Legs, fists, lungs working just fine. From the get-go he felt he was winning, lefts and rights pounding on Mason as he covered and crouched and hid behind his gloves and headgear. Triple E could hear Tozer Douglas shouting instructions, telling him to slow down, back off, pick his shots.

"Jayus, yew gonna blow a gasket!" shouted Tozer Douglas. "Set up now! Yew're hitt'n nawthin but his elbows, yew dumbbell bastrrrd!"

"I got him! I got him!" said Triple E, raining blows on Mason from all angles.

"Won't yew lissen? Back off, I tell yew!"

Triple E couldn't figure Tozer's problem. Mason hadn't thrown a punch, hadn't laid a glove on him. The boy was backpedaling, creeping away, hunched up like an old crone. Wham! what fun! Wham! Wham! Slamming him, slamming the bastard. Mighty blows, from mighty fists.

"Yew fuck'n ferlie!" shouted Tozer Douglas. "He's playin with yew! He's playin possum! Look at his eyes! Jayus, where do they get these ferlies they send me? Will yew slow down and see what yew're doin, Evans!"

It took a while, but Triple E was starting to get the message. As in his nightmares, his shots were doing no harm, and his breathing was getting harder and harsher, his lungs starting to blow and burn, his arms losing steam. No snap in his fists anymore. He had dropped his load pounding for two minutes on Mason, and Mason was peeking from behind his gloves, his eyes measuring Triple E. And with forty seconds to go on the digital clock, he was burned out. He couldn't understand how it happened.

He slowed down. He backed off. Gasping. His mouth felt as if it had been washed with lye, his heart was tripping. Thirty-five seconds. Thirty. His legs went watery.

I'm dead, he thought.

Mason came out of his shell and went to work on Triple E, giving him a clinic in technique for the rest of the round, while Triple E backed up, covered, and clinched and tried to recover his wind.

When the bell sounded, he went to his corner and Tozer Douglas berated him, saying he'd never seen such a dumb bastard in his life rush across the ring and burn himself out before half the round was over. What the hell had all the training been about? Had Triple E forgotten about protecting his wind? Had he forgotten how to slip punches and pick his shots? Tozer Douglas told him if he didn't go out in round two and fight a smart fight he was off the team. "No goddamn ferlie fucker gonna embarrass me," he said.

"Fuck that, man," muttered Triple E. "What do I care?"

Tozer was squatting in front of him, eyes filled with disgust. Triple E hated the man. Promised himself that one day he would punch Tozer—get a clean shot in and take him *out*.

When the warning buzzer sounded, Tozer gripped Triple E by the shoulders, forcing him to stand. "Get out there and kill that bastrrrd, yew fuckin heathen," he commanded. And then, inexplicably, he kissed Triple E on the forehead.

When the bell sounded, he went after Mason again, only this time more cautiously, sliding toward him and away, focusing on reflex, the ten thousands feints and punches he had practiced automatically countering what Mason could do. He threw a fake left hook, then went below to Mason's midsection, then hurriedly backed away as more jabs came at him, some just touching him, some hurting him. He let Mason come in, then stepped to the side quickly and threw a left at Mason's liver, brought a right into his breadbasket and threw the left again upstairs off the side of Mason's head. It worked well, a fine riff, all three punches landing, staggering Mason. It was a different round, moving and sticking, hitting, then slipping away.

At the end of it Tozer Douglas squeezed a wet sponge over Triple E's head, cooling his brain. "I knew I'd seen something in yew," Tozer said.

In the third round, he picked up the pace and drove Mason backwards for the entire three minutes and played with him, did the Ali shuffle and made faces at the crowd, who booed him, but when it was over, Triple E knew he had won, no doubt about it. Mason was bleeding from both nostrils, there was a welt beneath his left eye, foam and blood flecked his lower lip, he was gasping.

"You'll do," Mason said to him as they touched gloves and parted.

Tozer Douglas was sweet to Triple E afterward, raising his hand in triumph, hugging him, shouting in his face that he had big potential, a professional's touch. Triple E had never seen Tozer Douglas giddy like that. He walked Triple E to the lockers and bragged on him the whole time, calling him *toots,* patting him on the butt.

Stripped down naked, Triple E stepped in the shower and adjusted the valves. Tozer stood at the entrance, looking him up and down. "Look at yew. All muscle. Not an ounce of fuckin fat. A lean-mean fighting machine. My toots. My gift from the gods. My lightweight title. If yew learn to listen to me, we're gonna kill em, boyo!" He grinned and shook his head like he couldn't believe in his old age that he had gotten so lucky.

"I DON'T CARE, I never loved you, you sonofabitch," Triple E says. The flames leap like dancers. "I never loved you or her or Goodpasture, nobody, nothin . . . except her." He waves a hand in Jeanne's direction. His eyes won't focus. She swims in and out of sight.

He tries to throw some punches, tries to shuffle. He wants to stay on his feet, but his knees are weak and he keeps dipping like he's going to fall. His clothes are soaked in perspiration, and his teeth are chattering. His eyes sting. He wants to sleep, but he doesn't dare. He has to stay on guard, he has to be alert just in case.

"In case of what?" he says.

For a moment he is blind. And then he says, "Man, I'm sure pooped." There is static noise in his brain, dizziness, white spots coming at him, hitting him like soft stones. "I think I'm going to faint," he says.

And he does.

CHAPTER 12

WHEN MRS. BRIDGEWATER SAW him in the hall, she said, "Oh, Elbert Earl, your face!"

She went into Tozer's office and Triple E could hear her yelling all the way into the bay, where he had gone to shed his overalls and dress for dinner. She called Tozer Douglas a Neanderthal.

"You are feeding the worst in him!" she shouted.

"Nuts!" said Tozer.

"Do you have any idea? Do you know him?" Her voice went low and Triple E couldn't hear what she was telling Tozer.

She started pacing, her heels tap-tap-tapping. "Unforgivable," she kept muttering. "Unforgivable."

Tozer said, "Life ain't fair. Big deal. Be a man about it. Learn how to use it. I'm teaching him how to use it."

Things got quiet. Then Tozer said, "Yew don't know him like I do!" And he said she was full of horseshit, sentimental tosh, she was a dainty, pansy, pussy. He finished her off, saying, "God save me from messiahs, Jaysus fuckin Chrrrist!"

"I'm not a messiah, and there's not a sentimental bone in my body," she said. "It's hardheaded science I'm all about, and it tells me I have the tools to reshape him. I can fix the mistakes of the past."

"Go to Stone Garden, he's on every corner, hanging out, the insulted, the injured, the murderous. Try fixin their mistakes and they'll cut your throat, Bridgewater."

"He's not them," she said. And again there was a pause, and Triple E could hear their breaths mingling, fuming, and then she said, "I can only do one at a time."

"I can only do one at a time too," said Tozer.

They kept at it, tussling back and forth as if they had his soul between them. A moment later, something she said made Tozer shout so loud glass rattled in the door. He yelled at her that the goddamn likes of Elbert Earl were nothing subtle, not no pearl hiding in an oyster, but straightforward he was, not a thinker, not deep in no way. Pissed off he was and needed an outlet for his hate. Skid right over the surface of life, no goddamn depth at all, all of him wild, without judgment, not enough poetry or refinement in him to fill a thimble. Unable to govern himself without the fear of God and Tozer Douglas to keep him in line. "Action, Bridgewater, it's what the Elbert Earls of this world need. They're warriors. We need a war for them, a real war! It's what I give him. That ain't what you do and that's why your way don't fuckin fly!"

"I . . . ah god, it's like talking to a wall." Her heels tapped across the floor again and it sounded like she kicked the desk or the file cabinet, and she said, "Don't you dare tell me what I do! You're too stupid to know what I do!"

And that was it. Mrs. Bridgewater stomped out of the office. Slammed the door.

She came into the bay, to Triple E's locker, where he was putting on his tie. "Elbert Earl, it's up to you," she said. "He can't make you stay on the team. It's your decision."

She was shaking. Her cheeks scarlet. She held her arms like a fighter, elbows low, fists curled.

Triple E grinned and gave her a wink. "You gonna punch me, Mrs. B?" he asked.

Looking at her fists, she laughed. "People like him drive me wild," she said.

Their eyes lingered for a moment and he felt his blood surging. Reaching out he touched her shoulder. "Mrs. B," he said.

She took hold of his tie, crossed it, flipped it, and made a knot. She adjusted the knot neatly at his throat. He watched her face, he smelled her hair, smelled her lipstick, her sweet, humid breath. Her thick lenses made her eyes owlish. He wanted to remove her glasses. Take the bow out of her hair.

She took his hand, looked at his knuckles, rubbed them with her thumb. "Where are we?" she said. "What century is this? How far have we come if we can't stop using our fists?"

"Every century is the same," he told her.

She nodded. She said, "Kafka."

"He kicks ass," said Triple E. " 'The Penal Colony,' that one got me."

"What?" she said. She stared into his eyes and took a deep breath, like she was getting ready to hear an oracle.

He wanted to say something penetrating, something that

would make her happy and confirm her belief in him. Her face was bent upward, her lips parted, waiting. He wondered if he should kiss her, was that what she wanted?

"Sit down," she told him.

She pulled him to the bunk and they sat at an angle to each other, knee touching knee. She was holding his hands, looking at him, her eyes hopeful. This is what she liked best, when he would talk lit-crit. Interpreting it, digging out messages.

"Tell me," she said.

In his mind's eye, he saw the machine in Kafka's story, the one that carved on the prisoner, carving the sentence of the judge on his body, the needles going deeper and deeper until blood flowed fast and the condemned man died. "You learn it on your body," said Triple E. "You're sentenced by the judge, but he doesn't tell you what it is. The machine carves your sentence on your body. We all learn it on our bodies."

"On our bodies," she said.

"It's God, I think, or maybe Kafka's father carvin out the way he'd be. A symbol like that. Maybe they're the same thing, father and God. We get sentenced to a certain kind of life, and . . . and to a certain kind of death . . . and we don't know what it is we'll die of . . . until it's happenin, until the body is diseased or shot or whatever is meant for to happen. I don't know if Kafka means it's fixed that way, the fix is in the minute we're born, or it happens because of the way we lived, or what. But you don't know a thing till it's written on your body, because it's the body that fails you, it's the body that dies. We might have *cancer* written there," Triple E touched his head, "or a *heart attack,* or who knows? Maybe a bullet or a car accident. You can't tell until it happens, and then it happens and then you know."

"That's good," she said.

Triple E shrugged.

Kafka's words were there, but he didn't really know what they meant, not definitely. He took a stab at saying, that's all.

"But look at it this way," she said. And then, of course, she gave the right interpretation, which was on the money, her pitched penny always touching the wall. "The story is mostly about the difficulty of communication, how Kafka wishes he could communicate with his readers in such a way that his words would be written on their bodies, worked into them like the needles on the machine working into the prisoner's skin, until the words become a part of who he is. See what I mean? We think our words communicate just what we want, but they don't, they never do. The ear hears, but the brain creates infinite variety. It plops its luggage right in the middle of everything we say. But think if we could write the words into the skin, penetrate the soul. That would be total *communication*."

"I guess," he said.

"In there?"

"Uh-huh."

"Larger?"

"Way larger," he said. *Jesus,* he thought, *what are we talkin about?* His joebuck perked up when she touched his stomach.

She hesitated, her brows crimping, her mouth frowning. She told him she wished he was her son. "I wish I had raised you. If you had been my son . . ."

"Yeah?" he said.

"Your life would be different if you had been mine." She ran her hand over his prickly hair. Her palm slid lovingly over his ear, his cheek. "I have to tell you," she said. "I see a new you. Don't fear the new you. Don't fight him. He's the real Elbert Earl. He's what you were meant to be."

Not suppose to touch you, a voice told him.

He looked at the hem of her skirt. He could see two, three inches up her thigh. The pantyhose stretched tight over her knee in a slant of light. Glancing around, he searched the bay. They were all alone. Table 99 would be waiting for him in the mess hall.

"Listen, I want you to know somethin," he said. "I've known guys like Tozer Douglas all my life and I don't let them tell me nothin. You don't gotta worry about me turnin out like him. And listen here, if he tries messin with you, I'll be there. You never got to fear if Elbert Earl's near. I'll punch his goddamn lights out."

"None of that," she said. Then she said, "You're my boy," and she kissed his cheek. If he had seen it coming he would have whipped his lips to her, but she was too quick. She gave him a peck, then stood up and pulled him to his feet. His hard joebuck slid sideways under his pocket. It was aggravating.

"I'll tell Tozer Douglas you want to go back to your typewriter."

"Mrs. B—"

"I'll tell him you're done and he's to leave you alone." She squeezed his hand. "My best boy," she repeated.

She started to leave, but he pulled her back. "Don't do that," he said.

He was feeling two ways about it. He wanted to please her, but he wanted to fight too. "Look, I got to show what I can do. I got to prove that Elbert Earl Evans is no punk. I want to finish what I started, Mrs. B. I know I can do both things, what *you* want and what *he* wants. You keep givin me what to read, and we'll talk, and . . . you know what I'm sayin . . . we'll do our thing, me and you, and I promise boxing won't make a difference. It's somethin I do good. It's what I do. Guys in the ring know what I'm sayin. That title, it's what *I* want, you see. Not for Tozer Douglas. Not for Goodpasture." Triple E waved those notions away. "For me," he said. "So I can say, 'Here, this is what I'm made of.' And people will look at me and say, 'There he goes, the champ. Don't fool with him, he's Triple E.'"

She worked up a pout. Her lips chewy delicious. "I see," she said.

"I'm your best boy," he said. "Sure I am. Boxing can't change that." He leaned in to catch her eye, make her look at him. Just six inches separated their mouths. He could smell her breath sweet, like cherries, like she had been sucking on a cherry Life Saver. She licked her lips, making her mouth slick, getting it ready for him. He figured he knew what she wanted. Women weren't honest. They talked around what they really wanted.

"What you doin here?" said Tozer Douglas, bustling through the double doors. "Get to dinner, Evans!"

Reluctantly, Triple E let go of Mrs. Bridgewater's wrist. He gave it a squeeze, then let it drop and brushed by her and by Tozer waiting at the door, slid by and out. Went downstairs, his guts growling.

THE NEXT FIGHTER TO be matched against him was Rinehart from Golden's Correctional School for Boys. Triple E fought his own way again, paying little attention to Tozer, who was blowing gaskets and condemning Triple E, until he dropped Rinehart with an inside uppercut after fifteen seconds of the third round. And then Tozer said, "Well, yew do things your own way, don't you, kid? What the fuck am I here for if yew already know everything?"

Tony Sandoval followed the next week, and Triple E decisioned him. A guy named Hall quit in the first round the week after. Undefeated Marty Strick from Denver gave him a hard time, but Triple E got him on points. And Tozer's constant complaint was, "Yeah yew win, but yew don't listen. Yew never do what I tell yew to do." He bitched at Triple E after every fight, telling him not to show off, not to let his gloves hang and taunt his opponents and not to do the Ali shuffle. Someone was going to tag him and knock him on his ass, and then he'd quit that Ali shuffle shit. "Yew don't have no killer instinct," Tozer told him. "Yew beat a boyo just enough, then yew let up on him. I see yew do it all the time. Follow through, Evans. Yew gotta go in there feeling like a wrecking ball."

"I win, don't I?"

"Yeah, but yew shouldn't. Not the way yew fight."

Tozer grumbled, but Triple E didn't care. He had fun in the ring. Showing off was his thing. It was how Ali got so famous. But he was all business too, when he had to be. And that's what Triple E would do. Combine business and play. He would be the white man's Ali.

HE HAD LIFE WIRED. He got used to everything, even the ghostly Bridgewater voice over the intercom and all the sayings hanging on the walls, exerting him to meditation. He memorized the message on a sign over the chapel door—

THE TRAGEDY OF LIFE MAKES IT WORTHWHILE

—finding comfort in the truth of it. He felt he understood the purity of some of her sayings, her gushing and groaning over every book, over every insight into human behavior, every high thought, every low thought, every noble impulse, every horrid deed—it was all part of some place of wisdom she was building

222

for herself. And what he appreciated was that she never talked down to him. She said her job was to push him, to make him use his brain, to raise him up. Give him a standard. Make him *think*.

What he didn't appreciate was the way she got on her high horse too often, talking like she was the beginning and the ending. She couldn't *always* be right, could she? It was like she had the key tucked away in her genius brain. She had him figured out, and Tozer Douglas, and Mr. Shackly-sir, every mother's son at Goodpasture, every mother and every mother's son in the whole U.S. of A., had them all figured out. Her pride, it definitely provoked him, made him want to knock her down a peg. Nobody, he didn't care who it was, had the world in the palm of her hand the way she thought she did.

But even so, there were moments in her presence he felt as if something at his center were being opened, and he was getting more in tune with the riddles. It could happen, too, by reading a passage or a line in a book, when it would strike him just so much at the right angle that he would feel suddenly finer, suddenly full of potential, as if a metamorphosis were taking place, his wings opening, reaching, circling her world, encircling *her*. He watched, listened, waited, schemed his schemes and kept his antenna out for the right signals from Mrs. Bridgewater, which he knew would come because she was a woman with needs—the lips, the breasts, the pussy, and a mind that wouldn't quit. And when it happened as it would, as it should . . . then . . . then.

HE WAKES UP AND looks around, and there is Jeanne to her neck in hay and there is the fire and there is the broken window letting wind in. The sweat has dried cold on him. Running his palm over his face, he gathers up salt. He scoots backwards and sits on the hay next to Jeanne. He takes her pulse. It is racing. How long can a heart do that? he wonders.

"Jeanne, you want some water?" he asks.

She doesn't answer, but he melts snow in the can and dribbles water over her lips. She whines and won't drink it, so he drinks it himself. He's never been so thirsty in his life, not even when he finished a fight and was dying of thirst after. Water satisfied him then. It didn't satisfy him anymore. His mouth is always hot and dry no matter how much he pours down it.

He cooks another can of water and sips it. From his shirt pocket, he pulls out Jeanne's letters and shakes one open. In mid-December, using cousin Ava's address, Jeanne had started writing him, saying she had tried to forget him, but couldn't. She said he was in her. Her pulse beat Triple E—Triple E—Triple E.

He wrote back. They sent each other Christmas cards and continued from there. She kept insisting she wasn't dating or anything. She was saving herself for him. He wrote about being on the boxing team and how he was undefeated and the tournament was coming up at the end of February. His letters got longer and longer, giving her blow-by-blow accounts of his fights.

He unfolds one page and reads:

In the still of the night
I wish with all my might
For your lips and arms
For your loving charms
I miss thee
Triple E.

She told him there was no light or warmth or love with him gone. And in another letter she wrote:

> *Love is strange*
> *It's no game*
> *I want you so*
> *Can't let you go!*

And then in another it was—

Triple E,

Missing you a ton. Ten tons. A million. My life is a big fat zip without you. The moon is gone from my sky why oh why? What good is the moon if your love isn't here to share the moon with me? The stars hide their fires from my secret desires. The sun is cold as gold and I am feeling old. I hang thru each day and my Mom says I am an idiot but I don't give a you know what she thinks. She keeps telling me I'm not too big to spank. Just let her try! My Daddy tells me to snap out of it. What does he know about it? In my heart I tell him to jump off a cliff. They both harp that 15 is too young to know what love is. Ha! They are too old to remember what real love is. Who are they to say such things to me? I'm not 15 in my soul. Love makes me old as a million. I am old as the pyramids. You are right about us being eternal lovers, Triple E. I knew it from the first my soul was seeking yours. Hurry home to these hungry arms hungry for you.

Your Jeanne Marie

P.S. This letter entitles the bearer to one billion very sloppy kisses.

He remembers the thing about eternal lovers. He had picked it up from one of Mrs. Bridgewater's books and had written to Jeanne that there were eternal lovers who went on from life to life searching for each other.

He shuffles the pages, reads the final letter, the one he knows almost by heart:

My eyes are blurry with tears tonight. I feel so lonely for you how will I stand it how will it all end? What if you never came back to me, I would die! Will we ever see each other again do you think? It seems like not. But oh we must, we must! My heart is pounding your name, or maybe it is the pounding of our doom that I hear. I don't know, there are times I feel I must die without knowing true loves passion. I dont want to die. I want to be a woman for you right now right here this night here in my room. I dream you are in my arms again and I give myself to you and your kisses burn me to ashes like fire. I can't stand it! God Im so in love with you tonight. Come home!

You are the blood in my veins
til death we part,
Jeanne Marie

P.S. Remember that night in the back of that chevy when we both knew all the words to Love Struck Baby and we sang it together our lips touching? God, that was so incredible, Triple E. I think about it all the time.

He remembered: A quart of tequila, some grass, a stolen Camaro. Tom Patch was driving them east on 70, going nowhere. Ava next to him cuddling under his arm. Radio blasting Stevie Ray Vaughan while the car flew toward the big sleep and Jeanne clung to him, singing into his mouth, their voices and minds wild. How fine the moments burn! And when it was over, and the music's last whine was dying away, she said, "That's our song till the end of ever, Triple E."

"Yes, very definitely," he told her.

He looks at her. Brushes her hair back and strokes her cheek with the back of his hand. He pushes the hay aside, touches her legs. He runs his hand under her skirt and finds the crotch of her panties stiff. He keeps his fingers there feeling for warmth.

"I think I might be dyin now," he tells her. "This is it." His voice echoes inside his ears, like it is trapped in a barrel.

Getting up, he does his boxing ballet alone in the dim light, gliding window to window, forcing his heart to speed up, his breath to quicken, and he works toward a fantasy—he is inside her again in the car, her lips opening as she spreads her legs, and he plunges into her hot, wet, welcoming—"Oh, Jeanne. Oh, Jeanne."

But it doesn't work.

His fists move, his fists whiff the air, and he sees himself beating Bennie Bogs in the tournament, winning the trophy, taking the trophy to her, saying, *I did it for you, Jeanne.* Dressed in tight-tight sweater and tight-tight skirt, she holds out her arms to a real man. Tells him to come to her. The skirt rides up, her legs spread. A bush burning. He moves, he shuffles, he moves.

But it doesn't work.

Nothing works anymore.

He looks out the window and wonders if he will still be breathing at dawn. *Once there were children of the dawn,* said something he had read he wasn't sure where. It sounded holy, it had a Hansel and Gretel ending, *children of the dawn,* and there had been themes about atonement and pure light and a child outgrowing the sphere of the father. Maybe it was Kafka again? No. There wouldn't have been any children of the dawn in Kafka. Nothing like that. No peace in Kafka.

"Peace is reached when we stop feeding our fires," Mrs. Bridgewater said one day. She was sitting at her desk, her hands illuminated by the sun's rays plunging through the window. The light whitened her hair. She was a good lady, he knows that now. A sort of goddess of truth: *When we stop feeding our fires.*

CHAPTER 13

HE WAKES UP WITH a pounding headache. His mouth is dry. Every joint in his body is achy and stiff. Gingerly, he runs his fingers over his lips, over cracks and burning sores and pieces of skin clinging. The pain makes him wince. "Talk about chapped lips," he says, chuckling grimly. His eyeballs ache. Even his tongue aches.

The house is dark and freezing again. Embers glow wickedly inside the fireplace. Once more he feeds flooring to the fire. He has already torn up most of one room and a quarter of the living room itself. It is ridiculous how easily the wood breaks, how fast it burns. He clomps about on frozen feet, thinking of Frankenstein's monster, boom, boom, boom. He drags the wood. Slams it against the stone hearth, where it fractures into long splinters. His feet feel vague, detached. When he looks at them it's like they belong to someone else.

The flames eat wood, climb it, leap high, tongues of flame storming up the chimney. He looks at Jeanne and she seems dead, very definitely dead. Yellow light flickers over her face. Her mouth is open, the bottom lip twisted to one side, her eyelids delicate, almost translucent. The eyes peek out from under the lids. Faraway eyes. He bends his ear close and can hear her breathing in short raspy runs, straining for air as if her lungs are out of space.

"I've killed Jeanne," he whispers.

He cradles his head in his hands and tells himself he can't go on another minute. He wonders why he had to drive back to Stone Garden and find Jeanne at school. Why did she jump in the car and tell him she was going where he was going? It had sounded fine. It had sounded heroic, sort of. She was loyal to him. In love and loyal. But he should not have let her come. And not Tom nor Ava neither, bopping over and jumping in the car, like they were going on a picnic or something. What dorks! Thought he was some kind of big deal, Mr. Bad. It had been on the news about him escaping in a stolen car from Goodpasture, and they all looked at him like *wow*. But the whole thing was just pure dumb stupidity, brains running on empty.

"A no-brainer," he says aloud. "A no-brainer," he tells Jeanne. Her cheekbones shine. Her mouth hangs. Her half-lidded eyes see visions of the other side.

He wonders about cousin Ava, where did she go? And Tom. Did he make it through the snow, back to the highway, and is he on his way with help? And Mrs. Bridgewater. No, he doesn't want to think about her. Of Goodpasture, of Tozer Douglas, of Bennie Bogs, the fight, and the thing that happened in the third round, he doesn't want to think about any of it anymore. But he is drawn there—the closing of the ring.

TOZER BABBLED OF TITLES and trophies. Titles and trophies would justify him.

All of his fighters had been defeated in the semifinals. Each one a knife in the heart. "Don't let me down," he said to Triple E. "It's more than yew know," he said. "Yew're young, yew don't understand these things yet." He grabbed Triple E by the shoulders, his fingers desperate, demanding—almost threatening—and he said, *Only yew can do it now, son. My last hope. Do it for Papa Tozer. Do it for the old man.*

TRIPLE E STARES INTO the flames. "Do it for the old man," he tells himself. Echoes of the slaughterhouse. Little Triple E sitting on a fence. Watching frightened cattle. Tiny tongues of fire leaping from their hides as men zap them with electric prods, forcing them up the ramp to meet his father, and his father knocking them over, their bodies hitting the bloody, shit-strewn floor with a sound like padded trash cans falling.

And at one point Triple E was beckoned. Gimmee your hand, ordered his father, and he put the magic wand in his hand. Told him where to hit the cow, just an inch above the eyes, right in the middle, they won't feel a thing, don't miss and knock her eye out now. The other men were watching. His father prodded him with a finger, his elbow coaxed. Triple E tried to do it, but he couldn't. He kept worrying about knocking out the cow's eye and having to reload and the cow terrified and thrashing around, screaming and everything.

These are the necessities of life. This is what it is before your mother makes it into meatloaf. Do it clean, his father said. Make me proud, he said. But Triple E couldn't summon up the nerve. The cow stared at him, her eyes alive with wonder, and he handed the wand back and climbed down and walked away, and his father shouted at him, said—You never do one fuckin thing for your old man! Well, fuck you!

"HE CALLS ME DUST. And he says to me, 'You are not the son I wanted.' You remember that, Dad? How you think that makes me feel? I'll tell you somethin—you ain't the dad I wanted neither. Ain't no man nowhere. You nor Tozer Douglas, both of you a pair of users. One wants me to kill him a cow, the other wants me to win him a trophy. Pah!" Triple E spits. He leans back on the hay and thinks about what he did. And it makes him madder and madder. He doesn't know if he is mad at them or at himself. He made them pay for something, but he's not sure what, or if it was worth it, or anything.

"It was the showdown," he says. "Like a movie," he says, recalling the scarred eyebrows of Marlon Brando. It was an old movie on TV and Brando was a palooka who took a dive. Triple E sits up, his shoulders tight, ready to rock and roll.

THERE WAS SO MUCH noise in the arena, he could barely hear what Tozer Douglas was saying. Triple E just wanted to get the fight over. Bring him on. Bring on Bennie Bogs. Left hook, right cross, uppercut, feint, weave, bob, kaboom! Load up, hit him triple for one. Kill the body and the head will die. Little Ray was in Triple E's corner, the towel man, the stool man, the water man. Little Ray believed in Triple E. I love you, Triple E, he kept saying. Of course he did—everybody loved a boom-boom boxer.

The arena was full of people screaming for blood. Kill him! Kill him! They didn't care who got killed. When Bennie got hot, they screamed for Triple E's blood. When Triple E got hot, they screamed for Bennie's blood. They hated whoever was getting pounded. Triple E was their hero. Then Bennie was their hero.

In the crowd were men known as the Denver Dozen. They were big shots who had gotten together as a sponsoring group to back fighters from Colorado. They were willing to back Bennie Bogs if he won and was crowned Colorado's amateur lightweight champion again. The parole committee had agreed to put him on probation and turn him over to the sponsors so he could be trained as a pro. He was a lanky, muscular kid who had the bones of a heavyweight, though he was still only 130 pounds. The sponsoring group was betting that in four or five years he would give them a return on their money. Triple E had had the group pointed out to him, all of them in front-row seats. Spic and span in dress-down jeans and sweaters. Legs crossed. Neat little hands. Golden fingers. Perfect hair. Polished faces. Superior eyes. He hated them.

Tozer said that Bennie Bogs was fighting for his life, so Triple E should watch out, should use all the tools at his command and invent some new ones. What made a fighter great was when he rose to the challenge and went beyond himself when he had to. "Don't give a fuck what happens to him if he gits beat," said Tozer. "That's no your bizness, kid. Your bizness is to beat him any way yew can. Don't lighten up no matter what. Don't go soft. Be a wrecking ball. Give the bastrrrd hate and haymakers."

Triple E wondered what Tozer saw in him that made him think he would go soft or give a fuck about whether Bennie Bogs went back to Buena Vista or on to fame and glory.

"I'll kill that muther," Triple E told Tozer.

And Tozer said, "I'll love yew if yew do."

When the referee gave instructions to the two fighters, Triple E stood close, looking into Bennie's eyes. He and Bennie were duplicates of each other, except Bennie was black; but they were exactly the same height and weight, the same arm reach, fist size, chest, neck, and both undefeated.

Triple E watched Bennie's eyes skipping toward the Denver Dozen in the front row. His eyes never met Triple E's eyes, and it seemed to him that Bennie was so scared of losing he was practically paralyzed. It was Bennie's moment of truth. His whole life would be determined by how he performed for the next three rounds and he had already lost his concentration.

Geez, I'm gonna beat this guy easy, Triple E told himself.

WHEN THE BELL RANG, he stepped out and got off first, throwing two quick flicks, then a one-two combination, connecting so cleanly Bennie went down on one knee. He bounced right back up, but he was clearly worried. He came on cautiously, shuffling in, giving Triple E a peek-a-boo look. Triple E moved side to side, bouncing on his toes, the floor spongy beneath him. He had visions of fame and glory. The Denver Dozen signed *him*. He bought his love a Cadillac. He bought his love a house. His life stretched in front of him, filled with booze, pot, fast cars, Jeanne on his arm. Fame, fortune, worshiping fans. All the people who said he was a punk were eating their words. Sorry for doubting him. America would take him to its stone heart and call him king, immortal like Jack Johnson, Jack Dempsey, Muhammad Ali, Rocky Marciano—that's Triple E.

Bennie Bogs had that hard jab, though, and it kept Triple E off, that lightning jab and a sucker breadbasket fake that ended up a hook to the liver and then to the head. Triple E pressed in, letting Bogs jab away, wanting to get some shots at his midsection, get his arms down a bit.

At one point in the round, Bogs's jab seemed to be getting soft, feeling like a fist wrapped in wool, and Triple E got over-confident and went for the inside. Too late he realized that Bogs had been throwing puffs to get him to do just what he did, stepping in, his left poised to bring a shot to some juicy ribs, and *wham!* he got nailed by a right lead that unhinged him. He felt his jaw dislocate, felt his knees buckle, felt himself lurching sideways, then toppling over.

A moment later, he heard the ref counting, "One—two—three—"

Triple E rolled onto his stomach. His feet were trembling, the nerves shifting around as if looking for a circuit. He resettled his mouthpiece and heard something snap in his jaw. Hot pain ran up the back of his head and nested behind his eyes. He tasted morsels of blood and swallowed. At the count of eight he got up. In the far corner, Bogs stood slamming his fists together, waiting for the referee's decision. The ref cleaned Triple E's gloves and looked at him.

"What's your name?" said the ref.

"I'm okay," Triple E told him.

"What's your name?"

"Evans. I'm fine, c'mon."

The ref waved Bogs on. Triple E went to the ropes. He rolled his back along the ropes and covered up, while Bennie went to work, bringing it home, several shots to the ribs and when Triple E's elbows fell an inch to cover, Bennie went upstairs and worked on his head. Triple E didn't feel much pain, or much of anything except that his legs were wiggly. His legs weren't getting the signals he wanted to send them. He wanted his legs to move him off the ropes and away from Bennie's fists, but they wouldn't. He could hear the crowd going with Bennie, urging him to kill. Tozer's voice was coming through, screaming, "Uppercut him! Uppercut him, yew goddamn heathen!"

Triple E had just enough control to slip some punches and ward off others with his gloves and shoulders, and when the round ended he was able to stumble along the ropes to his corner and sit down. He felt water spraying his face. He took the sponge, sucked it. It reminded him of being a boy in the bathtub, sucking water out of the washrag.

"Fucker tagged me."

"Yew learned nothin I taught yew—nothin!"

Tozer scoured his palms back and forth over Triple E's thighs, coaxing life into them. He asked Triple E if he was a man. Was he a Goodpasture fighter or not? Was he gonna let the likes of Bennie Bogs beat him, that *bastrrrd,* was Triple E gonna fold? "Be a *white man!*" Tozer demanded. "Give it to him good! Make those fuckers in the front row notice yew! Take him down, bust his gut so bad he can't breathe! If yew can't do it for yourself, do it for Goodpasture, do it for me and your pals, do it for God and country, so yew can say once in your pissed-away life yew did something grand!"

Triple E's knee lusted after Tozer's chin. He despised the man, hated his ice-gray eyes, hated the mouth talking and talking. Everybody talked too much, him and Bridgewater—blah, blah, blah . . .

"I'm fightin my fight," he said. "Lemmee the fuck alone."

THE SECOND ROUND WAS better. He didn't fall for Bennie's fake to the inside and the right lead following over. Only one time would that trick work on Triple E. There was no showing off, no shuffle, no taunting. Triple E was all business.

Bennie went backwards as Triple E took him to task, getting shot after shot through his defenses. But he kept fighting, throwing punches, then crowding Triple E, using elbows and shoulders, on the inside, taking the bite out of Triple E's punches, then countering with uppercuts and shots to the back of the head, shots to the kidneys. Triple E absorbed everything and kept coming. He was swallowing blood again and it was hard to breathe. He was afraid to let the blood leak out. Enough blood and the ref would call the doctor for a look.

Triple E had seen it before, guys with lots of juice left, but bleeding so much the doc wouldn't let them fight. So Triple E swallowed. The blood was thick and it cut his wind. There was a steady pain running from the left side of his jaw to behind his left eye. Bogs's jabs were good. His jabs kept tapping Triple E's forehead. But he wasn't letting it stop him, was still moving in, his fists feeling like rocks, his arms coming on awhirl like an executioner with an ax, shoulders working tirelessly.

Bogs lost ground, he slid away, covering up, while Triple E worked methodically, a right cross over a jab, a left hook to the belly, followed by a hook to the head, followed by a right that glanced off Bennie's cheek and tore some skin, made him bleed. Triple E aimed for the blood.

He did not get excited, did not wear himself out throwing useless punches. His mind felt cold and competent. When he saw he couldn't get through to Bennie's torn cheek, he backed off and delivered textbook jabs and hooks. In the clench he dealt uppercuts, pounded the solar plexus, piled up points with the judges.

Bogs fought well in bursts, drove Triple E to the ropes.

Worked on his ribs, pounded on his arms and head. Triple E came back with a flurry, ending the round with Bogs ducking and covering and trying to bulldoze his way out of trouble.

TRIPLE E FIGURED IT was all but over. He figured the crown and the trophy were his and that in the year 2000, bad boys would still be reading his name in the trophy case. Elbert Earl Evans, a.k.a. Triple E, was here. He walked back to his corner and stood there waiting for the bell.

"It's about time yew listened to me!" said Tozer Douglas as he fanned Triple E with a towel. "He's yours. He's ready to go. He can't hardly stand up."

"I gotta headache would kill a cow," said Triple E. The pain behind his left eye was pulsing, making him feel like his eye was bleeding inside. He took the water bucket and spit into it, blood pouring from his mouth. He couldn't spit enough to get the blood out.

IN THE FIRST HALF of the third round, he kept hitting Bogs with rib shots, kidney shots to the deep-waist side, punches so hard that Bogs groaned and had to drop his arms to protect his body, and each time he hunched and his elbows pulled in, Triple E went to work on his head, hit him upstairs, then downstairs, then upstairs again. Hit him with a right hook so hard he went down on his butt, his mouthpiece flying out. He got to his hands and knees and waited till the count of eight before getting up. His corner put a fresh mouthpiece in and the ref waved him on. Triple E went after him, driving him to the ropes. But Bogs kept coming back, throwing shots of his own, hurting Triple E, making him give ground, making him dip and slip and move away.

He went in a circle. Looked for openings. Threw a pair of

jabs, then started with a right cross, and saw Bennie's fist lash out. A split second later, it was almost over. Bennie caught him on the chin, right on the button, and a lighter-than-air feeling entered Triple E's head. It was like the time Chuck Pump had suckered him, vacuumed his brain, and it was as if he lost his legs—but this time they were still under him, moving unaware. He didn't go down, he wasn't paralyzed. He felt like a floating vision, stepping in and out of vague worlds and timelines, his fists flicking at shadows of past and present, all one, no difference, his father's face, Tozer's, and a dozen sneering masks on Stone Garden streets, circles of boys howling, the air filled with defiance and pain and anger and pure, unprovoked hatred—everywhere enemies were falling at his feet, his fists bleeding, knuckles jammed and swollen, the gush of warm blood flowing over lips and chin.

Seconds later, his head cleared and he found himself staring into Bennie's eyes. He couldn't account for it. His mind had filled with infinite space, with death and the soul's terminal dream. He had been *out* on his feet. And yet never more aware of bodies interchanging, fists perpetual, repetitious worlds knitting lives together, the cycle going on at the same incurable pace. Dying and rebirth: spooky, awful. And wonderful too. Miraculous as loaves and fishes.

TWO MINUTES INTO THE round Bogs started hanging on more and more. Tozer Douglas was bellowing, telling him to tear the bastard's head off, saying Bogs was no man, that the sooty bastard was getting his, that when it was over they would have to pour him down the shithole where he belonged.

It seemed like every voice in the arena was in Triple E's favor, all those voices that had screamed for Bogs to murder Triple E were now screaming for him to murder Bogs. "Put him away! Murder that piece of shit!" Rabid faces is what he saw over Bogs' shoulder—pitiless eyes, terrible teeth. The loudest was Tozer Douglas, a happy ogre, grimacing and bellowing and pounding on the apron and saying, "Shovel shit, son! Shovel that shit!"

A minute to go and Bogs clutched Triple E again and Triple E could hear him breathing through his mouth, sucking up great sobs of air. Triple E was sobbing air too, swallowing blood and gasping, his lungs heaving. Blood was trickling from his nose, onto Bennie's back.

The referee stepped in and drove the boys apart. Triple E looked into Bennie's eyes once more. There was no quit in his eyes. Triple E went after him, and Bennie tried to dance, tried to get his legs going, but Triple E pursued him, hammering his body, and all Bennie could do was throw himself forward, smother the punches. Their chests sliding together. Bogs whispered, *I'm dead.* But he tried to fight on, tried to find something that would work. Bennie's punches were soft, but he was no quitter. He was a fighter. It was an honor to fight him.

For a few seconds, the two of them went toe to toe in the center of the ring, both swinging, both banging and getting banged. Then it was over and Bennie stumbled backwards, wrapping an elbow around the corner post, his eyes raking the crowd, then fixing on the ceiling overhead as if it were a way out. He was gasping for air. He opened himself to Triple E's finishing punches, arms stretching wide-crucified resting on the ropes. Triple E was panting, swallowing and panting. His fists were down near his hips, his gloves heavy as horseshoes. Bennie waited for him to end it.

It was an odd moment for Triple E. He wanted to tell Bennie about it, wanted to say, "Bennie you're okay, man." And he wanted to say, "We done good, Bennie," but it would have been too dumb, and so he just stood there in the center of the ring, half-smiling, alone, isolated, cocooned.

It was a neat feeling, a still point in a turning world. The j.d's, the faculty, the counselors, the parents who had come, the admin people, the janitors, the sponsors, all of them were outside and irrelevant to what he and Bennie were, the two of them remote, meeting the call to action, the ordeal, the trial, coming through, and then the oneness. He found himself not wanting to end it, not wanting Bennie or himself crowned. No trophy for nobody. Why can't we just walk away now? he asked himself. It's enough. We've done enough.

"Hey, Bennie," he said.

"Get that faggot!" cried Tozer. "Sic'm, yew goddamn heathen! No quarter!"

A murmur of voices started up, tiny grumblings at first that soon grew into a flood of insults:

"Cheesewiz!"

"Punks!"

"Whussies!"

"Pussies!"

"Skags!"

"No heart! No heart!"

He glanced at the sea of faces urging him to kill. His head pounded, his vision blurred, blood clung like syrup inside his mouth. He wanted out of there. Who were they, those people? What gave them the right? Fuck them and all motherfuckers like them. He figured he and Bennie could whip all their asses. Wade out there side by side and clean their clocks. He doubted if any of them would get in the ring with him or Bennie, go three rounds. Could they stand toe to toe, pound the piss out of each other like he and Bennie had? They screamed and carried on, but Triple E knew them. All mouth.

Not one soul-cool like Bennie Bogs. Not one bone-bad as Elbert Earl Evans. Thumbs-down they were giving him, the crowd giving him thumbs-down. Where did they think they were? What century were they in?

The referee looked confused. He glanced at the judges, then asked the boys if they wanted to continue fighting. Twenty-three seconds to go. Twenty. Nineteen. Tozer bawled at Triple E, ordering him to finish Bogs. Triple E stood at arm's length. Bogs had not moved. He leaned on the ropes, breathing. Seventeen. Sixteen. He shrugged and put his gloves up. Triple E did not respond. Bogs waved him in. *"C'mon,"* he said.

Fourteen. Thirteen . . .

"Goddamn you, Evans! What the hell yew think this is!" screamed Tozer. "Who the hell yew think yew are!"

TRIPLE E'S MIND HAD seemed a *sure thing*—a born fighter, pitiless in the ring—but something changed in his head, a switch went off. His heart began to calm down. His lungs pumped slower. His muscles relaxed.

There was no more need. It was over. And he couldn't say exactly why. Maybe it was Bennie's unrepentant eyes and the moment so cool he didn't want to spoil it. Or maybe it was something else, something too deep to know.

"How about that?" he said.

"Hunh?" said Bennie, his head cocking sideways.

Tozer kept hooting, "Sic em, yew sonofabitch! Goddamn yew, Evans, don't punk out, yew bastrrrd!"

The crowd cursed and booed and demanded satisfaction.

But Triple E couldn't have cared less about them. He thought about the Olympic rebel, the gold-medal winner, his black-fisted glove raised in defiance as the "Star-Spangled Ban-

ner" played. Triple E raised his fist straight overhead. The boo-
ing got louder.

Tozer screamed, "I knew it! I knew yew'd fuck it up!"

Triple E walked away, parted the ropes, jumped to the
floor and went up the aisle, his teeth ripping at the tape over
his glove strings. The bell ending the round rang and a deafen-
ing din of boos and curses fell on his head. For a moment he
felt wrong. And then he felt right.

At the door to the locker room, he turned around and saw
the referee talking to the judges, his hands gesturing. Bennie
was looking at the Denver Dozen. Tozer was still beside the
ring, pounding the apron with his head. The crowd was howling. Some of the boys were fighting. The counselors and guards
were running back and forth, grabbing arms and necks, shov-
ing boys into their seats, hauling some of them up the aisles. It
was pandemonium.

"Kill each other. Kill each other, you mungos." All this
mess because of him. Always causing trouble everywhere he
went. Trouble with a capital *T*. "You got a kind of chaotic
power," he told himself.

LATER WHEN J.D.'S ASKED him why he had walked away,
he didn't know what to say. All he could say was fuck that shit,
or fuck Tozer Douglas and fuck stupid trophies and fuck titles
and fuck everything and everybody. "I do what I want! I'm my
own man!" he told them.

Tozer quit talking to Triple E. Triple E got shit details from
then on, latrine duty every day and shoveling snow and washing trays in the kitchen till ten at night, and hours spent cleaning the barn gutters with a scoop shovel, all the gutters, all by
himself. Triple E's ten cows were taken away, given to a better

boy. His fellow boxers on the team ignored him. He overheard comments about what a pisser he was, how he had a tapioca heart. Couldn't even finish Bogs off. Left the ring with eleven seconds to go. Disqualified himself, forfeited the match.

He could hear them in the halls: *There's the guy, the punk who quit, the one they call Triple E.*

THE FIRE CRACKLES AND unloads an ember that almost lands in the hay. He crushes the ember with his heel, smears it back and forth over the floor. He is lying next to Jeanne, holding her hand, the fight with Bogs hitting rewind in his head. He is trying to figure out what possessed him to quit. He really doesn't know for sure. It seemed like the right thing to do. To say no to everything and walk away. And so he did, and that was it. And boxing was over. He wonders how far he could have gone with it. To the top? A career of breaking heads, of learning how to give pain, take pain. "A real man conquers it and learns how to use it," Tozer had said.

"That's true," says Triple E. "You turn it into anger, and anger makes you mean." He looks toward the frosted window. He shivers. He tastes blood seeping from his ragged lips. Every joint in his body aches. He feels bruised and broken. "Makes you able to take this kind of shit," he says.

He gives up thinking about it. He doesn't want anger anymore, he wants peace. From his pocket he takes the booklet of poems and leafs through them, reads aloud in the faint light, hoping the rhythm of the words will keep Jeanne's brain alive, maybe bring her back, make her open her eyes and look at him in recognition.

Farm poet Chouinard had had a tough time. The poems tell about it, how his farm was failing and his cows getting sick, endless rain spoiling the mowed hay, the hay bleaching in the fields. His debt load sinking him. And then he had a heart attack. It is all there, the ordeal of Chouinard's life laid out in words without compromise.

But some of the poems are not so dark. Some talk about his love for the land and for his cattle and his wife and daughter. One poem calls his daughter "A northern light, flowering clean and strong." Another says that he loves his wife with "the simple passion of the thought that you are mine, / have been mine for a silver span of years."

Triple E wonders if poet Chouinard made it, was he mean enough, defiant enough? Is he still farming? Or has he gone the way of all the others, the small farms failing, being steam-rollered by the big corporations? The last poem gives a hint, it says:

> this weary heart (hush
> walk softly here)
> sleeps.

Did that mean it was over for him? Maybe so. Everything flows to its end somewhere. That's what the sign over Mrs. Bridgewater's door said: *Even the weariest river winds somewhere safe to sea.*

He puts the poems back in his pocket and stares into the fire and thinks of how calm and resigned he feels. Nothing is scary anymore. He's going to go to sleep and die. Him and Jeanne, and that's the way. They are weary rivers flowing to the sea. So fuck it. He looks around at the decaying house and realizes how appropriate it is for the transition about to take place. Like an unbending book. Like a Kafka ending.

AFTER A WHILE HE nods off, dozes a bit, dreams that he is falling, wakes up with a jolt. He gathers more wood to keep the fire fed. He stuffs the chimney with as much wood as it can take. The flames roar like a massive engine. Minutes later, he falls asleep again.

An hour passes, maybe less, when he is awakened by the sensation of something stinging his cheek. A piece of charred wood tumbles over his shoulder and into the hay. When he looks up, he sees the roof on fire, embers trickling down. It takes a moment to sink in. Fire. The house is burning.

"What the goddamn hell!" he says.

Grabbing Jeanne by the collar, he skids her across the floor and outside onto the snow, away from the flames.

AN HOUR LATER, HE sits dazed and disbelieving, watching as the roof collapses, watching the fire chew up their last chance of survival. Jeanne's head is on his lap. Thick smoke billows into the soft dawn, filling it with ashes. The chimney crown bursts, sending stones into the sky. Ashes rain on the snow and on himself and Jeanne. Stones hit them. He leans over and covers Jeanne's face, while bits of stone pepper his back.

The fire consumes the entire house, pumping warmth into the air until midmorning. Triple E stays until only the foundation and charred wood remains. Smoke billows from the burned-out socket, smoke rising lazily into the sky.

Jeanne is mumbling. She thrashes around. She keeps saying his name, but when he answers she tells him she doesn't want him, she wants Mommy. When the sun is overhead, he puts her back on the hood and starts off. The snow squeaks beneath his feet, the hood pulls easy. Then the angle gets steeper and he is slowed to a crawl. The bare bushes around him shudder. Their arms sheathed in ice. The blankness of the white world beyond the brush fills him with rage. He refuses to look at it. He turns his back to the long grade in front of him and starts jerking the hood uphill by digging in his heels and pulling. Then sitting down, scooting up and digging in his heels again, inch by inch moving his load out of the valley.

THE SUN IS FAR west when they get back to the car. She can stand and move if he helps her. He is staggering with exhaustion, but he manages to tumble her through the window and onto the front seat. Then himself. When he tries to start the car, the battery is dead. He yanks up the backseat and stuffs it through the shattered window in back. He closes everything up tight as he can get it. The sun is coming through the front glass, magnified, making him too warm, but he knows it won't be for very long. He knows that when the sun falls off the edge of the earth, he and Jeanne will go with it.

On the floor he finds a broken Oreo and eats it, washes it down with snow.

The earth which fed you, now will eat you echoes in his mind. That's what a lady chanted at his grandfather's funeral. And she meant it kindly, meant it as a good thing, tit for tat: *The earth which fed you, now will eat you.* He looks out the window, watching the sun disappear. Another hour it will be dark, the wind will be cold, it will freeze everything it touches.

A pair of birds, maybe the same pair he has seen twice before, flies by. He watches them dip down and skim the snow and recede far into the white, until they reach the vanishing point. Bits of song click on and off inside his head, *Oh say can you see, by the dawn's early light* . . . He feels crazy. "I'm crazy," he says.

247

Jeanne's voice, soft as feathers, whispers for him to turn on the heater. "The key," she says. "The key . . ."

The outline of the road is in front of him, all of it together running at an angle, sloping like a river, fierce rays of pink-shrimp twilight leading the way. Jeanne is sitting upright, her long hair spreading over the back of the seat. He lays his head on her lap and listens to her mumble. She wants her mommy, her daddy. She wants to be warm. Turn the key on. Gimme heat . . . hugs. Turn the key.

MRS. BRIDGEWATER HAD GONE around for days gloating about what Triple E had done. Sensing, she said, that her methods had gotten through to him. She was proud. She was even writing a paper about it for *Hybrid Science*. Her gloating spoiled what he had done *not* for her, but for a reason way beyond anything he could name. It had been special, something for him and Bennie and all the rebels who refused to be ruled.

Yet after a while, he started wondering if maybe she really did have something to do with his quitting. It depressed him, the whole thing, her and Tozer and losing the title and the way everybody looked at him like he was some kind of freak.

Mrs. Bridgewater was invited to be on National Public Radio, and Triple E got to hear her bragging about her methods, her use of certain books and edifying quotes and herself as sensitive counselor learning what was wrong in each boy's life and using her skills to *enlighten,* and thereby salvage, those with unrealized potential. She said right out that Triple E was an example of how good her methods were, how her methods worked on the right kind of mind.

When she came to work the next day, he was shoveling snow off the steps in front, and she smiled at him, ta-ta'd her fingers and walked on. He watched her mount the steps in tight pants and a short jacket that showed rolling buttocks and thick legs. She had heavy flesh. She's a cow, he told himself. Her fat ass is for fucking. She goes home and fucks her husband. Gets off on how terrific she is saving that bad-bones Triple E.

That night, he lay on his bunk and watched a faceless man and Renee Bridgewater go at it, she over his knees, him spanking her big bare ass. Howling and howling. He opened the door. He peeked inside. "Hit her!" he told the man. "Hit her hard!"

DARK VISIONS ATE AT Triple E's heart, made him go a little bit, or more than a little bit, insane.

And then one day in her office, smug and confident, knowing all, she ordered him to harness his anger, use it for good, and if he would do that he would move mountains. While she was jabbering, showing cleavage, her blouse tight provocative, he looked at the only mountains he cared about moving. Mountains saying, Suck these, young man, these pink pretties. You can fuck me if you want.

No, they hadn't said that. They said . . . she said: "We've made tremendous progress. I want you to listen to me. I want you to believe in yourself. I'm so proud of you, Elbert Earl." And when she kissed the top of his head, he smelled her, the hollow of her breasts breathing out of her blouse, and that's what triggered him. He jumped out of the chair and hugged her. *"Love me,"* he whispered. *"Love me, somebody."*

She said: "You're such a sweetie." And she hugged him back.

He pressed against her and . . . and she froze. "Kiss me," he commanded. "Kiss me, Mrs. B, you know you want to. You gotta be lovin me now, after what I did for you." He locked his lips on hers. Juicy stuff. There was a second of surrender in her, he felt it, he felt her knees watery, her lips slackly sucking. "Love, Mrs. B. Love."

He kissed deep in her neck. The little dent in her throat, gave it a lick. The earring, a bauble of gold, kissed that. Bottom lip crushed with pink lipstick, smelled it, nibbled it. Palmed her breast, ran his hands up and down her, squeezed her big, rubbery ass.

"Now, listen," she said, her voice phlegmy.

There was a pink bow in her hair. He untied it and her hair puffed. She backpedaled, backing herself against the bookshelf, where he clutched her hips and started dry-fucking her.

"All right, that's enough!" she said.

He was all over her, and she was starting to fight back. She loved him. She knew in her heart she loved him. They would shack up and ball their brains out every night.

"If I've done anything to lead you on," she said breathlessly.

He took her glasses off, set them on the shelf. "I love your eyes," he said.

She wasn't smug now, she wasn't knowing. "Take your hands off me!" she said. He grabbed her groin, grabbed her right where she lived. He knew that if he could get a finger in her, she would melt and go for him and have to have him.

"Have you lost your mind?" she said, her voice shrill.

He dug into her crotch, he broke her waistband and jerked her pants down, grabbed at her panties, tugging at them, clawing.

"Oh, my God!" she cried.

"Shut up!" he said. And he hit her one-two, stunned her with a pair of shots that would have had Bogs pausing. She slumped to her knees, her face even with his lap, her hands

250

clutching his legs. He thought he might beat her to death. His fists rose above her head. Her head rocked back and forth. She thrust her mouth at him, bit his thigh.

"That's right, do that!" he said. He admired her grit, that she would bite him. It made him smile. He looked her over carefully. She was an interesting specimen. Nose bleeding. A welt rising on her cheekbone. Eyes rolling, teeth gnawing. Roughly he pushed her away and her head bumped the floor. He stretched her out, slid her pants over her ankles, tore her underpants to pieces. She was groaning, kicking, trying to cover up, murmuring—"Nuh, nuhhhh . . ."

She didn't want him? How could she not want him? He cocked his fists again. "I could kill you," he said. "Pound you to pieces."

Her head flopped backwards, her eyelids fluttered open. She looked at him. "Why?" she whispered.

He told her: "Because you don't know shit, Mrs. B. You think you're some kind of genius, but you don't know shit. You act like I'm somethin, but it's just you and your books and gettin on the radio, your big name, you care about. I'm nothin to you, you big phony. You're just as fucked as Tozer."

"Not true," she said.

"Nothin but somethin to trot out and take bows over. You been playin with me like a rat in a cage . . . yeah, a white rat in a cage. Dr. Bridgewater's latest experiment. How many shots of Kafka will it take to drive the devil outta Triple E? Bet you got it all writ down like a scientist, haven't you? Your data. Then you can publish another book and everybody be jealous of you, look at all her books, what a smart lady! She found what will cure the mean streets—books'll do it! Art'll do it! Words'll do it. Hand em out with condoms and you've cured everything. Words, words, words. Blah, blah, blah . . . Jesus-fuck, it scares me to think how full the world is of dumbshits like you!"

"You don't know," she said. "You don't know about the words. They're in you, they won't go away."

"What's wrong with me?" he said, pressing his fingers to his head. "My head don't feel right."

"You're broke," she said. "You need help." Her eyes were filled with tears. Slack lips. Nose trickling blood onto her upper lip, blood playing with the corner of her mouth, like a deep red worm trying to burrow in. Purple welt on her cheek. A woman. Face lopsided, wiggly with lines like Tozer's had been at the fight—faces made of clay and he, Triple E the sculptor, had been thumbing them this way and that way, shaping them. She was just an old lady, a frightened old lady who knew only that she was over her head now, that words meant nothing now, that fine phrases were nothing now. His fists scattered words, broke them into molecules.

"Elbert Earl," she said, whispering his name like a prayer.

"Don't Elbert Earl me. I'm Triple E, bad as I can be!" He slammed his palms over his ears, squeezed hard. "Jesus, I don't know what's goin on," he said.

"You haven't understood," she said, her voice wooden, as if her tongue had gone numb. "You haven't understood my meaning."

"Maybe that's right," he said.

Her voice moved in a mechanical rhythm and she said, "I've tried my best with you."

"Fuck that, I'm still the same incorrigible, rotten-nasty-no-account I always been."

She shook her head and she said, "One day you'll see."

"You really think so?"

"Yeah . . . yes."

"You're just runnin off the mouth. How about I smack you some more? Want a nose like mine? Would you like my nose, lady?"

Her eyes looked burned out, smoky. She shrugged. Too weary to answer.

His hands were shaky. He didn't know what he wanted to do with his hands. If he wrapped his fingers around her neck, his hands would steady. "I'm comin apart," he said. "I'm blowin a gasket," he told her. His heart was slamming around like a fist, he could feel it punching his lungs, his ears, his brain. "Pieces of Triple E gonna fly all over this room."

"Let's talk," she said.

"Like talkin cures a goddamn thing! I don't want to talk. It's talk that's done me. Things were simple till you and your bullshit talk. Don't know if I'm comin or goin. Don't know, can't tell."

Everything was a wall and a locked door with a space beyond leading to nothing. Again and again he had felt it. Living his life in the dark, thrashing around, unable to see where he was going, unable to feel his way through. It was dark before and after. He wanted one moment back, the second or two after Bennie had punched him so hard—when the web of life got sutured together—he wanted that again, the little miracle in the ring.

Was it Triple E thinking this way—or was it someone else? Maybe he was possessed. Maybe that was the thing, his whole trouble. "You gimmee a cuckoo brain, Bridgewater." He looked at the window, the glass throwing back fragments of himself.

"We can work it out," she said. "No one has to know what happened. This is just between you and me." She opened her mouth and words came out. It was as if prerecorded sentences had clicked on in her head. This is what you say in this situation. You say: we can work it out. No one has to know. It is between you and me.

"You don't know your ass from your elbow, Mrs. B. It's changed between us. Changed fundamental."

"Triple E is broken. He doesn't know what he's doing," she said.

"I never have. I never fuckin have."

She was half-sitting, leaning her head and shoulders against a cabinet, her palms on the braided rug. Her ass flattened out beneath her like soft pastry. Her legs were slightly bent, one knee turned inward. Just above her hairs was a horizontal scar. He wondered if her female organs had been removed. She had no children. *If you had been my son,* she had said once.

"You still want me to be your son?" he said.

She looked at him, her eyes rimmed in red. Tears trickled down her cheeks. The blood beneath her nose, over her mouth and chin, looked like a crushed flower. "I wanted you to be worth the effort."

"You and Tozer . . . you, me, everybody—we all don't know shit from shinola, I'm convinced of that. Everybody's talkin past everybody. Nothin else goin on in this world but empty talkin past. My eyes different from your eyes, your eyes different from Tozer's eyes, Tozer's eyes different from both our eyes. Nobody sees nothin the same, not even if you carve the words in. You got off on my life, but its just a tickle up the ass for you. Fun with Triple E, but you don't see nothin the way I do."

She shook her head. "Everybody suffers, Elbert Earl."

"That's true too," he said. "Everything's true."

"I don't need to be beaten. I just need to know what suffering is. Who hasn't suffered?"

"Well, I'm just sayin . . . Jesus fuck me, I don't know what I'm sayin." He looked away from her, out the window at the snow coming down at an angle. "I gotta get outta here," he said.

"Maybe so," she said, mumbling at him, wanting to be rid of him.

He set his brows in an icy line. "You shut up. You zip it. I'm sayin what's what, not you. For once in your life, you don't have the answers. I got the answers." He yanked her to her feet, shoved her toward the closet. She went gratefully, it seemed, hurrying to the closet on stiff legs, her hands searching in front of her like a blind person. He locked the door behind her and leaned against it for a moment, trying to think. He could hear her muffled sobs.

"Gotta go," he said.

He took her keys and money, her cigarettes and matches, and went out the window. He walked like nobody's business to the parking lot. He stole her Oldsmobile, driving it out the archway announcing GOODPASTURE CORRECTIONAL FA-CILITY and turning southeast toward Alta. The wipers worked hard, while flakes of snow, like dying white moths, settled over the windshield and the evergreens, the aspens, the wooden fence, the fallen trees, the rotting logs, the uneven land. Great breaths of wind swept over the road. Boundaries vanished.

CHAPTER 14

Excerpt from "Rise and Walk," an article in the *Grand Junction Chronicle*, Grand Junction, Colorado, Sunday, Social News Section, March 12, 1984, by Cissy Caffery, staff writer.

THE AFTERNOON OF THE day the house caught fire, Kempis was standing in the bed of his four-wheel-drive truck, tossing hay to his cattle. Kempis had thrown the last of the bales over the side when, as he tells it, "I took a breather and I looked around and I saw the smoke and knew right away Wes Johnson's old farm was on fire. So I headed over there to see what was going on."

Kempis came upon the Johnson house burned to the ground. "The remains looking like charred bones," Kempis said. Kempis also noticed footprints in the snow, and the track of what might have been a very wide toboggan, and, in his own words, "The Cosmic Christ who determines our destiny touched my heart and I got a strong spiritual feeling from the place, and I knew somebody was lost in the wilderness and needing me."

Kempis hurried home and told his wife, Ruthie, about what he had seen. Ruthie had dinner ready and knowing they might be searching in the freezing cold all night, she made her husband sit down and eat. It was dark before they set out in their four-wheeler.

An hour later they came upon the stranded car, an Oldsmobile Cutlass Ciera half-buried in the snow. "Its iced windows bounced light at us before the rest come into view," said Kempis.

Kempis positioned his truck so that its headlights fell upon the stranded vehicle from several yards away, then he and Ruthie made their way to the car, wading knee-deep in snow. Kempis shined his flashlight on the car's windshield, but the ice was so thick that everything was distorted and they couldn't see anything inside the car. The side windows were the same and the doors wouldn't open, so Kempis and Ruthie had to go around to the trunk, where they tried to peer through the back window. But the glass was broken out and a car seat had been crammed in the window frame to keep the weather out. Kempis and Ruthie pushed the obstruction aside and looked in. The beam from the flashlight caught something shiny up ahead. Ruthie said it looked like frosted hair, which is what it was, the frosted-over hair of a young girl sitting bolt upright, her face facing toward the windshield. But Kempis saw something different. In his court affidavit he said:

When I first seen that head covered in white like that, seemed to me I was looking at a dove with its wings drooping down. It was her hair fanning out, but it looked like a dove's drooping wings. There was an inch of frost over that little girl's hair. The car lights were playing tricks on the glass, and the light was making a kind of bright tunnel, and for a second I seen this vision of dove's wings. It was a beautiful, pious thing. I'm a spiritual man. I believe in Jesus and Mary, blessed be their holy names, and I believe my visions come for a reason. But then, of course, the vision faded, and I seen it wasn't a dove. It was her.

We prayed for her, an Act of Contrition—just in case the soul was standing judgment and an Act of Contrition might help—and in the middle of prayin' this boy peeks his head up and looks at me, I seen his eyes over the rim of the seat, and he whispers in a croaky voice, he says, "Could you help us, sir?" I almost had a heart attack. It was a moment I'm not likely to ever forget.

Me and Ruthie have talked it over and we agree angels were there that night. You could feel a mighty presence, the tunnel and the lights and everything shiny and those dove wings drooping. All signs from above, just like the pillar of smoke rising from Wes Johnson's place. Moses saw a cloud pillar across the Red Sea, you know. Believe what you want, but I know what these mountains can do and what a body can stand in winter. No one should've survived what them two babies survived—fifty-plus hours in zero-degree windchill and no food and both of them dressed like they were going window-shopping at the mall. Crazy fool kids. It wasn't just luck they had, I'll tell you true. Heaven was on their side. Angels brought me and Ruthie to them, that's the way we see it. The Power that runs the cosmos held His hand over those two lost youngins till we could get there and rescue them. "They will rise and walk," the angels said to me. And that's what they did, they rose from the dead and they walked. May the Almighty strike me down if one word I've said ain't gospel.

Ava After

WHEN AVA LEFT THE car in Gunnison, she walked around until she found a public phone in a laundromat and called her mother collect. She told her mother where she was. Her mother told her to sit tight, she was coming. It was midnight when she got there and woke Ava, who was still in the laundromat, lying on a row of chairs, her head cradled on her arm, her thumb in her mouth. They slept in the car the rest of the night, running the heater to keep warm. In the morning they went to a café, had breakfast, and then drove home to Stone Garden.

It was a week before they learned of Triple E and Jeanne getting rescued.

Tom Patch was never found. It is understood that Patch perished in the cold somewhere and those who keep the wild lands tidy devoured his flesh, scattered his bones.

Jeanne and Triple E spent several days in a hospital, where Triple E lost most of his toes and a good bit of skin from his ears and cheeks, leaving him looking weathered and scarred and old before his time. After he was well enough, he was sent south to the Buena Vista Correctional Facility, where he served six quiet months. Then he was put on probation with the stipulation that he leave Colorado and not return until he was at least twenty-one.

His parents came up with the money to send him to an aunt and uncle in Minnesota, where he was to serve out his probation period. But he didn't stay there. He jumped probation and went west. People wrote him off, another loser, another sad statistic. Probably dead or doing drugs in an L.A. alley, they would say. But maybe not. Maybe his ambivalent heart found something to do that fits his talents. There must be some place where Triple E belongs. Some place where the better features of his nature can be put to use. When Ava last heard from him, he was in California—but heading for Alaska, he told her. Heading for the last frontier is what he said.

As for Jeanne, it was touch and go in the hospital. She stayed in a stupor and near death for days. It took blood transfusions, followed by dialysis, to clean the toxins out of her and get her lungs and kidneys functioning right. She was fighting pneumonia as well. But finally she pulled through. She was a different person afterward. She wasn't rebellious anymore. She became the quiet, thoughtful, grateful daughter her parents had always wanted. Grateful to be alive and warm and safe in her own bed.

By the time Triple E got out of Buena Vista, Jeanne had disappeared from Stone Garden. He tried to call her before he left for Minnesota, but her phone was disconnected. In order to keep Jeanne away from Triple E for good, her father had put in for a transfer, and she was living somewhere in Germany, but nobody knew where exactly. She and Triple E, world-class eternal lovers though they were, never met again.

THREE YEARS AFTER HER little adventure, Ava married a man who was thirty-three. She was seventeen at the time. They live now at the edge of the prairie, where the prairie begins and where the last townlet of Denver ends, that in-between point that doesn't commit them to either town or country. They have two children, a boy whose Christian name is Triple E and a girl called Jeanne Marie. The poetic sound of her children's names pleases Ava very much. When she calls them into dinner, she sings out, "Jeanne Marie and Triple E! . . . Triple E and Jeanne Marie! . . . Dinner!" And two scruffy youngsters show up, wild-eyed and dirty, but as healthy in mind and body as any mother can hope for them to be.

Ava's man is steady. He dotes on his children. He loves his wife and she loves him. A girl like Ava might easily have become another Colfax floater, but she didn't. Kids grow up and they fool you. Some of them do anyway.

When she thinks of Tom Patch these days, she can't figure out what drew her to him, can't understand why she loved him so much, and she'll tell you that her only excuse is *youth*. She was young. And everybody knows that young love doesn't have to make sense—*to make sense*.

Her favorite pastime now is reading. Like Renee Bridgewater, she searches in books for wisdom. She wants to know mostly how best to raise her children, so they won't be needy and hungry for love and turn foolish and self-destructive like she did. To enable her to not forget what it was like to be young, she reads the *experts,* and they tell her all about it. But mostly she uses her own good common sense, which started accumulating when she got out of that stolen Oldsmobile on a freezing winter's day in Gunnison, Colorado.

HERE'S AN OFFER. IF you take East Colfax out of Aurora and Stone Garden till it ends and turns into the frontage road paralleling Highway 70 heading toward Kansas, between the towns of Watkins and Bennett you'll come to dried-up Kiowa Creek. Up ahead you should see a pistachio green water tower. Take the first dirt road north after you cross the dry Kiowa. Within fifty yards you will come to a driveway on the right. A sign will say Cherry Road. Go up to the house: a white frame house with asphalt shingle roof and yellow trim and yellow planter boxes with cherries painted on them, a picket fence and two tail-wagging mutts in front. There is a large porch and a butter-yellow swing.

That's the place. You're there. Knock on the gate and Ava will come out. She looks older than you think, so don't wonder if it's her mother you're looking at. It's not. Her mother died from heart failure a couple years ago. Ask Ava if she's got a minute. Use my name if you want. Tell her I sent you. And she'll tell you to come sit. She'll put the coffee on. Then when you're comfortable and ready to hear it, show her this book, ask her about the story you've just read. Ava knows what's missing and she'll understand why you're there. She'll nod like she does and she'll say, "Ah yes, them yes." She's good with the truth. You'll like her. And she'll like you for taking so much trouble, driving so far out. And she'll tell you what you need to know.